The Fearful Pit

Dante Alighieri, one of the greatest poets of all time, belongs in the immortal company of Homer, Virgil, Milton, and Shakespeare. His poetic masterpiece, the *Inferno,* is an intense and moving human drama, an unforgettable visionary journey through the horrors of Hell, a vivid pageant of the Middle Ages, and the way of an individual soul from sin to purgatory.

The *Inferno* describes Dante's visit to the lower realms of the next world. He passes through the giant gates with their prophetic inscription: *Abandon All Hope Ye Who Enter Here,* through the nine circles of Hell, where anguished men and women expiate earthly sins of lust and greed, malice and betrayal, in varying degrees of torment.

John Ciardi, a distinguished American poet, has brilliantly rendered the *Inferno* into modern English, bringing it alive again, with all the burning clarity and universal relevance with which the thirteenth century genius originally endowed it.

"Fresh and sharp . . . I think this version of Dante will be in many respects the best we have seen."—*John Crowe Ransom*

DANTE ALIGHIERI

THE INFERNO

a verse rendering for the modern reader
by JOHN CIARDI

Historical Introduction by Archibald T. MacAllister

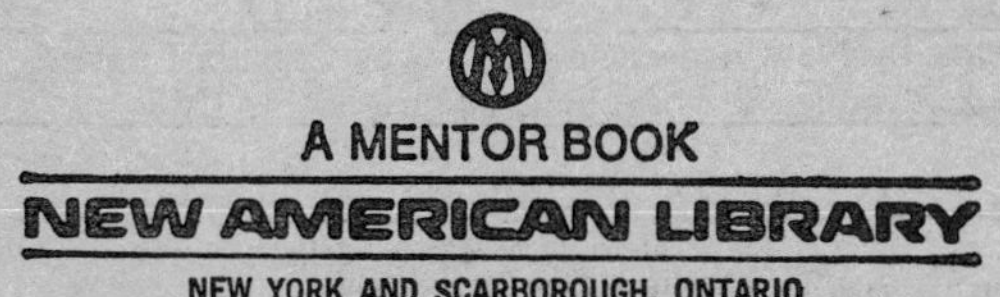

This book is also available in a clothbound edition published by Rutgers University Press.

MENTOR TRADEMARK REG. U.S. PAT. OFF. AND FOREIGN COUNTRIES
REGISTERED TRADEMARK—MARCA REGISTRADA
HECHO EN CHICAGO, U.S.A.

SIGNET, SIGNET CLASSIC, MENTOR, PLUME, MERIDIAN AND NAL BOOKS are published *in the United States* by
New American Library,
1633 Broadway, New York, New York 10019,
in Canada by New American Library of Canada Limited,
81 Mack Avenue, Scarborough, Ontario M1L 1M8

35 36 37 38 39 40 41

PRINTED IN THE UNITED STATES OF AMERICA

Contents

ILLUSTRATIONS

To Judith

Cosi n'andammo infino alla lumiera,
parlando cose, che il tacere è bello,
sì com' era il parlar colà dov' era.

Translator's Note

When the violin repeats what the piano has just played, it cannot make the same sounds and it can only approximate the same chords. It can, however, make recognizably the same "music," the same air. But it can do so only when it is as faithful to the self-logic of the violin as it is to the self-logic of the piano.

Language too is an instrument, and each language has its own logic. I believe that the process of rendering from language to language is better conceived as a "transposition" than as a "translation," for "translation" implies a series of word-for-word equivalents that do not exist across language boundaries any more than piano sounds exist in the violin.

The notion of word-for-word equivalents also strikes me as false to the nature of poetry. Poetry is not made of words but of word-complexes, elaborate structures involving, among other things, denotations, connotations, rhythms, puns, juxtapositions, and echoes of the tradition in which the poet is writing. It is difficult in prose and impossible in poetry to juggle such a complex intact across the barrier of language. What must be saved, even at the expense of making four strings do for eighty-eight keys, is the total feeling of the complex, its *gestalt*.

The only way I could see of trying to preserve that *gestalt* was to try for a language as close as possible to Dante's, which is in essence a sparse, direct, and idiomatic language, distinguishable from prose only in that it transcends every known notion of prose. I do not imply that Dante's is the language of common speech. It is a much better thing than that: it is what common speech would be if it were made perfect.

One of the main sources of the tone of Dante's speech is his revolt from the Sicilian School of Elegance. Nothing would be more misleading than to say that Dante's language is simple. Overwhelmingly, however, it seeks to avoid elegance simply for the sake of elegance. And overwhelmingly it is a spoken tongue.

I have labored therefore for something like idiomatic English in the present rendering. And I have foregone the use of Dante's triple rhyme because it seemed clear that one rendering into English might save the rhyme or save the tone of the language, but not both. It requires approximately 1500 triple rhymes to render The *Inferno* and even granted that many of these combinations can be used and re-used, English has no such resources of rhyme. Inevitably the language must be inverted, distorted, padded, and made unspeakable in order to force the line to come out on that third all-consuming rhyme. In Italian, where it is only a slight exaggeration to say that everything rhymes with everything else or a variant form of it, the rhyme is no problem: in English it is disaster.

At the same time some rhyme is necessary, I think, to approximate Dante's way of going, and the three line stanzas seem absolutely indispensable because the fact that Dante's thought tends to conclude at the end of each tercet (granted a very large number of run-on tercets) clearly determines the "pace" of the writing, *i.e.*, the rate at which it reveals itself to the reader. These were my reasons for deciding on the present form. Moreover, I have not hesitated to use a deficient rhyme when the choice seemed to lie between forcing an exact rhyme and keeping the language more natural.

For my interpretation of many difficult passages I have leaned heavily on the Biagi commentaries, and even more heavily on the Vandelli-Scartazzini. A number of these interpretations are at odds with those set forth in some of the more familiar English versions of The *Inferno*, but, subject to my own error, this rendering is consistent at all points with Vandelli's range of arguments.

I have also leaned heavily on the good will and knowledge of a number of scholars. Dudley Fitts read patiently through the whole manuscript and made detailed, and usually legible, notes on it. Professor A. T.

MacAllister not only gave me the benefit of another complete set of detailed notes, but agreed to undertake the historical introduction so important to a good understanding of Dante, and so brilliantly presented here.

Professor Giorgio di Santillana gave me sound and subtle advice on many points. My major regret is that he left for Italy before I could take further advantage of his patience and of his profound understanding of Dante. I wish to thank also Professor C. S. Singleton for some useful disapproval at a few points, Professor Irwin Swerdlow and Professor Richard W. B. Lewis for hours of patient listening, and my sister, Mrs. Thomas W. Fennessey, for typing through many drafts. I think, too, I should acknowledge a debt of borrowed courage to all other translators of Dante; without their failures I should never have attempted my own.

John Ciardi
Rutgers University

Introduction

The *Divine Comedy* is one of the few literary works which have enjoyed a fame that was both immediate and enduring. Fame might indeed be said not to have awaited its completion, shortly before the author's death in 1321, for the first two parts, including the *Inferno* here presented, had already in a very few years achieved a reputation tinged with supernatural awe. Within two decades a half-dozen commentaries had been written, and fifty years later it was accorded the honor of public readings and exposition—an almost unheard-of tribute to a work written in the humble vernacular.

The six centuries through which the poem has come to us have not lessened its appeal nor obscured its fame. All of them have not, of course, been unanimous in their appreciation: for a fifteenth-century Latinist, Dante was a poet "fit for cobblers"; eighteenth-century worshipers of Reason could not be wholly sympathetic to a poet who insisted on the limitations of reason and philosophy. It was the effete mid-sixteenth century which in spite of certain reservations, first proclaimed "divine" the work its author had called simply his "Comedy." The significant fact is that the *Divine Comedy* has demanded critical consideration of each successive age and every great writer; and the nature of their reaction could well serve as a barometer of taste and a measure of their greatness.

By that standard the present age should prove truly great, for its interest in the *Comedy* has rarely been matched. Credit for the nineteenth-century rediscovery of Dante in the English-speaking world belongs to Coleridge, who was ably seconded in this country by Longfellow and Norton. Contemporary enthusiasm was touched off by T. S. Eliot's *Essay on Dante* and has grown, in some quarters, to the proportions of a cult.

What is this work which has displayed such persistent

vitality? It is a narrative poem whose greatest strength lies in the fact that it does not so much narrate as dramatize its episodes. Dante had doubtless learned from experience how soporific a long narrative could be. He also firmly believed that the senses were the avenues to the mind and that sight was the most powerful ("noblest," he would have said) of these. Hence his art is predominantly visual. He believed also that the mind must be moved in order to grasp what the senses present to it; therefore he combines sight, sound, hearing, smell and touch with fear, pity, anger, horror and other appropriate emotions to involve his reader to the point of seeming actually to experience his situations and not merely to read about them. It is really a three-dimensional art.

The *Divine Comedy* is also an allegory. But it is fortunately that special type of allegory wherein every element must first correspond to a literal reality, every episode must exist coherently in itself. Allegoric interpretation does not detract from the story as told but is rather an added significance which one may take or leave. Many readers, indeed, have been thrilled by the *Inferno's* power with hardly an awareness of further meanings. Dante represents mankind, he represents the "Noble Soul," but first and always he is Dante Alighieri, born in thirteenth-century Florence; Virgil represents human reason, but only after he has been accepted as the poet of ancient Rome. The whole poem purports to be a vision of the three realms of the Catholic otherworld, Hell, Purgatory and Paradise, and a description of "the state of the soul after death"; yet it is peopled with Dante's contemporaries and, particularly in the materialistic realism of the *Inferno,* it is torn by issues and feuds of the day, political, religious and personal. It treats of the most universal values—good and evil, man's responsibility, free will and predestination; yet it is intensely personal and political, for it was written out of the anguish of a man who saw his life blighted by the injustice and corruption of his times.

The *Divine Comedy* is classically referred to as the

epitome, the supreme expression of the Middle Ages. If by this is meant that many typically medieval attitudes are to be found in it, it is true: the reasoning is scholastic, the learning, the mysticism are those of the author's time. But if from such a statement one is to infer (as is frequently done) that the poem is a hymn to its times, a celebration and glorification of them, as Virgil's *Aeneid* was of Rome, then nothing could be more misleading. The *Comedy* is a glorification of the ways of God, but it is also a sharp and great-minded protest at the ways in which men have thwarted the divine plan. This plan, as Dante conceived it, was very different from the typically medieval view, which saw the earthly life as a "vale of tears," a period of trial and suffering, an unpleasant but necessary preparation for the after-life where alone man could expect to enjoy happiness. To Dante such an idea was totally repugnant. He gloried in his God-given talent, his well disciplined faculties, and it seemed inconceivable to him that he and mankind in general should not have been intended to develop to the fullest their specifically human potential. The whole *Comedy* is pervaded by his conviction that man should seek earthly immortality by his worthy actions here, as well as prepare to merit the life everlasting. His theory is stated explicitly in his Latin treatise, *De Monarchia*:

> "Ineffable Providence has thus designed two ends to be contemplated of man: first, the happiness of this life, which consists in the activity of his natural powers, and is prefigured by the Earthly Paradise; and then the blessedness of life everlasting . . . . which may be symbolized by the Celestial Paradise."

To us, reading his masterpiece at the comfortable distance of six hundred years, it may well seem that few men have better realized their potential than Dante; to him, a penniless exile convicted of a felony, separated under pain of death from home, family and friends, his life seemed to have been cut off in the middle.

It was Dante's pride—and the root of his misfortune—

to have been born in the free commune of Florence, located near the center of the Italian peninsula, during the turbulent thirteenth century. It is important that we remember to think of it, not as an Italian city, but as a sovereign country, a power in the peninsula and of growing importance internationally. It had its own army, its flag, its ambassadors, its foreign trade, its own coinage; the florin, in fact, was on its way to becoming the standard of international exchange, the pound sterling or dollar of its day. Its control was a prize worth fighting for, and the Florentines were nothing loth to fight, especially among themselves. Internal strife had begun long before, as the weakening of the Empire had left its robber-baron representatives increasingly vulnerable to attack and eventual subjection by the townsfolk. They had become unruly citizens at best in their fortress-like houses, and constituted a higher nobility whose arrogance stirred the resentment of the lesser nobility, the merchants and artisans. The history of the republic for many years is the story of the bloody struggle among these groups, with the gradual triumph of the lower classes as flourishing trade brought them unheard-of prosperity. Early in Dante's century the struggle acquired color and new ferocity. In 1215 the jilting of an Amidei girl was avenged by the murder of the offending member of the Buondelmonti family, which, according to the chronicler Villani, originated the infamous Guelf-Ghibelline factions. But the lines had already long been drawn on the deeper issues, with the Ghibellines representing the old Imperial aristocracy and the Guelfs the burghers, who, in international politics, favored the Pope. In 1248, with the aid of Frederick II, the Ghibellines expelled the Guelfs; in 1251 the latter returned and drove out the Ghibellines, who were again defeated in 1258. In 1260 the Ghibellines amassed a formidable army under the leadership of Farinata degli Uberti and overwhelmed the Guelfs at Montaperti, where the Arbia ran red with the blood of the six thousand slain, and sixteen thousand were taken prisoner. The very existence of Florence hung momentarily in the balance as the triumphant Ghibellines listened to the urgings of their allies from neighboring Siena that they wipe out the city; only Farinata's resolute opposition saved it. Gradually the Guelfs recovered, and in 1266 they completely and finally crushed their enemies at Benevento. Thus ended the worst of this partisan strife from which, as Machiavelli was to write, "there resulted more murders, banishments and destruction of families than ever in any city known to history."

Dante Alighieri had been born the preceding year, 1265, toward the end of May; he was a year old when his family (a typically Guelf mixture of lesser nobility and burgher) must have joined in the celebration of their party's victory. His whole impressionable childhood was undoubtedly filled with stories of the struggle so recently ended. The fascination it had for him is evident in the *Comedy*, where it is an important factor in the *Inferno* and the lower, "material" portion of *Purgatory*.

Our actual knowledge of Dante's life is disappointingly small, limited to a few documents of record. The biographies, beginning with Boccaccio's about fifty years after his death, are largely hearsay, legend and deductions based on his works and the meager references scattered through them. We know that his mother died when he was very young, that his father remarried, and that Dante was completely orphaned in adolescence. This is thought to account for a certain hunger for parental affection which can be noted in the *Comedy*. He doubtless received the normal education of the day for his class, and perhaps more, for his bent must have been clearly intellectual and literary. That he took an early interest in the vernacular lyric only recently borrowed from the Provençal is demonstrated by poems dating from his middle or late 'teens. It was through this activity that he made his closest friendship, that with Guido Cavalcanti, who was a gifted poet some years Dante's senior.

Most of our impressions about his youth are gleaned from his first work, in the planning of which Cavalcanti had a part. Called *La Vita Nuova* ("The New Life"), it was deliberately written in the vernacular in 1292 to celebrate the most important influence in Dante's life, his love for Beatrice Portinari. It is made up of sonnets and longer lyrics interspersed with prose passages which explain and narrate the circumstances under which the poems had been composed years earlier. An astonishing feature of the book is the careful symmetry of its arrangement where the balance of three, nine and ten foreshadows the elaborate design which will be worked out in the *Comedy*. Very briefly, it is the story of a boy of nine suddenly awaking to love at the sight of a girl of almost the same age; of a second encounter at the age of 18 when a greeting is exchanged; of tribulations and misunderstandings leading to her disapproval; of her sudden death when the poet was 25, his grief and attempted consolation by another girl; finally of a "marvelous vision" of his Beatrice when he was 27, thus completing the trinity of "nines" and determining him to write no more of her until he could do so worthily. Although it is autobiographical, the *Vita Nuova* is not an autobiography; it is a delicate and sensitive analysis of emotions. Such facts as enter into it assume an air of strange unreality.

From our small array of factual data we learn that Dante's life in this period included other things than tremulous sighs and visions. In 1289 he took part in the battle of Campaldino and the capture of Caprona. In 1295 appears the first record of his political activity. In the same year he made himself eligible for public office by enrolling in a guild, the Apothecaries', where the books of that day were sold. In the following year it is recorded that he spoke in the "Council of the Hundred." By 1299 he had advanced to fill a minor ambassadorship. In the meantime he married Gemma, sister of his friend Forese Donati and of the hot-tempered Corso. As the mature but still youthful Alighieri was playing an ever more prominent role in politics, familiar tensions were once again building up within the republic. Thirty years without a serious threat from their common enemy put too great a strain on Guelf unity; and again it was a murder, though in nearby Pistoia, which precipitated open conflict. The Florentines took sides and in the late spring of 1300 the two parties, called "Blacks" and "Whites," fought in the streets. It was at this particular moment that Dante's political career was crowned with the highest success and he was elected one of the six supreme magistrates, called priors. Himself a moderate White, he found it necessary during the two-month term to join in banishing his brother-in-law, Corso Donati, and his "first friend," Guido Cavalcanti, as ringleaders respectively of the Blacks and Whites. (Cavalcanti died very soon of an illness contracted during his banishment.) As friction continued, the Blacks conspired for the intervention of the Pope, Boniface VIII, who was delighted with the chance to strengthen the Papacy's claim on Tuscany. In spite of frantic White opposition he sent Charles of Valois ostensibly as impartial arbitrator and peacemaker. What the Pope's secret orders were became instantly apparent when Charles was admitted in November 1301, for he set upon the Whites, admitted the banished Blacks and stood by as they gave themselves over to murder and pillage. The matter was then legitimized by a series of "purge trials" of the sort only too familiar to us. Among those accused, and of course convicted, of graft and corruption in office was Dante Alighieri. Fortunately he had been absent and had stayed away; but from early in 1302 his voluntary absence became exile under penalty of being burned alive.

We know even less of the remaining 19 years except that they were spent largely with a series of patrons in various courts of Italy. The exile had no funds, no reputation as yet, no powerful friends. He stayed at various times with the Scala family, then with the Malaspinas; tradition has it that he studied at Paris, and even at Oxford. As time passed and his reputation grew, his way became easier and his last years were spent in relative comfort at Ravenna as the honored guest of Guido Novello da Polenta, nephew of Francesca da Rimini. On the way back from a diplomatic mission to Venice he fell ill and died soon after his return. In *Paradise XVII* he left one of the most poignant descriptions of life in exile ever written: "Thou shalt prove how salty tastes another's bread, and how hard a path it is to go up and down another's stairs."

That Dante had ample reason to feel that the political chaos of his day was a prime menace to man's pursuit of happiness should be quite apparent. It should also be understandable that he used the *Comedy* to protest this evil and to suggest a remedy. His analysis and conclusions took years of reading and meditation, during which he denounced all existing parties, Whites, Blacks, Guelfs, and Ghibellines, in order to "make a party by himself." As his compatriot Machiavelli was to do two hundred years later and from very similar motives, he sought his material in the literature of Ancient Rome, with the difference that the later scholar had the advantage of the humanistic revival and the free inquiry of the Renaissance, whereas Dante was a pioneer circumscribed by scholasticism. He had already begun his study of ancient philosophy a few years after the *Vita Nuova* and before his political disaster. In his next work, the *Convivio* or *Banquet,* he tells how difficult he had found it: the Latin he had learned proved quite different from that of Boethius' *Consolations of Philosophy.* Cicero's urbane and complex style was much harder and, more confusing still, his whole mode of thought, his concepts, viewpoints, allusions were as if from a different world. The young explorer from medieval Christendom went doggedly on from one work to another which he had seen mentioned, without adequate teachers, courses, reference works, or indeed, the works themselves, except as he could beg or borrow the manuscripts. Eventually he mastered and assimilated all the learning available in Latin or Latin translations, from the *Timaeus* of Plato, Cicero, Virgil, Horace, Ovid, Statius and Lucan through St. Augustine and other Fathers of the Church, to Averröes, St. Thomas and the great mystics. But the wastefulness, the needless difficulties, the groping aroused his indignation, as injustice always did. He had been "educated" but how much had it helped him in the pursuit of real learning? He knew that there were others, too, who longed for such knowledge but lacked his extraordinary mental equipment (he allowed himself no false modesty) and thus failed to win through. What was lacking were real schools with competent teachers and high standards, available to all who had the talent and the desire to learn. But what agency would set them up and maintain them? Not the Church; for, though it was no longer ignorant of philosophy, the Church was suspicious of it and not inclined to grant it that primacy in the conduct of human affairs which Dante assigned to it. This was another problem, to be studied along with that of political instability and strife. In the meantime he, Dante Alighieri, could contribute the fruits of his own efforts in the form of an encyclopaedia or compendium of knowledge which would at the same time earn for him badly needed prestige. Not only would it gather together the knowledge which he had found scattered piecemeal in many works and in different forms, it would make that knowledge accessible by use of the vernacular instead of Latin. Such a thing was revolutionary in the first decade of the fourteenth century and called for an explanation which Dante gave in the form of an impassioned defense of what we call Italian. He concluded with the following prophetic words, referring to the new language as

> ". . . a new light, a new sun, which shall rise whereas the accustomed one (Latin) shall set, and which shall give light to those who are in darkness because the accustomed sun does not give them light."

The *Banquet* was to consist of fifteen sections: an introduction and fourteen of Dante's longer philosophical lyrics, each followed by an expository prose passage. Only four sections were completed. Among the possible reasons for its abandonment, two in particular seem valid. First, the work is a failure in organization and style, typically medieval in its discursive rambling. Second, it was written to exalt philosophy, "most noble daughter of the Emperor of the Universe," and thus constituted a perilous deviation for a medieval Christian. It is at least possible that this frame of mind was included in the "Dark

Wood" in which the *Comedy* begins, and it almost certainly inspired the repeated warnings against over-dependence on philosophy and human wisdom which the poem contains.

Evidence that Dante had already begun to formulate his solution to the evils of his day may be found in the *Banquet,* but it is in the *De Monarchia,* last of his more important minor works, that we find the full statement of his theories. This is the best organized and most complete of his treatises. He probably composed it in the last decade of his life and chose Latin as a medium rather deliberately, I suspect, for discretion's sake. It is certain, at any rate, that copies of it were sought out for burning by the Papacy some years after the author's death, and it was among the first books placed on the *Index.* The Church, struggling to wrest from the enfeebled Empire its supremacy as a temporal power, had made it a matter of dogma that the emperors were as dependent on the popes as was the moon on the sun. The *De Monarchia* denied and denounced this position, affirming that the two powers were rather like two equal suns, each dependent only on God and designed to guide man toward his two goals: peace and happiness in this world and spiritual salvation in the next.

> "To these states of blessedness, just as to diverse conclusions, man must come by diverse means. To the former we come by the teachings of philosophy . . . in conformity with the moral and intellectual virtues; to the latter through spiritual teachings which transcend human reason . . . in conformity with the theological virtues . . . . Now the former end and means are made known to us by human reason . . . and the latter by the Holy Spirit . . . . Nevertheless, human passion would cast all these behind, were not men, like wild horses in their brutishness, held to the road by bit and rein.
>
> "Wherefore a twofold directive agent was necessary to man in accordance with the twofold end: the Supreme Pontiff to lead the human race by means of

revelation, and the Emperor to guide it to temporal felicity by means of philosophic education."

Failure of the two guides to cooperate prevented peace and bred injustice. Part of the blame rested on the Empire for neglecting its duties, but the larger share fell on the Papacy. In its greed for temporal power, which Dante believed rooted in the ill-conceived "Donation of Constantine," it not only deprived mankind of a strong civil government but neglected its proper task of spiritual guidance, so that most men were damned not only in this life but in the life to come. Dante's ideas have long been ridiculed as quixotic, yet history has seen a Declaration affirming man's right to "the pursuit of happiness," the separation of Church and State, education secularized and rendered accessible to the public, while to many today the idea of peace and justice through a world government seems not so much chimerical as indispensable.

Whatever fate might have befallen the *De Monarchia* would have mattered little, for its essential thesis was preserved in the enduring beauty of the *Divine Comedy,* interwoven with the other themes, expressed at times openly, at other times merely implicit in the structure. For the same reason it was unimportant that the *Banquet* lay unfinished, for all the erudition Dante had planned to present in that indigestible work found much nobler, more convincing expression in the poetry of the *Comedy.* Even the beautiful little youthful work, the *Vita Nuova,* found itself continued and sublimated on the slopes and summit of *Purgatory,* where Beatrice reappears in womanly glory first to confront and then to guide her lover. For one of the marvels of this great poem is the way in which all of Dante's learning, his speculations, observations and experiences were blended together in its intricate fabric.

The poem's complex structure is itself a marvelous thing. Before we examine it briefly we should, however, remember that Dante lived in a Catholic world or, rather, universe, in which every slightest thing was encompassed in the will and knowledge of an omnipotent and omniscient Deity and that the supreme attribute of that Deity was the mystery of His Trinity and Unity. Evidences of that mystery were sought and found everywhere and such numerical symbolism was not as today comical abracadabra but a serious and even sacred matter.

Now let us look at the *Comedy*. It is made up of three nearly equal parts which are distinct yet carefully interrelated to form a unified whole. Each part moreover is the expression of one Person of the Trinity: *Inferno,* the Power of the Father, *Purgatory,* the Wisdom of the Son, *Paradise,* the Love of the Holy Spirit. Each part, or *cántica,* contains 33 cantos for a total of 99. If we add the first, introductory, canto we obtain a grand total of 100 which is the square of 10; 10 is the perfect number, for it is composed solely of the square of the Trinity plus 1 which represents the Unity of God. Even the rhyme scheme itself is the *terza rima* or "third rhyme" which Dante invented for his purpose. There are other symmetries and correspondences, but this should suffice to demonstrate that Dante planned his own creation in as close an imitation of a divinely created and controlled universe as was possible to the mind of man. Almost literally nothing was left to chance.

We today are more than inclined to despise such concern with what seem to us trifles, externals, Victorian gingerbread, because we are convinced that the mind preoccupied with them cannot have much of importance to say. In our utilitarian scorn we are in danger of forgetting that a certain preoccupation with form (and even today's straight line betrays such a preoccupation) is essential to beauty. In the *Divine Comedy* we must remember that Dante had for his subject the whole world, the entire universe, all of man's history, his learning, his beliefs, plus his own particular messages. To him preoccupation with form was not extrinsic, not a luxury; it was his salvation. As Mr. Gilbert Highet points out, it is this that sets Dante apart from his contemporaries, this was the great lesson he had learned from his master and author, Virgil. The medieval digressions which infest the *Ban-*

quet have been eliminated by the "fren dell'arte." I doubt whether there is another work of this size which is so economical in its use of words. The reader always has, as Mr. Ciardi aptly puts it, ". . . a sense of the right-choice-always-being-made"; and this applies to everything from the smallest word to the harmonious interrelation of the principal divisions.

This awareness of intelligence at work is clearly felt throughout the *Inferno*. This is the realm—or condition—of the "dead people," those who have rejected spiritual values by yielding to bestial appetites or violence, or by perverting their human intellect to fraud or malice against their fellowmen. As subject matter it is the lowest, ugliest, most materialistic of the whole poem. Now in his unfinished treatise on the vernacular, *De Vulgari Eloquentia,* Dante had established a basic rule that the poet must make his style match his material. In accordance with this we should expect the style of the *Inferno* to be lower than that of the other divisions—and that is exactly what we find. The poet has used throughout it a low level of diction, common, everyday words and constructions and relatively simple figures. Yet with this prosaic equipment he has obtained incomparable effects, from the poignant sensuality of Francesca (V), the dignity of Farinata (X), the pathos of Ser Brunetto (XV), to demoniac farce (XXI) and revolting ugliness (XXIX). He employed not only ordinary words but, where he thought it useful, those which in our language seem to require only four letters.

It is Mr. Ciardi's great merit to be one of the first American translators to have perceived this special quality of the *Inferno* and the first to have reproduced it successfully in English. In order to achieve this he has abandoned any attempt to reproduce Dante's complicated rhyme scheme and has even had to do some slight violence to conventional poetic usage. The resulting effect to the ear, which must be the supreme judge in these matters, is a good likeness of the original. It may also be something of a shock to those who insist on a uniformly hieratic approach to all things Dantesque; let them come really to know the vigorous, uncompromising Florentine who, even in *Paradise,* wrote:

"E lascia pur grattar dov'è la rogna!"

("And let them go ahead and scratch where it itches.")

Archibald T. MacAllister

Princeton, New Jersey
July 14, 1953

Canto I

The Dark Wood of Error

Midway in his allotted threescore years and ten, Dante comes to himself with a start and realizes that he has strayed from the True Way into the Dark Wood of Error (Worldliness). As soon as he has realized his loss, Dante lifts his eyes and sees the first light of the sunrise (the Sun is the Symbol of Divine Illumination) lighting the shoulders of a little hill (The Mount of Joy). It is the Easter Season, the time of resurrection, and the sun is in its equinoctial rebirth. This juxtaposition of joyous symbols fills Dante with hope and he sets out at once to climb directly up the Mount of Joy, but almost immediately his way is blocked by the Three Beasts of Worldliness: THE LEOPARD OF MALICE AND FRAUD, THE LION OF VIOLENCE AND AMBITION, and THE SHE-WOLF OF INCONTINENCE. These beasts, and especially the She-Wolf, drive him back despairing into the darkness of error. But just as all seems lost, a figure appears to him. It is the shade of VIRGIL, Dante's symbol of HUMAN REASON.

Virgil explains that he has been sent to lead Dante from error. There can, however, be no direct ascent past the beasts: the man who would escape them must go a longer and harder way. First he must descend through Hell (The Recognition of Sin), then he must ascend through Purgatory (The Renunciation of Sin), and only then may he reach the pinnacle of joy and come to the Light of God. Virgil offers to guide Dante, but only as far as Human Reason can go. Another guide (BEATRICE, symbol of DIVINE LOVE) must take over for the final ascent, for Human Reason is self-limited. Dante submits himself joyously to Virgil's guidance and they move off.

Midway in our life's journey, I went astray
from the straight road and woke to find myself
alone in a dark wood. How shall I say

what wood that was! I never saw so drear,
so rank, so arduous a wilderness!
Its very memory gives a shape to fear.

Death could scarce be more bitter than that place!
But since it came to good, I will recount
all that I found revealed there by God's grace.

How I came to it I cannot rightly say,
so drugged and loose with sleep had I become
when I first wandered there from the True Way.

But at the far end of that valley of evil
whose maze had sapped my very heart with fear!
I found myself before a little hill

and lifted up my eyes. Its shoulders glowed
already with the sweet rays of that planet
whose virtue leads men straight on every road,

and the shining strengthened me against the fright
whose agony had wracked the lake of my heart
through all the terrors of that piteous night.

Just as a swimmer, who with his last breath
flounders ashore from perilous seas, might turn
to memorize the wide water of his death—

so did I turn, my soul still fugitive
from death's surviving image, to stare down
that pass that none had ever left alive.

And there I lay to rest from my heart's race
till calm and breath returned to me. Then rose
and pushed up that dead slope at such a pace

each footfall rose above the last. And lo!
almost at the beginning of the rise
I faced a spotted Leopard, all tremor and flow

and gaudy pelt. And it would not pass, but stood
so blocking my every turn that time and again
I was on the verge of turning back to the wood.

This fell at the first widening of the dawn
as the sun was climbing Aries with those stars
that rode with him to light the new creation.

Thus the holy hour and the sweet season
of commemoration did much to arm my fear
of that bright murderous beast with their good omen.

Yet not so much but what I shook with dread
at sight of a great Lion that broke upon me
raging with hunger, its enormous head

held high as if to strike a mortal terror
into the very air. And down his track,
a She-Wolf drove upon me, a starved horror

ravening and wasted beyond all belief.
She seemed a rack for avarice, gaunt and craving.
Oh many the souls she has brought to endless grief!

She brought such heaviness upon my spirit
at sight of her savagery and desperation,
I died from every hope of that high summit.

And like a miser—eager in acquisition
but desperate in self-reproach when Fortune's wheel
turns to the hour of his loss—all tears and attrition

I wavered back; and still the beast pursued,
forcing herself against me bit by bit
till I slid back into the sunless wood.

And as I fell to my soul's ruin, a presence
gathered before me on the discolored air,
the figure of one who seemed hoarse from long silence.

At sight of him in that friendless waste I cried:
"Have pity on me, whatever thing you are,
whether shade or living man." And it replied:

"Not man, though man I once was, and my blood
was Lombard, both my parents Mantuan.
I was born, though late, *sub Julio,* and bred

in Rome under Augustus in the noon
of the false and lying gods. I was a poet
and sang of old Anchises' noble son

who came to Rome after the burning of Troy.
But you—why do *you* return to these distresses
instead of climbing that shining Mount of Joy

which is the seat and first cause of man's bliss?"
"And are you then that Virgil and that fountain
of purest speech?" My voice grew tremulous:

"Glory and light of poets! now may that zeal
and love's apprenticeship that I poured out
on your heroic verses serve me well!

For you are my true master and first author,
the sole maker from whom I drew the breath
of that sweet style whose measures have brought me honor.

See there, immortal sage, the beast I flee.
For my soul's salvation, I beg you, guard me from her,
for she has struck a mortal tremor through me."

And he replied, seeing my soul in tears:
"He must go by another way who would escape
this wilderness, for that mad beast that fleers

before you there, suffers no man to pass.
She tracks down all, kills all, and knows no glut,
but, feeding, she grows hungrier than she was.

She mates with any beast, and will mate with more
before the Greyhound comes to hunt her down.
He will not feed on lands nor loot, but honor

and love and wisdom will make straight his way.
He will rise between Feltro and Feltro, and in him
shall be the resurrection and new day

of that sad Italy for which Nisus died,
and Turnus, and Euryalus, and the maid Camilla.
He shall hunt her through every nation of sick pride

till she is driven back forever to Hell
whence Envy first released her on the world.
Therefore, for your own good, I think it well

you follow me and I will be your guide
and lead you forth through an eternal place.
There you shall see the ancient spirits tried

in endless pain, and hear their lamentation
as each bemoans the second death of souls.
Next you shall see upon a burning mountain

souls in fire and yet content in fire,
knowing that whensoever it may be
they yet will mount into the blessed choir.

To which, if it is still your wish to climb,
a worthier spirit shall be sent to guide you.
With her shall I leave you, for the King of Time,

who reigns on high, forbids me to come there
since, living, I rebelled against his law.
He rules the waters and the land and air

and there holds court, his city and his throne.
  Oh blessed are they he chooses!" And I to him:
  "Poet, by that God to you unknown,

lead me this way. Beyond this present ill
  and worse to dread, lead me to Peter's gate
  and be my guide through the sad halls of Hell."

And he then: "Follow." And he moved ahead
in silence, and I followed where he led.

Notes

1. *midway in our life's journey:* The Biblical life span is threescore years and ten. The action opens in Dante's thirty-fifth year, i.e., 1300 A.D.

17. *that planet:* The sun. Ptolemaic astronomers considered it a planet. It is also symbolic of God as He who lights man's way.

31. *each footfall rose above the last:* The literal rendering would be: "So that the fixed foot was ever the lower." "Fixed" has often been translated "right" and an ingenious reasoning can support that reading, but a simpler explanation offers itself and seems more competent: Dante is saying that he climbed with such zeal and haste that every footfall carried him above the last despite the steepness of the climb. At a slow pace, on the other hand, the rear foot might be brought up only as far as the forward foot. This device of selecting a minute but exactly-centered detail to convey the whole of a larger action is one of the central characteristics of Dante's style.

THE THREE BEASTS: These three beasts undoubtedly are taken from *Jeremiah* v, 6. Many additional and incidental interpretations have been advanced for them, but the central interpretation must remain as noted. They foreshadow the three divisions of Hell (incontinence, violence, and fraud) which Virgil explains at length in Canto XI, 16-111. I am not at all sure but what the She-Wolf is better interpreted as Fraud and the Leopard as Incontinence. Good arguments can be offered either way.

38-9. *Aries . . . that rode with him to light the new creation:* The medieval tradition had it that the sun was in Aries at the time of the Creation. The significance of the astronomical and religious conjunction is an important part of Dante's intended allegory. It is just before dawn of Good Friday 1300 A.D. when he awakens in the Dark Wood. Thus his new life begins under Aries, the sign of creation, at dawn (rebirth) and in the Easter season (resurrection).

Moreover the moon is full and the sun is in the equinox, conditions that did not fall together on any Friday of 1300. Dante is obviously constructing poetically the perfect Easter as a symbol of his new awakening.

69. *sub Julio:* In the reign of Julius Caesar.

95. *The Greyhound . . . Feltro and Feltro:* Almost certainly refers to Can Grande della Scala (1290-1329), great Italian leader born in Verona, which lies between the towns of Feltre and Montefeltro.

100-101. *Nisus, Turnus, Euryalus, Camilla:* All were killed in the war between the Trojans and the Latians when, according to legend, Aeneas led the survivors of Troy into Italy. Nisus and Euryalus (*Aeneid* IX) were Trojan comrades-in-arms who died together. Camilla (*Aeneid* XI) was the daughter of the Latian king and one of the warrior women. She was killed in a horse charge against the Trojans after displaying great gallantry. Turnus (Aeneid XII) was killed by Aeneas in a duel.

110. *the second death:* Damnation. "This is the second death, even the lake of fire." (*Revelation* xx, 14)

118. *forbids me to come there since, living, etc.:* Salvation is only through Christ in Dante's theology. Virgil lived and died before the establishment of Christ's teachings in Rome, and cannot therefore enter Heaven.

125. *Peter's gate:* The gate of Purgatory. (See *Purgatorio* IX, 76 ff.) The gate is guarded by an angel with a gleaming sword. The angel is Peter's vicar (Peter, the first Pope, symbolized all Popes; i.e., Christ's vicar on earth) and is entrusted with the two great keys.

Some commentators argue that this is the gate of Paradise, but Dante mentions no gate beyond this one in his ascent to Heaven. It should be remembered, too, that those who pass the gate of Purgatory have effectively entered Heaven.

The three great gates that figure in the entire journey are: the gate of Hell (Canto III, 1-11), the gate of Dis (Canto VIII, 79-113, and Canto IX, 86-87), and the gate of Purgatory, as above.

Canto II

The Descent

It is evening of the first day (Friday). Dante is following Virgil and finds himself tired and despairing. How can he be worthy of such a vision as Virgil has described? He hesitates and seems about to abandon his first purpose.

To comfort him Virgil explains how Beatrice descended to him in Limbo and told him of her concern for Dante. It is she, the symbol of Divine Love, who sends Virgil to lead Dante from error. She has come into Hell itself on this errand, for Dante cannot come to Divine Love unaided; Reason must lead him. Moreover Beatrice has been sent with the prayers of the Virgin Mary (COMPASSION), and of Saint Lucia (DIVINE LIGHT). Rachel (THE CONTEMPLATIVE LIFE) also figures in the heavenly scene which Virgil recounts.

Virgil explains all this and reproaches Dante: how can he hesitate longer when such heavenly powers are concerned for him, and Virgil himself has promised to lead him safely?

Dante understands at once that such forces cannot fail him, and his spirits rise in joyous anticipation.

The light was departing. The brown air drew down
all the earth's creatures, calling them to rest
from their day-roving, as I, one man alone,

prepared myself to face the double war
of the journey and the pity, which memory
shall here set down, nor hesitate, nor err.

O Muses! O High Genius! Be my aid!
O Memory, recorder of the vision,
here shall your true nobility be displayed!

Thus I began: "Poet, you who must guide me,
before you trust me to that arduous passage,
look to me and look through me—can I be worthy?

You sang how the father of Sylvius, while still
in corruptible flesh won to that other world,
crossing with mortal sense the immortal sill.

But if the Adversary of all Evil
weighing his consequence and who and what
should issue from him, treated him so well—

that cannot seem unfitting to thinking men,
since he was chosen father of Mother Rome
and of her Empire by God's will and token.

Both, to speak strictly, were founded and foreknown
as the established Seat of Holiness
for the successors of Great Peter's throne.

In that quest, which your verses celebrate,
he learned those mysteries from which arose
his victory and Rome's apostolate.

There later came the chosen vessel, Paul,
bearing the confirmation of that Faith
which is the one true door to life eternal.

But I—how should I dare? By whose permission?
I am not Aeneas. *I* am not Paul.
Who could believe me worthy of the vision?

How, then, may I presume to this high quest
and not fear my own brashness? You are wise
and will grasp what my poor words can but suggest."

As one who unwills what he wills, will stay
strong purposes with feeble second thoughts
until he spells all his first zeal away—

so I hung back and balked on that dim coast
till thinking had worn out my enterprise,
so stout at starting and so early lost.

"I understand from your words and the look in your eyes,"
that shadow of magnificence answered me,
"your soul is sunken in that cowardice

that bears down many men, turning their course
and resolution by imagined perils,
as his own shadow turns the frightened horse.

To free you of this dread I will tell you all
of why I came to you and what I heard
when first I pitied you. I was a soul

among the souls of Limbo, when a Lady
so blessed and so beautiful, I prayed her
to order and command my will, called to me.

Her eyes were kindled from the lamps of Heaven.
Her voice reached through me, tender, sweet, and low.
An angel's voice, a music of its own:

'O gracious Mantuan whose melodies
live in earth's memory and shall live on
till the last motion ceases in the skies,

my dearest friend, and fortune's foe, has strayed
onto a friendless shore and stands beset
by such distresses that he turns afraid

from the True Way, and news of him in Heaven
rumors my dread he is already lost.
I come, afraid that I am too-late risen.

Fly to him and with your high counsel, pity,
  and with whatever need be for his good
  and soul's salvation, help him, and solace me.

It is I, Beatrice, who send you to him.
  I come from the blessed height for which I yearn.
  Love called me here. When amid Seraphim

I stand again before my Lord, your praises
  shall sound in Heaven.' She paused, and I began:
  'O Lady of that only grace that raises

feeble mankind within its mortal cycle
  above all other works God's will has placed
  within the heaven of the smallest circle;

so welcome is your command that to my sense,
  were it already fulfilled, it would yet seem tardy.
  I understand, and am all obedience.

But tell me how you dare to venture thus
  so far from the wide heaven of your joy
  to which your thoughts yearn back from this abyss.'

'Since what you ask,' she answered me, 'probes near
  the root of all, I will say briefly only
  how I have come through Hell's pit without fear.

Know then, O waiting and compassionate soul,
  that is to fear which has the power to harm,
  and nothing else is fearful even in Hell.

I am so made by God's all-seeing mercy
  your anguish does not touch me, and the flame
  of this great burning has no power upon me.

There is a Lady in Heaven so concerned
  for him I send you to, that for her sake
  the strict decree is broken. She has turned

and called Lucia to her wish and mercy
saying: 'Thy faithful one is sorely pressed;
in his distresses I commend him to thee.'

Lucia, that soul of light and foe of all
cruelty, rose and came to me at once
where I was sitting with the ancient Rachel,

saying to me: 'Beatrice, true praise of God,
why dost thou not help him who loved thee so
that for thy sake he left the vulgar crowd?

Dost thou not hear his cries? Canst thou not see
the death he wrestles with beside that river
no ocean can surpass for rage and fury?

No soul of earth was ever as rapt to seek
its good or flee its injury as I was—
when I had heard my sweet Lucia speak—

to descend from Heaven and my blessed seat
to you, laying my trust in that high speech
that honors you and all who honor it.'

She spoke and turned away to hide a tear
that, shining, urged me faster. So I came
and freed you from the beast that drove you there,

blocking the near way to the Heavenly Height.
And now what ails you? Why do you lag? Why
this heartsick hesitation and pale fright

when three such blessed Ladies lean from Heaven
in their concern for you and my own pledge
of the great good that waits you has been given?"

As flowerlets drooped and puckered in the night
turn up to the returning sun and spread
their petals wide on his new warmth and light—

just so my wilted spirits rose again
  and such a heat of zeal surged through my veins
  that I was born anew. Thus I began:

"Blesséd be that Lady of infinite pity,
  and blesséd be thy taxed and courteous spirit
  that came so promptly on the word she gave thee.

Thy words have moved my heart to its first purpose.
  My Guide! My Lord! My Master! Now lead on:
  one will shall serve the two of us in this."

He turned when I had spoken, and at his back
I entered on that hard and perilous track.

Notes

13-30. AENEAS AND THE FOUNDING OF ROME.
Here is a fair example of the way in which Dante absorbed pagan themes into his Catholicism.

According to Virgil, Aeneas is the son of mortal Anchises and of Venus. Venus, in her son's interest, secures a prophecy and a promise from Jove to the effect that Aeneas is to found a royal line that shall rule the world. After the burning of Troy, Aeneas is directed by various signs to sail for the Latian lands (Italy) where his destiny awaits him. After many misadventures, he is compelled (like Dante) to descend to the underworld of the dead. There he finds his father's shade, and there he is shown the shades of the great kings that are to stem from him. (*Aeneid* VI, 921 ff.) Among them are Romulus, Julius Caesar, and Augustus Caesar. The full glory of the Roman Empire is also foreshadowed to him.

Dante, however, continues the Virgilian theme and includes in the predestination not only the Roman Empire but the Holy Roman Empire and its Church. Thus what Virgil presented as an arrangement of Jove, a concession to the son of Venus, becomes part of the divine scheme of the Catholic God, and Aeneas is cast as a direct forerunner of Peter and Paul.

13. *father of Sylvius:* Aeneas.

51-52. *I was a soul among the souls in Limbo:* See Canto IV, lines 31-45, where Virgil explains his state in Hell.

78. *the heaven of the smallest circle:* The moon. "Heaven" here is used in its astronomical sense. All within that circle is the earth. According to the Ptolemaic system the earth was the center of creation and was surrounded by nine heavenly spheres (nine heavens) concentrically placed around it. The moon was the first of these, and therefore the smallest. A cross section of this universe could be represented by drawing nine concentric circles (at varying distances about the earth as a center). Going outward from the center these circles would indicate, in order, the spheres of

The Moon
Mercury
Venus
The Sun
Mars
Jupiter
Saturn
The Fixed Stars
The Primum Mobile

Beyond the Primum Mobile lies the Empyrean.

97. *Lucia:* (Loo-TCHEE-yah) Allegorically she represents Divine Light. Her name in Italian inevitably suggests "luce" (light), and she is the patron saint of eyesight. By a process quite common in medieval religion, the special powers attributed to Lucia seem to have been suggested by her name rather than her history. (In France, by a similar process, St. Clair is the patroness of sight.)

102. *Rachel:* Represents the Contemplative Life.

A note on "thee" and "thou": except for the quotations from the souls in Heaven, and for Dante's fervent declamation to Virgil, I have insisted on "you" as the preferable pronoun form. I have used "thee" and "thou" in these cases with the idea that they might help to indicate the extraordinary elevation of the speakers and of the persons addressed.

Canto III

AU

THE VESTIBULE OF HELL ***The Opportunists***

The Poets pass the Gate of Hell and are immediately assailed by cries of anguish. Dante sees the first of the souls in torment. They are THE OPPORTUNISTS, those souls who in life were neither for good nor evil but only for themselves. Mixed with them are those outcasts who took no sides in the Rebellion of the Angels. They are neither in Hell nor out of it. Eternally unclassified, they race round and round pursuing a wavering banner that runs forever before them through the dirty air; and as they run they are pursued by swarms of wasps and hornets, who sting them and produce a constant flow of blood and putrid matter which trickles down the bodies of the sinners and is feasted upon by loathsome worms and maggots who coat the ground.

The law of Dante's Hell is the law of symbolic retribution. As they sinned so are they punished. They took no sides, therefore they are given no place. As they pursued the ever-shifting illusion of their own advantage, changing their courses with every changing wind, so they pursue eternally an elusive, ever-shifting banner. As their sin was a darkness, so they move in darkness. As their own guilty conscience pursued them, so they are pursued by swarms of wasps and hornets. And as their actions were a moral filth, so they run eternally through the filth of worms and maggots which they themselves feed.

Dante recognizes several, among them POPE CELESTINE V, but without delaying to speak to any of these souls, the Poets move on to ACHERON, the first of the rivers of Hell. Here the newly-arrived souls of the damned gather and wait for monstrous CHARON to ferry them over to punishment. Charon recognizes Dante as a living man and angrily refuses him passage. Virgil forces Charon to serve them, but Dante swoons with terror, and does not reawaken until he is on the other side.

I AM THE WAY INTO THE CITY OF WOE.
I AM THE WAY TO A FORSAKEN PEOPLE.
I AM THE WAY INTO ETERNAL SORROW.

SACRED JUSTICE MOVED MY ARCHITECT.
I WAS RAISED HERE BY DIVINE OMNIPOTENCE,
PRIMORDIAL LOVE AND ULTIMATE INTELLECT.

ONLY THOSE ELEMENTS TIME CANNOT WEAR
WERE MADE BEFORE ME, AND BEYOND TIME I STAND.
ABANDON ALL HOPE YE WHO ENTER HERE.

These mysteries I read cut into stone
above a gate. And turning I said: "Master,
what is the meaning of this harsh inscription?"

And he then as initiate to novice:
"Here must you put by all division of spirit
and gather your soul against all cowardice.

This is the place I told you to expect.
Here you shall pass among the fallen people,
souls who have lost the good of intellect."

So saying, he put forth his hand to me,
and with a gentle and encouraging smile
he led me through the gate of mystery.

Here sighs and cries and wails coiled and recoiled
on the starless air, spilling my soul to tears.
A confusion of tongues and monstrous accents toiled

in pain and anger. Voices hoarse and shrill
and sounds of blows, all intermingled, raised
tumult and pandemonium that still

whirls on the air forever dirty with it
as if a whirlwind sucked at sand. And I,
holding my head in horror, cried: "Sweet Spirit,

what souls are these who run through this black haze?"
And he to me: "These are the nearly soulless
whose lives concluded neither blame nor praise.

They are mixed here with that despicable corps
of angels who were neither for God nor Satan,
but only for themselves. The High Creator

scourged them from Heaven for its perfect beauty,
and Hell will not receive them since the wicked
might feel some glory over them." And I:

"Master, what gnaws at them so hideously
their lamentation stuns the very air?"
"They have no hope of death," he answered me,

"and in their blind and unattaining state
their miserable lives have sunk so low
that they must envy every other fate.

No word of them survives their living season.
Mercy and Justice deny them even a name.
Let us not speak of them: look, and pass on."

I saw a banner there upon the mist.
Circling and circling, it seemed to scorn all pause.
So it ran on, and still behind it pressed

a never-ending rout of souls in pain.
I had not thought death had undone so many
as passed before me in that mournful train.

And some I knew among them; last of all
I recognized the shadow of that soul
who, in his cowardice, made the Great Denial.

At once I understood for certain: these
were of that retrograde and faithless crew
hateful to God and to His enemies.

These wretches never born and never dead
ran naked in a swarm of wasps and hornets
that goaded them the more the more they fled,

and made their faces stream with bloody gouts
of pus and tears that dribbled to their feet
to be swallowed there by loathsome worms and maggots.

Then looking onward I made out a throng
assembled on the beach of a wide river,
whereupon I turned to him: "Master, I long

to know what souls these are, and what strange usage
makes them as eager to cross as they seem to be
in this infected light." At which the Sage:

"All this shall be made known to you when we stand
on the joyless beach of Acheron." And I
cast down my eyes, sensing a reprimand

in what he said, and so walked at his side
in silence and ashamed until we came
through the dead cavern to that sunless tide.

There, steering toward us in an ancient ferry
came an old man with a white bush of hair,
bellowing: "Woe to you depraved souls! Bury

here and forever all hope of Paradise:
I come to lead you to the other shore,
into eternal dark, into fire and ice.

And you who are living yet, I say begone
from these who are dead." But when he saw me stand
against his violence he began again:

"By other windings and by other steerage
shall you cross to that other shore. Not here! Not here!
A lighter craft than mine must give you passage."

And my Guide to him: "Charon, bite back your spleen:
this has been willed where what is willed must be,
and is not yours to ask what it may mean."

The steersman of that marsh of ruined souls,
who wore a wheel of flame around each eye,
stifled the rage that shook his woolly jowls.

But those unmanned and naked spirits there
turned pale with fear and their teeth began to chatter
at sound of his crude bellow. In despair

they blasphemed God, their parents, their time on earth,
the race of Adam, and the day and the hour
and the place and the seed and the womb that gave them birth.

But all together they drew to that grim shore
where all must come who lose the fear of God.
Weeping and cursing they come for evermore,

and demon Charon with eyes like burning coals
herds them in, and with a whistling oar
flails on the stragglers to his wake of souls.

As leaves in autumn loosen and stream down
until the branch stands bare above its tatters
spread on the rustling ground, so one by one

the evil seed of Adam in its Fall
cast themselves, at his signal, from the shore
and streamed away like birds who hear their call.

So they are gone over that shadowy water,
and always before they reach the other shore
a new noise stirs on this, and new throngs gather.

"My son," the courteous Master said to me,
"all who die in the shadow of God's wrath
converge to this from every clime and country.

And all pass over eagerly, for here
Divine Justice transforms and spurs them so
their dread turns wish: they yearn for what they fear.

No soul in Grace comes ever to this crossing;
therefore if Charon rages at your presence
you will understand the reason for his cursing."

When he had spoken, all the twilight country
shook so violently, the terror of it
bathes me with sweat even in memory:

the tear-soaked ground gave out a sigh of wind
that spewed itself in flame on a red sky,
and all my shattered senses left me. Blind,

like one whom sleep comes over in a swoon,
I stumbled into darkness and went down.

Notes

7-8. *Only those elements time cannot wear:* The Angels, the Empyrean, and the First Matter are the elements time cannot wear, for they will last to all time. Man, however, in his mortal state, is not eternal. The Gate of Hell, therefore, was created before man. The theological point is worth attention. The doctrine of Original Sin is, of course, one familiar to many creeds. Here, however, it would seem that the preparation for damnation predates Original Sin. True, in one interpretation, Hell was created for the punishment of the Rebellious Angels and not for man. Had man not sinned, he would never have known Hell. But on the other hand, Dante's God was one who knew all, and knew therefore that man would indeed sin. The theological problem is an extremely delicate one.

It is significant, however, that having sinned, man lives out his days on the rind of Hell, and that damnation is forever below his feet. This central concept of man's sinfulness, and, opposed to it, the doctrine of Christ's ever-abounding mercy, are central to all of Dante's theology. Only as man surrenders himself to Divine Love may he hope for salvation, and salvation is open to all who will surrender themselves.

8. *and to all time I stand:* So odious is sin to God that there can be no end to its just punishment.

9. *Abandon all hope ye who enter here:* The admonition, of course, is to the damned and not to those who come on Heaven-sent errands. The Harrowing of Hell (see Canto IV, note to l. 53)

provided the only exemption from this decree, and that only through the direct intercession of Christ.

57. *who, in his cowardice, made the Great Denial:* This is almost certainly intended to be Celestine V, who became Pope in 1294. He was a man of saintly life, but allowed himself to be convinced by a priest named Benedetto that his soul was in danger since no man could live in the world without being damned. In fear for his soul he withdrew from all worldly affairs and renounced the papacy. Benedetto promptly assumed the mantle himself and became Boniface VIII, a Pope who became for Dante a symbol of all the worst corruptions of the church. Dante also blamed Boniface and his intrigues for many of the evils that befell Florence. We shall learn in Canto XIX that the fires of Hell are waiting for Boniface in the pit of the Simoniacs, and we shall be given further evidence of his corruption in Canto XXVII. Celestine's great guilt is that his cowardice (in selfish terror for his own welfare) served as the door through which so much evil entered the church.

80. *an old man:* Charon. He is the ferryman of dead souls across the Acheron in all classical mythology.

88-90. *By other windings:* Charon recognizes Dante not only as a living man but as a soul in grace, and knows, therefore, that the Infernal Ferry was not intended for him. He is probably referring to the fact that souls destined for Purgatory and Heaven assemble not at his ferry point, but on the banks of the Tiber, from which they are transported by an Angel.

100. *they blasphemed God:* The souls of the damned are not permitted to repent, for repentance is a divine grace.

123. *they yearn for what they fear:* Hell (allegorically Sin) is what the souls of the damned really wish for. Hell is their actual and deliberate choice, for divine grace is denied to none who wish for it in their hearts. The damned must, in fact, deliberately harden their hearts to God in order to become damned. Christ's grace is sufficient to save all who wish for it.

133-34 DANTE'S SWOON: This device (repeated at the end of Canto V) serves a double purpose. The first is technical: Dante uses it to cover a transition. We are never told how he crossed Acheron, for that would involve certain narrative matters he can better deal with when he crosses Styx in Canto VII. The second is to provide a point of departure for a theme that is carried through the entire descent: the theme of Dante's emotional reaction to Hell. These two swoons early in the descent show him most susceptible to the grief about him. As he descends, pity leaves him, and he even goes so far as to add to the torments of one sinner. The allegory is clear: we must harden ourselves against every sympathy for sin.

HELL

FIRST SEVEN CIRCLES

GATE OF HELL

VESTIBULE: OPPORTUNISTS

ACHERON: CHARON

CIRCLE I (LIMBO) VIRTUOUS PAGANS AND UNBAPTIZED CHILDREN

MINOS

CIRCLE II: THE CARNAL

CERBERUS

CIRCLE III: THE GLUTTONOUS

PLUTUS

CIRCLE IV: HOARDERS AND WASTERS

THE GREAT TOWER

CIRCLE V (STYX): WRATHFUL AND SULLEN

PHLEGYAS

WALLS OF DIS (FIENDS AND FURIES)

CIRCLE VI: HERETICS

THE MINOTAUR

CENTAURS

PHLEGETHON (ROUND I OF CIRCLE VII)

WOOD OF SUICIDES (ROUND II OF CIRCLE VII) HARPIES

BURNING PLAIN (ROUND III OF CIRCLE VII)

GERYON

WATERFALL

X = STATIONS OF MONSTERS

Canto IV

CIRCLE ONE: *Limbo* *The Virtuous Pagans*

Dante wakes to find himself across Acheron. The Poets are now on the brink of Hell itself, which Dante conceives as a great funnel-shaped cave lying below the northern hemisphere with its bottom point at the earth's center. Around this great circular depression runs a series of ledges, each of which Dante calls a CIRCLE. Each circle is assigned to the punishment of one category of sin.

As soon as Dante's strength returns, the Poets begin to cross the FIRST CIRCLE. Here they find the VIRTUOUS PAGANS. They were born without the light of Christ's revelation, and, therefore, they cannot come into the light of God, but they are not tormented. Their only pain is that they have no hope.

Ahead of them Dante sights a great dome of light, and a voice trumpets through the darkness welcoming Virgil back, for this is his eternal place in Hell. Immediately the great Poets of all time appear—HOMER, HORACE, OVID, and LUCAN. They greet Virgil, and they make Dante a sixth in their company.

With them Dante enters the Citadel of Human Reason and sees before his eyes the Master Souls of Pagan Antiquity gathered on a green, and illuminated by the radiance of Human Reason. This is the highest state man can achieve without God, and the glory of it dazzles Dante, but he knows also that it is nothing compared to the glory of God.

A monstrous clap of thunder broke apart
  the swoon that stuffed my head; like one awakened
  by violent hands, I leaped up with a start.

And having risen; rested and renewed,
I studied out the landmarks of the gloom
to find my bearings there as best I could.

And I found I stood on the very brink of the valley
called the Dolorous Abyss, the desolate chasm
where rolls the thunder of Hell's eternal cry,

so depthless-deep and nebulous and dim
that stare as I might into its frightful pit
it gave me back no feature and no bottom.

Death-pale, the Poet spoke: "Now let us go
into the blind world waiting here below us.
I will lead the way and you shall follow."

And I, sick with alarm at his new pallor,
cried out, "How can I go this way when you
who are my strength in doubt turn pale with terror?"

And he: "The pain of these below us here,
drains the color from my face for pity,
and leaves this pallor you mistake for fear.

Now let us go, for a long road awaits us."
So he entered and so he led me in
to the first circle and ledge of the abyss.

No tortured wailing rose to greet us here
but sounds of sighing rose from every side,
sending a tremor through the timeless air,

a grief breathed out of untormented sadness,
the passive state of those who dwelled apart,
men, women, children—a dim and endless congress.

And the Master said to me: "You do not question
what souls these are that suffer here before you?
I wish you to know before you travel on

that these were sinless. And still their merits fail,
for they lacked Baptism's grace, which is the door
of the true faith *you* were born to. Their birth fell

before the age of the Christian mysteries,
and so they did not worship God's Trinity
in fullest duty. I am one of these.

For such defects are we lost, though spared the fire
and suffering Hell in one affliction only:
that without hope we live on in desire."

I thought how many worthy souls there were
suspended in that Limbo, and a weight
closed on my heart for what the noblest suffer.

"Instruct me, Master and most noble Sir,"
I prayed him then, "better to understand
the perfect creed that conquers every error:

has any, by his own or another's merit,
gone ever from this place to blessedness?"
He sensed my inner question and answered it:

"I was still new to this estate of tears
when a Mighty One descended here among us,
crowned with the sign of His victorious years.

He took from us the shade of our first parent,
of Abel, his pure son, of ancient Noah,
of Moses, the bringer of law, the obedient.

Father Abraham, David the King,
Israel with his father and his children,
Rachel, the holy vessel of His blessing,

and many more He chose for elevation
among the elect. And before these, you must know,
no human soul had ever won salvation."

We had not paused as he spoke, but held our road
and passed meanwhile beyond a press of souls
crowded about like trees in a thick wood.

And we had not traveled far from where I woke
when I made out a radiance before us
that struck away a hemisphere of dark.

We were still some distance back in the long night,
yet near enough that I half-saw, half-sensed,
what quality of souls lived in that light.

"O ornament of wisdom and of art,
what souls are these whose merit lights their way
even in Hell. What joy sets them apart?"

And he to me: "The signature of honor
they left on earth is recognized in Heaven
and wins them ease in Hell out of God's favor."

And as he spoke a voice rang on the air:
"Honor the Prince of Poets; the soul and glory
that went from us returns. He is here! He is here!"

The cry ceased and the echo passed from hearing;
I saw four mighty presences come toward us
with neither joy nor sorrow in their bearing.

"Note well," my Master said as they came on,
"that soul that leads the rest with sword in hand
as if he were their captain and champion.

It is Homer, singing master of the earth.
Next after him is Horace, the satirist,
Ovid is third, and Lucan is the fourth.

Since all of these have part in the high name
the voice proclaimed, calling me Prince of Poets,
the honor that they do me honors them."

So I saw gathered at the edge of light
the masters of that highest school whose song
outsoars all others like an eagle's flight.

And after they had talked together a while,
they turned and welcomed me most graciously,
at which I saw my approving Master smile.

And they honored me far beyond courtesy,
for they included me in their own number,
making me sixth in that high company.

So we moved toward the light, and as we passed
we spoke of things as well omitted here
as it was sweet to touch on there. At last

we reached the base of a great Citadel
circled by seven towering battlements
and by a sweet brook flowing round them all.

This we passed over as if it were firm ground.
Through seven gates I entered with those sages
and came to a green meadow blooming round.

There with a solemn and majestic poise
stood many people gathered in the light,
speaking infrequently and with muted voice.

Past that enameled green we six withdrew
into a luminous and open height
from which each soul among them stood in view.

And there directly before me on the green
the master souls of time were shown to me.
I glory in the glory I have seen!

Electra stood in a great company
among whom I saw Hector and Aeneas
and Caesar in armor with his falcon's eye.

I saw Camilla, and the Queen Amazon
across the field. I saw the Latian King
seated there with his daughter by his throne.

And the good Brutus who overthrew the Tarquin:
Lucrezia, Julia, Marcia, and Cornelia;
and, by himself apart, the Saladin.

And raising my eyes a little I saw on high
Aristotle, the master of those who know,
ringed by the great souls of philosophy.

All wait upon him for their honor and his.
I saw Socrates and Plato at his side
before all others there. Democritus

who ascribes the world to chance, Diogenes,
and with him there Thales, Anaxagoras,
Zeno, Heraclitus, Empedocles.

And I saw the wise collector and analyst—
Dioscorides I mean. I saw Orpheus there,
Tully, Linus, Seneca the moralist,

Euclid the geometer, and Ptolemy,
Hippocrates, Galen, Avicenna,
and Averrhoës of the Great Commentary.

I cannot count so much nobility;
my longer theme pursues me so that often
the word falls short of the reality.

The company of six is reduced by four.
My Master leads me by another road
out of that serenity to the roar

and trembling air of Hell. I pass from light
into the kingdom of eternal night.

Notes

13 ff. *death-pale:* Virgil is most likely affected here by the return to his own place in Hell. "The pain of these below" then (line 19) would be the pain of his own group in Limbo (the Virtuous Pagans) rather than the total of Hell's suffering.

31 ff. *You do not question:* A master touch of characterization. Virgil's *amour propre* is a bit piqued at Dante's lack of curiosity about the position in Hell of Virgil's own kind. And it may possibly be, by allegorical extension, that Human Reason must urge the soul to question the place of reason. The allegorical point is conjectural, but such conjecture is certainly one of the effects inherent in the use of allegory; when well used, the central symbols of the allegory continue indefinitely to suggest new interpretations and shades of meaning.

53. *a Mighty One:* Christ. His name is never directly uttered in Hell.

53. *descended here:* The legend of the Harrowing of Hell is Apocryphal. It is based on I *Peter* iii, 19: "He went and preached unto the spirits in prison." The legend is that Christ in the glory of His resurrection descended into Limbo and took with Him to Heaven the first human souls to be saved. The event would, accordingly, have occurred in 33 or 34 A.D. Virgil died in 19 B.C.

102. *making me sixth in that high company:* Merit and self-awareness of merit may well be a higher thing than modesty. An additional point Dante may well have had in mind, however, is the fact that he saw himself as one pledged to continue in his own times the classic tradition represented by these poets.

103-105. These lines amount to a stylistic note. It is good style (*'l tacere è bello* where *bello* equals "good style") to omit this discussion, since it would digress from the subject and, moreover, his point is already made. Every great narrator tends to tell his story from climax to climax. There are times on the other hand when Dante delights in digression. (See General Note to Canto XX.)

106. A GREAT CITADEL. The most likely allegory is that the Citadel represents philosophy (that is, human reason without the light of God) surrounded by seven walls which represent the seven liberal arts, or the seven sciences, or the seven virtues. Note that Human Reason makes a light of its own, but that it is a light in darkness and forever separated from the glory of God's light. The *sweet brook flowing* round them all has been interpreted in many ways. Clearly fundamental, however, is the fact that it divides those in the Citadel (those who wish to know) from those in the outer darkness.

109. *as if it were firm ground:* Since Dante still has his body, and since all others in Hell are incorporeal shades, there is a recurring narrative problem in the *Inferno* (and through the rest of the *Commedia*): how does flesh act in contact with spirit? In the *Purgatorio* Dante attempts to embrace the spirit of Casella and his arms pass through him as if he were empty air. In the Third Circle, below (Canto VI, 34-36), Dante steps on some of the spirits lying in the slush and his foot passes right through them. (The original lines offer several possible readings of which I have preferred this one.) And at other times Virgil, also a spirit, picks Dante up and carries him bodily.

It is clear, too, that Dante means the spirits of Hell to be weightless. When Virgil steps into Phlegyas' bark (Canto VIII) it does not settle into the water, but it does when Dante's living body steps aboard. There is no narrative reason why Dante should not sink into the waters of this stream and Dante follows no fixed rule in dealing with such phenomena, often suiting the physical action to the allegorical need. Here, the moat probably symbolizes some requirement (The Will to Know) which he and the other poets meet without difficulty.

THE INHABITANTS OF THE CITADEL. They fall into three main groups:

1. *The heroes and heroines:* All of these it must be noted were associated with the Trojans and their Roman descendants. (See note on AENEAS AND THE FOUNDING OF ROME, Canto II.) The Electra Dante mentions here is not the sister of Orestes (see Euripides' *Electra*) but the daughter of Atlas and the mother of Dardanus, the founder of Troy.

2. *The philosophers:* Most of this group is made up of philosophers whose teachings were, at least in part, acceptable to church scholarship. Democritus, however, "who ascribed the world to chance," would clearly be an exception. The group is best interpreted, therefore, as representing the highest achievements of Human Reason unaided by Divine Love. *Plato and Aristotle:* Through a considerable part of the Middle Ages Plato was held to be the fountainhead of all scholarship, but in Dante's time practically all learning was based on Aristotelian theory as interpreted through the many commentaries. *Linus:* the Italian is "Lino" and for it some commentators read "Livio" (Livy).

3. *The naturalists:* They are less well known today. In Dante's time their place in scholarship more or less corresponded to the role of the theoretician and historian of science in our universities. *Avicenna* (his major work was in the eleventh century) and *Avverhoës* (twelfth century) were Arabian philosophers and physicians especially famous in Dante's time for their commentaries on Aristotle. *Great Commentary:* has the force of a title, i.e., The Great Commentary as distinguished from many lesser commentaries.

The Saladin: This is the famous Saladin who was defeated by Richard the Lion-Heart, and whose great qualities as a ruler became a legend in medieval Europe.

Canto V

CIRCLE TWO *The Carnal*

The Poets leave Limbo and enter the SECOND CIRCLE. Here begin the torments of Hell proper, and here, blocking the way, sits MINOS, the dread and semi-bestial judge of the damned who assigns to each soul its eternal torment. He orders the Poets back; but Virgil silences him as he earlier silenced Charon, and the Poets move on.

They find themselves on a dark ledge swept by a great whirlwind, which spins within it the souls of the CARNAL, those who betrayed reason to their appetites. Their sin was to abandon themselves to the tempest of their passions: so they are swept forever in the tempest of Hell, forever denied the light of reason and of God. Virgil identifies many among them. SEMIRAMIS is there, and DIDO, CLEOPATRA, HELEN, ACHILLES, PARIS, and TRISTAN. Dante sees PAOLO and FRANCESCA swept together, and in the name of love he calls to them to tell their sad story. They pause from their eternal flight to come to him, and Francesca tells their history while Paolo weeps at her side. Dante is so stricken by compassion at their tragic tale that he swoons once again.

So we went down to the second ledge alone;
  a smaller circle of so much greater pain
  the voice of the damned rose in a bestial moan.

There Minos sits, grinning, grotesque, and hale.
  He examines each lost soul as it arrives
  and delivers his verdict with his coiling tail.

That is to say, when the ill-fated soul
appears before him it confesses all,
and that grim sorter of the dark and foul

decides which place in Hell shall be its end,
then wraps his twitching tail about himself
one coil for each degree it must descend.

The soul descends and others take its place:
each crowds in its turn to judgment, each confesses,
each hears its doom and falls away through space.

"O you who come into this camp of woe,"
cried Minos when he saw me turn away
without awaiting his judgment, "watch where you go

once you have entered here, and to whom you turn!
Do not be misled by that wide and easy passage!"
And my Guide to him: "That is not your concern;

it is his fate to enter every door.
This has been willed where what is willed must be,
and is not yours to question. Say no more."

Now the choir of anguish, like a wound,
strikes through the tortured air. Now I have come
to Hell's full lamentation, sound beyond sound.

I came to a place stripped bare of every light
and roaring on the naked dark like seas
wracked by a war of winds. Their hellish flight

of storm and counterstorm through time foregone,
sweeps the souls of the damned before its charge.
Whirling and battering it drives them on,

and when they pass the ruined gap of Hell
through which we had come, their shrieks begin anew.
There they blaspheme the power of God eternal.

And this, I learned, was the never ending flight
of those who sinned in the flesh, the carnal and lusty
who betrayed reason to their appetite.

As the wings of wintering starlings bear them on
in their great wheeling flights, just so the blast
wherries these evil souls through time foregone.

Here, there, up, down, they whirl and, whirling, strain
with never a hope of hope to comfort them,
not of release, but even of less pain.

As cranes go over sounding their harsh cry,
leaving the long streak of their flight in air,
so come these spirits, wailing as they fly.

And watching their shadows lashed by wind, I cried:
"Master, what souls are these the very air
lashes with its black whips from side to side?"

"The first of these whose history you would know,"
he answered me, "was Empress of many tongues.
Mad sensuality corrupted her so

that to hide the guilt of her debauchery
she licensed all depravity alike,
and lust and law were one in her decree.

She is Semiramis of whom the tale is told
how she married Ninus and succeeded him
to the throne of that wide land the Sultans hold.

The other is Dido; faithless to the ashes
of Sichaeus, she killed herself for love.
The next whom the eternal tempest lashes

is sense-drugged Cleopatra. See Helen there,
from whom such ill arose. And great Achilles,
who fought at last with love in the house of prayer.

And Paris. And Tristan." As they whirled above
he pointed out more than a thousand shades
of those torn from the mortal life by love.

I stood there while my Teacher one by one
named the great knights and ladies of dim time;
and I was swept by pity and confusion.

At last I spoke: "Poet, I should be glad
to speak a word with those two swept together
so lightly on the wind and still so sad."

And he to me: "Watch them. When next they pass,
call to them in the name of love that drives
and damns them here. In that name they will pause."

Thus, as soon as the wind in its wild course
brought them around, I called: "O wearied souls!
if none forbid it, pause and speak to us."

As mating doves that love calls to their nest
glide through the air with motionless raised wings,
borne by the sweet desire that fills each breast—

Just so those spirits turned on the torn sky
from the band where Dido whirls across the air;
such was the power of pity in my cry.

"O living creature, gracious, kind, and good,
going this pilgrimage through the sick night,
visiting us who stained the earth with blood,

were the King of Time our friend, we would pray His peace
on you who have pitied us. As long as the wind
will let us pause, ask of us what you please.

The town where I was born lies by the shore
where the Po descends into its ocean rest
with its attendant streams in one long murmur.

Love, which in gentlest hearts will soonest bloom
seized my lover with passion for that sweet body
from which I was torn unshriven to my doom.

Love, which permits no loved one not to love,
took me so strongly with delight in him
that we are one in Hell, as we were above.

Love led us to one death. In the depths of Hell
Caïna waits for him who took our lives."
This was the piteous tale they stopped to tell.

And when I had heard those world-offended lovers
I bowed my head. At last the Poet spoke:
"What painful thoughts are these your lowered brow covers?"

When at length I answered, I began: "Alas!
What sweetest thoughts, what green and young desire
led these two lovers to this sorry pass."

Then turning to those spirits once again,
I said: "Francesca, what you suffer here
melts me to tears of pity and of pain.

But tell me: in the time of your sweet sighs
by what appearances found love the way
to lure you to his perilous paradise?"

And she: "The double grief of a lost bliss
is to recall its happy hour in pain.
Your Guide and Teacher knows the truth of this.

But if there is indeed a soul in Hell
to ask of the beginning of our love
out of his pity, I will weep and tell:

On a day for dalliance we read the rhyme
of Lancelot, how love had mastered him.
We were alone with innocence and dim time.

Pause after pause that high old story drew
  our eyes together while we blushed and paled;
  but it was one soft passage overthrew

our caution and our hearts. For when we read
  how her fond smile was kissed by such a lover,
  he who is one with me alive and dead

breathed on my lips the tremor of his kiss.
  That book, and he who wrote it, was a pander.
  That day we read no further." As she said this,

the other spirit, who stood by her, wept
  so piteously, I felt my senses reel
  and faint away with anguish. I was swept

by such a swoon as death is, and I fell,
as a corpse might fall, to the dead floor of Hell.

Notes

2. *a smaller circle:* The pit of Hell tapers like a funnel. The circles of ledges accordingly grow smaller as they descend.

4. *Minos:* Like all the monsters Dante assigns to the various offices of Hell, Minos is drawn from classical mythology. He was the son of Europa and of Zeus who descended to her in the form of a bull. Minos became a mythological king of Crete, so famous for his wisdom and justice that after death his soul was made judge of the dead. Virgil presents him fulfilling the same office at Aeneas' descent to the underworld. Dante, however, transforms him into an irate and hideous monster with a tail. The transformation may have been suggested by the form Zeus assumed for the rape of Europa—the monster is certainly bullish enough here—but the obvious purpose of the brutalization is to present a figure symbolic of the guilty conscience of the wretches who come before it to make their confessions. Dante freely reshapes his materials to his own purposes.

8. *it confesses all:* Just as the souls appeared eager to cross Acheron, so they are eager to confess even while they dread. Dante is once again making the point that sinners elect their Hell by an act of their own will.

27. *Hell's full lamentation:* It is with the second circle that the real tortures of Hell begin.

34. *the ruined gap of Hell:* See note to Canto II, 53. At the time of the Harrowing of Hell a great earthquake shook the underworld shattering rocks and cliffs. Ruins resulting from the same shock are noted in Canto XII, 34, and Canto XXI, 112 ff. At the beginning of Canto XXIV, the Poets leave the *bolgia* of the Hypocrites by climbing the ruined slabs of a bridge that was shattered by this earthquake.

THE SINNERS OF THE SECOND CIRCLE (THE CARNAL): Here begin the punishments for the various sins of Incontinence (The sins of the She-Wolf). In the second circle are punished those who sinned by excess of sexual passion. Since this is the most natural sin and the sin most nearly associated with love, its punishment is the lightest of all to be found in Hell proper. The Carnal are whirled and buffeted endlessly through the murky air (symbolic of the beclouding of their reason by passion) by a great gale (symbolic of their lust).

53. *Empress of many tongues:* Semiramis, a legendary queen of Assyria who assumed full power at the death of her husband, Ninus.

61. *Dido:* Queen and founder of Carthage. She had vowed to remain faithful to her husband, Sichaeus, but she fell in love with Aeneas. When Aeneas abandoned her she stabbed herself on a funeral pyre she had had prepared.

According to Dante's own system of punishments, she should be in the Seventh Circle (Canto XIII) with the suicides. The only clue Dante gives to the tempering of her punishment is his statement that "she killed herself for love." Dante always seems readiest to forgive in that name.

65. *Achilles:* He is placed among this company because of his passion for Polyxena, the daughter of Priam. For love of her, he agreed to desert the Greeks and to join the Trojans, but when he went to the temple for the wedding (according to the legend Dante has followed) he was killed by Paris.

74. *those two swept together:* Paolo and Francesca (PAH-oe-loe: Frahn-CHAY-ska).

Dante's treatment of these two lovers is certainly the tenderest and most sympathetic accorded any of the sinners in Hell, and legends immediately began to grow about this pair.

The facts are these. In 1275 Giovanni Malatesta (Djoe-VAH-nee Mahl-ah-TEH-stah) of Rimini, called Giovanni the Lame, a somewhat deformed but brave and powerful warrior, made a political marriage with Francesca, daughter of Guido da Polenta of Ravenna. Francesca came to Rimini and there an amour grew between her and Giovanni's younger brother Paolo. Despite the fact that Paolo had married in 1269 and had become the father of two daughters by 1275, his affair with Francesca continued for many years. It was sometime between 1283 and 1286 that Giovanni surprised them in Francesca's bedroom and killed both of them.

Around these facts the legend has grown that Paolo was sent by Giovanni as his proxy to the marriage, that Francesca thought he was her real bridegroom and accordingly gave him her heart irrevocably at first sight. The legend obviously increases the pathos, but nothing in Dante gives it support.

102. *that we are one in Hell, as we were above:* At many points of *The Inferno* Dante makes clear the principle that the souls of the damned are locked so blindly into their own guilt that none can feel sympathy for another, or find any pleasure in the presence of another. The temptation of many readers is to interpret this line romantically: *i.e.,* that the love of Paolo and Francesca survives Hell itself. The more Dantean interpretation, however, is that they add to one another's anguish (a) as mutual reminders of their sin, and (b) as insubstantial shades of the bodies for which they once felt such great passion.

104. *Caïna waits for him:* Giovanni Malatesta was still alive at the writing. His fate is already decided, however, and upon his death, his soul will fall to Caïna, the first ring of the last circle (Canto XXXII), where lie those who performed acts of treachery against their kin.

124-5. *the rhyme of Lancelot:* The story exists in many forms. The details Dante makes use of are from an Old French version.

126. *dim time:* The original simply reads "We were alone, suspecting nothing." "Dim time" is rhyme-forced, but not wholly outside the legitimate implications of the original, I hope. The old courtly romance may well be thought of as happening in the dim ancient days. The apology, of course, comes after the fact: one does the possible then argues for justification, and there probably is none.

134. *that book, and he who wrote it, was a pander:* "Galeotto," the Italian word for "pander," is also the Italian rendering of the name of Gallehault, who in the French Romance Dante refers to here, urged Lancelot and Guinevere on to love.

Canto VI

CIRCLE THREE ***The Gluttons***

Dante recovers from his swoon and finds himself in the THIRD CIRCLE. A great storm of putrefaction falls incessantly, a mixture of stinking snow and freezing rain, which forms into a vile slush underfoot. Everything about this Circle suggests a gigantic garbage dump. The souls of the damned lie in the icy paste, swollen and obscene, and CERBERUS, the ravenous three-headed dog of Hell, stands guard over them, ripping and tearing them with his claws and teeth.

These are the GLUTTONS. In life they made no higher use of the gifts of God than to wallow in food and drink, producers of nothing but garbage and offal. Here they lie through all eternity, themselves like garbage, half-buried in fetid slush, while Cerberus slavers over them as they in life slavered over their food.

As the Poets pass, one of the speakers sits up and addresses Dante. He is CIACCO, THE HOG, a citizen of Dante's own Florence. He recognizes Dante and asks eagerly for news of what is happening there. With the foreknowledge of the damned, Ciacco then utters the first of the political prophecies that are to become a recurring theme of the Inferno. The Poets then move on toward the next Circle, at the edge of which they encounter the monster Plutus.

My senses had reeled from me out of pity
  for the sorrow of those kinsmen and lost lovers.
  Now they return, and waking gradually,

I see new torments and new souls in pain
  about me everywhere. Wherever I turn
  away from grief I turn to grief again.

I am in the Third Circle of the torments.
Here to all time with neither pause nor change
the frozen rain of Hell descends in torrents.

Huge hailstones, dirty water, and black snow
pour from the dismal air to putrefy
the putrid slush that waits for them below.

Here monstrous Cerberus, the ravening beast,
howls through his triple throats like a mad dog
over the spirits sunk in that foul paste.

His eyes are red, his beard is greased with phlegm,
his belly is swollen, and his hands are claws
to rip the wretches and flay and mangle them.

And they, too, howl like dogs in the freezing storm,
turning and turning from it as if they thought
one naked side could keep the other warm.

When Cerberus discovered us in that swill
his dragon-jaws yawed wide, his lips drew back
in a grin of fangs. No limb of him was still.

My Guide bent down and seized in either fist
a clod of the stinking dirt that festered there
and flung them down the gullet of the beast.

As a hungry cur will set the echoes raving
and then fall still when he is thrown a bone,
all of his clamor being in his craving,

so the three ugly heads of Cerberus,
whose yowling at those wretches deafened them,
choked on their putrid sops and stopped their fuss.

We made our way across the sodden mess
of souls the rain beat down, and when our steps
fell on a body, they sank through emptiness.

All those illusions of being seemed to lie
drowned in the slush; until one wraith among them
sat up abruptly and called as I passed by:

"O you who are led this journey through the shade
of Hell's abyss, do you recall this face?
You had been made before I was unmade."

And I: "Perhaps the pain you suffer here
distorts your image from my recollection.
I do not know you as you now appear."

And he to me: "Your own city, so rife
with hatred that the bitter cup flows over
was mine too in that other, clearer life.

Your citizens nicknamed me Ciacco, The Hog:
gluttony was my offense, and for it
I lie here rotting like a swollen log.

Nor am I lost in this alone; all these
you see about you in this painful death
have wallowed in the same indecencies."

I answered him: "Ciacco, your agony
weighs on my heart and calls my soul to tears;
but tell me, if you can, what is to be

for the citizens of that divided state,
and whether there are honest men among them,
and for what reasons we are torn by hate."

And he then: "After many words given and taken
it shall come to blood; White shall rise over Black
and rout the dark lord's force, battered and shaken.

Then it shall come to pass within three suns
that the fallen shall arise, and by the power
of one now gripped by many hesitations

Black shall ride on White for many years,
loading it down with burdens and oppressions
and humbling of proud names and helpless tears.

Two are honest, but none will heed them. There,
pride, avarice, and envy are the tongues
men know and heed, a Babel of despair."

Here he broke off his mournful prophecy.
And I to him: "Still let me urge you on
to speak a little further and instruct me:

Farinata and Tegghiaio, men of good blood,
Jacopo Rusticucci, Arrigo, Mosca,
and the others who set their hearts on doing good—

where are they now whose high deeds might be-gem
the crown of kings? I long to know their fate.
Does Heaven soothe or Hell envenom them?"

And he: "They lie below in a blacker lair.
A heavier guilt draws them to greater pain.
If you descend so far you may see them there.

But when you move again among the living,
oh speak my name to the memory of men!
Having answered all, I say no more." And giving

his head a shake, he looked up at my face
cross-eyed, then bowed his head and fell away
among the other blind souls of that place.

And my Guide to me: "He will not wake again
until the angel trumpet sounds the day
on which the host shall come to judge all men.

Then shall each soul before the seat of Mercy
return to its sad grave and flesh and form
to hear the edict of Eternity."

So we picked our slow way among the shades
and the filthy rain, speaking of life to come.
"Master," I said, "when the great clarion fades

into the voice of thundering Omniscience,
what of these agonies? Will they be the same,
or more, or less, after the final sentence?"

And he to me: "Look to your science again
where it is written: the more a thing is perfect
the more it feels of pleasure and of pain.

As for these souls, though they can never soar
  to true perfection, still in the new time
  they will be nearer it than they were before."

And so we walked the rim of the great ledge
  speaking of pain and joy, and of much more
  that I will not repeat, and reached the edge

where the descent begins. There, suddenly,
we came on Plutus, the great enemy.

Notes

13. *Cerberus:* In classical mythology Cerberus appears as a three-headed dog. His master was Pluto, king of the Underworld. Cerberus was placed at the Gate of the Underworld to allow all to enter, but none to escape. His three heads and his ravenous disposition make him an apt symbol of gluttony.

14. *like a mad dog:* Cerberus *is* a dog in classical mythology, but Dante seems clearly to have visualized him as a half-human monster. The beard (line 16) suggests that at least one of his three heads is human, and many illuminated manuscripts so represent him.

38. *until one wraith among them:* As the Poets pass, one of the damned sits up and asks if Dante recognizes him. Dante replies that he does not, and the wraith identifies himself as a Florentine nicknamed Ciacco, *i.e.*, The Hog.

Little is known about Ciacco (TCHA-koe). Boccaccio refers to a Florentine named Ciacco (Decameron IX, 8), and several conflicting accounts of him have been offered by various commentators. All that need be known about him, however, is the nature of his sin and the fact that he is a Florentine. Whatever else he may have been does not function in the poem.

42. *You had been made before I was unmade:* That is, "you were born before I died." The further implication is that they must have seen one another in Florence, a city one can still walk across in twenty minutes, and around in a very few hours. Dante certainly would have known everyone in Florence.

61. CIACCO'S PROPHECY: This is the first of the political prophecies that are to become a recurring theme of the *Inferno.* (It is the second if we include the political symbolism of the Greyhound in Canto I.) Dante is, of course, writing after these events have all

taken place. At Easter time of 1300, however, the events were in the future.

The Whites and the Blacks of Ciacco's prophecy should not be confused with the Guelphs and the Ghibellines. The internal strife between the Guelphs and the Ghibellines ended with the total defeat of the Ghibellines. By the end of the 13th century that strife had passed. But very shortly a new feud began in Florence between White Guelphs and Black Guelphs. A rather gruesome murder perpetrated by Focaccio de' Cancellieri (Foe-KAH-tchoe day Khan-tchell-YAIR-ee) became the cause of new strife between two branches of the Cancellieri family. On May 1 of 1300 the White Guelphs (Dante's party) drove the Black Guelphs from Florence in bloody fighting. Two years later, however ("within three suns"), the Blacks, aided by Dante's detested Boniface VIII, returned and expelled most of the prominent Whites, among them Dante; for he had been a member of the Priorate (City Council) that issued a decree banishing the leaders of both sides. This was the beginning of Dante's long exile from Florence.

70. *two are honest:* In the nature of prophecies this remains vague. The two are not identified.

76-77. FARINATA will appear in Canto X among the Heretics: TEGGHIAIO and JACOPO RUSTICUCCI, in Canto XVI with the homosexuals, MOSCA in Canto XXVIII with the sowers of discord. ARRIGO does not appear again and he has not been positively identified. Dante probably refers here to Arrigo (or Oderigo) dei Fifanti, one of those who took part in the murder of Buondelmonte (Canto XXVIII, line 106, note).

87. *speak my name:* Excepting those shades in the lowest depths of Hell whose sins are so shameful that they wish only to be forgotten, all of the damned are eager to be remembered on earth. The concept of the family name and of its survival in the memories of men were matters of first importance among Italians of Dante's time, and expressions of essentially the same attitude are common in Italy today.

103. *your science:* "Science" to the man of Dante's time meant specifically "the writings of Aristotle and the commentaries upon them."

Canto VII

CIRCLE FOUR *The Hoarders and the Wasters*

CIRCLE FIVE *The Wrathful and the Sullen*

PLUTUS menaces the Poets, but once more Virgil shows himself more powerful than the rages of Hell's monsters. The Poets enter the FOURTH CIRCLE and find what seems to be a war in progress.

The sinners are divided into two raging mobs, each soul among them straining madly at a great boulder-like weight. The two mobs meet, clashing their weights against one another, after which they separate, pushing the great weights apart, and begin over again.

One mob is made up of the HOARDERS, the other of the WASTERS. In life, they lacked all moderation in regulating their expenses; they destroyed the light of God within themselves by thinking of nothing but money. Thus in death, their souls are encumbered by dead weights (mundanity) and one excess serves to punish the other. Their souls, moreover, have become so dimmed and awry in their fruitless rages that there is no hope of recognizing any among them.

The Poets pass on while Virgil explains the function of DAME FORTUNE in the Divine Scheme. As he finishes (it is past midnight now of Good Friday) they reach the inner edge of the ledge and come to a Black Spring which bubbles murkily over the rocks to form the MARSH OF STYX, which is the FIFTH CIRCLE, the last station of the UPPER HELL.

Across the marsh they see countless souls attacking one another in the foul slime. These are the WRATHFUL and the symbolism of their punishment is obvious. Virgil also points out to Dante certain bubbles rising from the slime and informs him that below that mud lie entombed the souls of the SULLEN. In life they refused to welcome the sweet light of the Sun (Divine Illumination) and in death they are buried forever below the stinking waters of the Styx, gargling the words of an endless chant in a grotesque parody of singing a hymn.

"Papa Satán, Papa Satán, aleppy,"
  Plutus clucked and stuttered in his rage;
  and my all-knowing Guide, to comfort me:

"Do not be startled, for no power of his,
  however he may lord it over the damned,
  may hinder your descent through this abyss."

And turning to that carnival of bloat
  cried: "Peace, you wolf of Hell. Choke back your bile
  and let its venom blister your own throat.

Our passage through this pit is willed on high
  by that same Throne that loosed the angel wrath
  of Michael on ambition and mutiny."

As puffed out sails fall when the mast gives way
  and flutter to a self-convulsing heap—
  so collapsed Plutus into that dead clay.

Thus we descended the dark scarp of Hell
  to which all the evil of the Universe
  comes home at last, into the Fourth Great Circle

and ledge of the abyss. O Holy Justice,
  who could relate the agonies I saw!
  What guilt is man that he can come to this?

Just as the surge Charybdis hurls to sea
  crashes and breaks upon its countersurge,
  so these shades dance and crash eternally.

Here, too, I saw a nation of lost souls,
far more than were above: they strained their chests
against enormous weights, and with mad howls

rolled them at one another. Then in haste
they rolled them back, one party shouting out:
"Why do you hoard?" and the other: "Why do you waste?"

So back around that ring they puff and blow,
each faction to its course, until they reach
opposite sides, and screaming as they go

the madmen turn and start their weights again
to crash against the maniacs. And I,
watching, felt my heart contract with pain.

"Master," I said, "what people can these be?
And all those tonsured ones there on our left—
is it possible they *all* were of the clergy?"

And he: "In the first life beneath the sun
they were so skewed and squinteyed in their minds
their misering or extravagance mocked all reason.

The voice of each clamors its own excess
when lust meets lust at the two points of the circle
where opposite guilts meet in their wretchedness.

These tonsured wraiths of greed were priests indeed,
and popes and cardinals, for it is in these
the weed of avarice sows its rankest seed."

And I to him: "Master, among this crew
surely I should be able to make out
the fallen image of some soul I knew."

And he to me: "This is a lost ambition.
In their sordid lives they labored to be blind,
and now their souls have dimmed past recognition.

All their eternity is to butt and bray:
one crew will stand tight-fisted, the other stripped
of its very hair at the bar of Judgment Day.

Hoarding and squandering wasted all their light
and brought them screaming to this brawl of wraiths.
You need no words of mine to grasp their plight.

Now may you see the fleeting vanity
of the goods of Fortune for which men tear down
all that they are, to build a mockery.

Not all the gold that is or ever was
under the sky could buy for one of these
exhausted souls the fraction of a pause."

"Master," I said, "tell me—now that you touch
on this Dame Fortune—what *is* she, that she holds
the good things of the world within her clutch?"

And he to me: "O credulous mankind,
is there one error that has wooed and lost you?
Now listen, and strike error from your mind:

That king whose perfect wisdom transcends all,
made the heavens and posted angels on them
to guide the eternal light that it might fall

from every sphere to every sphere the same.
He made earth's splendors by a like decree
and posted as their minister this high Dame,

the Lady of Permutations. All earth's gear
she changes from nation to nation, from house to house,
in changeless change through every turning year.

No mortal power may stay her spinning wheel.
The nations rise and fall by her decree.
None may foresee where she will set her heel:

she passes, and things pass. Man's mortal reason
cannot encompass her. She rules her sphere
as the other gods rule theirs. Season by season

her changes change her changes endlessly,
and those whose turn has come press on her so,
she must be swift by hard necessity.

And this is she so railed at and reviled
that even her debtors in the joys of time
blaspheme her name. Their oaths are bitter and wild,

but she in her beatitude does not hear.
Among the Primal Beings of God's joy
she breathes her blessedness and wheels her sphere.

But the stars that marked our starting fall away.
We must go deeper into greater pain,
for it is not permitted that we stay."

And crossing over to the chasm's edge
we came to a spring that boiled and overflowed
through a great crevice worn into the ledge.

By that foul water, black from its very source,
we found a nightmare path among the rocks
and followed the dark stream along its course.

Beyond its rocky race and wild descent
the river floods and forms a marsh called Styx,
a dreary swampland, vaporous and malignant.

And I, intent on all our passage touched,
made out a swarm of spirits in that bog
savage with anger, naked, slime-besmutched.

They thumped at one another in that slime
with hands and feet, and they butted, and they bit
as if each would tear the other limb from limb.

And my kind Sage: "My son, behold the souls
of those who lived in wrath. And do you see
the broken surfaces of those water-holes

on every hand, boiling as if in pain?
There are souls beneath that water. Fixed in slime
they speak their piece, end it, and start again:

'Sullen were we in the air made sweet by the Sun;
in the glory of his shining our hearts poured
a bitter smoke. Sullen were we begun;

sullen we lie forever in this ditch.'
This litany they gargle in their throats
as if they sang, but lacked the words and pitch."

Then circling on along that filthy wallow,
we picked our way between the bank and fen,
keeping our eyes on those foul souls that swallow

the slime of Hell. And so at last we came
to foot of a Great Tower that has no name.

Notes

1. *Papa Satán, Papa Satán, aleppy:* Virgil, the all-knowing, may understand these words, but no one familiar with merely human languages has deciphered them. In Canto XXXI the monster Nimrod utters a similar meaningless jargon, and Virgil there cites it as evidence of the dimness of his mind. Gibberish is certainly a characteristic appropriate to monsters, and since Dante takes pains to make the reference to Satan apparent in the gibberish, it is obviously infernal and debased, and that is almost certainly all he intended.

The word "papa" as used here probably means "Pope" rather than "father." "Il papa santo" is the Pope. "Papa Satán" would be his opposite number. In the original the last word is "aleppe." On the assumption that jargon translates jargon I have twisted it a bit to rhyme with "me."

2. *Plutus:* In Greek mythology, Plutus was the God of Wealth. Many commentators suggest that Dante confused him with Pluto, the son of Saturn and God of the Underworld. But in that case, Plutus

would be identical with Lucifer himself and would require a central place in Hell, whereas the classical function of Plutus as God of Material Wealth makes him the ideal overseer of the miserly and the prodigal.

22. *Charybdis:* A famous whirlpool in the Straits of Sicily.

68. *Dame Fortune:* A central figure in medieval mythology. She is almost invariably represented as a female figure holding an ever-revolving wheel symbolic of Chance. Dante incorporates her into his scheme of the Universe, ranking her among the angels, and giving her a special office in the service of the Catholic God. This is the first of many passages in the *Commedia* in which Dante sets forth the details of the Divine Ordering of the universe.

84. *none may foresee where she will set her heel:* A literal translation of the original would be "She is hidden like a snake in the grass." To avoid the comic overtone of that figure in English, I have substituted another figure which I believe expresses Dante's intent without destroying his tone.

87. *the other gods:* Dante can only mean here "the other angels and ministers of God."

97. *But the stars that marked our starting fall away:* It is now past midnight of Good Friday.

101. *a black spring:* All the waters of Hell derive from one source (see Canto XIV, lines 12 following). This black spring must therefore be the waters of Acheron boiling out of some subterranean passage.

THE FIFTH CIRCLE (THE WRATHFUL AND THE SULLEN)

Dante's symbolism here is self-evident, but his reaction to these sinners is different from any we have observed thus far. Up to now he has either been appalled, or overcome by pity. In his ironic description of the Sullen he ridicules the damned for the first time. And in the next Canto he is to take pleasure (if only a passing pleasure) in increasing the sufferings of Filippo Argenti.

Dante will again be moved to pity as he descends the slopes of Hell. In fact, Virgil will find it necessary to scold him for pitying those whom God in His infinite wisdom has damned. Gradually, however, Dante's heart hardens against the damned as he descends lower and lower into Hell, and this development should be followed through the *Inferno* along with many other themes Dante carries and builds upon. There is no way of grasping the genius of Dante's architectonic power without noting his careful development of such themes. Even beyond the brilliance of his details, Dante's power is structural: everything relates to everything else.

107. *Styx:* The river Styx figures variously in classic mythology, but usually (and in later myths always) as a river of the Underworld. Dante, to heighten his symbolism, makes it a filthy marsh.

This marsh marks the first great division of Hell. Between Acheron and Styx are punished the sins of Incontinence (the Sins of the She-Wolf). This is the Upper Hell. Beyond Styx rise the flaming walls of the infernal city of Dis, within which are punished Violence and Fraud (the sins of the Lion, and the Sins of the Leopard). It is symbolically fitting that the approaches to the city of Hell should be across the filthiest of marshes.

131. *a Great Tower:* No special significance need be attributed to the Tower. It serves as a signaling point for calling the ferryman from Dis.

Canto VIII

CIRCLE FIVE: *Styx* — *The Wrathful, Phlegyas*

CIRCLE SIX: *Dis* — *The Fallen Angels*

The Poets stand at the edge of the swamp, and a mysterious signal flames from the great tower. It is answered from the darkness of the other side, and almost immediately the Poets see PHLEGYAS, the Boatman of Styx, racing toward them across the water, fast as a flying arrow. He comes avidly, thinking to find new souls for torment, and he howls with rage when he discovers the Poets. Once again, however, Virgil conquers wrath with a word and Phlegyas reluctantly gives them passage.

As they are crossing, a muddy soul rises before them. it is FILIPPO ARGENTI, one of the Wrathful. Dante recognizes him despite the filth with which he is covered, and he berates him soundly, even wishing to see him tormented further. Virgil approves Dante's disdain and, as if in answer to Dante's wrath, Argenti is suddenly set upon by all the other sinners present, who fall upon him and rip him to pieces.

The boat meanwhile has sped on, and before Argenti's screams have died away, Dante sees the flaming red towers of Dis, the Capital of Hell. The great walls of the iron city block the way to the Lower Hell. Properly speaking, all the rest of Hell lies within the city walls, which separate the Upper and the Lower Hell.

Phlegyas deposits them at a great Iron Gate which they find to be guarded by the REBELLIOUS ANGELS. These creatures of Ultimate Evil, rebels against God Himself, refuse to let the Poets pass. Even Virgil is powerless against them, for Human Reason by itself cannot cope with the essence of Evil. Only Divine Aid can bring hope. Virgil accordingly sends up a prayer for assistance and waits anxiously for a Heavenly Messenger to appear.

Returning to my theme, I say we came
to the foot of a Great Tower; but long before
we reached it through the marsh, two horns of flame

flared from the summit, one from either side,
and then, far off, so far we scarce could see it
across the mist, another flame replied.

I turned to that sea of all intelligence
saying: "What is this signal and counter-signal?
Who is it speaks with fire across this distance?"

And he then: "Look across the filthy slew:
you may already see the one they summon,
if the swamp vapors do not hide him from you."

No twanging bowspring ever shot an arrow
that bored the air it rode dead to the mark
more swiftly than the flying skiff whose prow

shot toward us over the polluted channel
with a single steersman at the helm who called:
"So, do I have you at last, you whelp of Hell?"

"Phlegyas, Phlegyas," said my Lord and Guide,
"this time you waste your breath: you have us only
for the time it takes to cross to the other side."

Phlegyas, the madman, blew his rage among
those muddy marshes like a cheat deceived,
or like a fool at some imagined wrong.

My Guide, whom all the fiend's noise could not nettle,
boarded the skiff, motioning me to follow:
and not till I stepped aboard did it seem to settle

into the water. At once we left the shore,
that ancient hull riding more heavily
than it had ridden in all of time before.

And as we ran on that dead swamp, the slime
rose before me, and from it a voice cried:
"Who are you that come here before your time?"

And I replied: "If I come, I do not remain.
But you, who are *you,* so fallen and so foul?"
And he: "I am one who weeps." And I then:

"May you weep and wail to all eternity,
for I know you, hell-dog, filthy as you are."
Then he stretched both hands to the boat, but warily

the Master shoved him back, crying, "Down! Down!
with the other dogs!" Then he embraced me saying:
"Indignant spirit, I kiss you as you frown.

Blessed be she who bore you. In world and time
this one was haughtier yet. Not one unbending
graces his memory. Here is his shadow in slime.

How many living now, chancellors of wrath,
shall come to lie here yet in this pigmire,
leaving a curse to be their aftermath!"

And I: "Master, it would suit my whim
to see the wretch scrubbed down into the swill
before we leave this stinking sink and him."

And he to me: "Before the other side
shows through the mist, you shall have all you ask.
This is a wish that should be gratified."

And shortly after, I saw the loathsome spirit
so mangled by a swarm of muddy wraiths
that to this day I praise and thank God for it.

"After Filippo Argenti!" all cried together.
The maddog Florentine wheeled at their cry
and bit himself for rage. I saw them gather.

And there we left him. And I say no more.
But such a wailing beat upon my ears,
I strained my eyes ahead to the far shore.

"My son," the Master said, "the City called Dis
lies just ahead, the heavy citizens,
the swarming crowds of Hell's metropolis."

And I then: "Master, I already see
the glow of its red mosques, as if they came
hot from the forge to smolder in this valley."

And my all-knowing Guide: "They are eternal
flues to eternal fire that rages in them
and makes them glow across this lower Hell."

And as he spoke we entered the vast moat
of the sepulchre. Its wall seemed made of iron
and towered above us in our little boat.

We circled through what seemed an endless distance
before the boatman ran his prow ashore
crying: "Out! Out! Get out! This is the entrance."

Above the gates more than a thousand shades
of spirits purged from Heaven for its glory
cried angrily: "Who is it that invades

Death's Kingdom in his life?" My Lord and Guide
advanced a step before me with a sign
that he wished to speak to some of them aside.

They quieted somewhat, and one called, "Come,
but come alone. And tell that other one,
who thought to walk so blithely through death's kingdom,

he may go back along the same fool's way
he came by. Let him try his living luck.
You who are dead can come only to stay."

Reader, judge for yourself, how each black word
fell on my ears to sink into my heart:
I lost hope of returning to the world.

"O my beloved Master, my Guide in peril,
who time and time again have seen me safely
along this way, and turned the power of evil,

stand by me now," I cried, "in my heart's fright.
And if the dead forbid our journey to them,
let us go back together toward the light."

My Guide then, in the greatness of his spirit:
"Take heart. Nothing can take our passage from us
when such a power has given warrant for it.

Wait here and feed your soul while I am gone
on comfort and good hope; I will not leave you
to wander in this underworld alone."

So the sweet Guide and Father leaves me here,
and I stay on in doubt with yes and no
dividing all my heart to hope and fear.

I could not hear my Lord's words, but the pack
that gathered round him suddenly broke away
howling and jostling and went pouring back,

slamming the towering gate hard in his face.
That great Soul stood alone outside the wall.
Then he came back; his pain showed in his pace.

His eyes were fixed upon the ground, his brow
had sagged from its assurance. He sighed aloud:
"Who has forbidden me the halls of sorrow?"

And to me he said: "You need not be cast down
by my vexation, for whatever plot
these fiends may lay against us, we will go on.

This insolence of theirs is nothing new:
they showed it once at a less secret gate
that still stands open for all that they could do—

the same gate where you read the dead inscription;
and through it at this moment a Great One comes.
Already he has passed it and moves down

ledge by dark ledge. He is one who needs no guide,
and at his touch all gates must spring aside."

Notes

1. *Returning to my theme:* There is evidence that Dante stopped writing for a longer or shorter period between the seventh and eighth Cantos. None of the evidence is conclusive but it is quite clear that the plan of the *Inferno* changes from here on. Up to this point the Circles have been described in one canto apiece. If this was Dante's original plan, Hell would have been concluded in five more Cantos, since there are only Nine Circles in all. But in the later journey the Eighth Circle alone occupies thirteen Cantos. Dante's phrase may be simply transitional, but it certainly marks a change in the plan of the poem.

19. *Phlegyas:* Mythological King of Boeotia. He was the son of Ares (Mars) by a human mother. Angry at Apollo, who had seduced his daughter (Aesculapius was born of this union), he set fire to Apollo's temple at Delphi. For this offense, the God killed him and threw his soul into Hades under sentence of eternal torment. Dante's choice of a ferryman is especially apt. Phlegyas is the link between the Wrathful (to whom his paternity relates him) and the Rebellious Angels who menaced God (as he menaced Apollo).

27. *and not till I stepped aboard did it seem to settle:* Because of his living weight.

32. *Filippo Argenti:* (Ahr-DJEN-tee) One of the Adimari family, who were bitter political enemies of Dante. Dante's savagery toward

him was probably intended in part as an insult to the family. He pays them off again in the Paradiso when he has Cacciaguida (Kah-tchah-GWEE-da) call them "The insolent gang that makes itself a dragon to chase those who run away, but is sweet as a lamb to any who show their teeth—or their purse."

43. *Blessed be she who bore you:* These were Luke's words to Christ. To have Virgil apply them to Dante after such violence seems shocking, even though the expression is reasonably common in Italian. But Dante does not use such devices lightly. The *Commedia,* it must be remembered, is a vision of the progress of man's soul toward perfection. In being contemptuous of Wrath, Dante is purging it from his soul. He is thereby growing nearer to perfection, and Virgil, who has said nothing in the past when Dante showed pity for other sinners (though Virgil will later take him to task for daring to pity those whom God has shut off from pity), welcomes this sign of relentless rejection. Only by a ruthless enmity toward evil may the soul be purified, and as Christ is the symbol of ultimate perfection by rejection of Evil, so the birth of that rejection in Dante may aptly be greeted by the words of Luke, for it is from this that the soul must be reborn. Righteous indignation, moreover (*giusto sdegno*), is one of the virtues Christ practiced (e.g., against the money changers) and is the golden mean of right action between the evil extremes of wrath and sullenness.

64. *Dis:* Pluto, King of the Underworld of ancient mythology, was sometimes called Dis. This, then, is his city, the metropolis of Satan. Within the city walls lies all the Lower Hell; within it fire is used for the first time as a torment of the damned; and at its very center Satan himself stands fixed forever in a great ice cap.

68. *mosques:* To a European of Dante's time a mosque would seem the perversion of a church, the impious counterpart of the House of God, just as Satan is God's impious counterpart. His city is therefore architecturally appropriate, a symbolism that becomes all the more terrible when the mosques are made of red-hot iron.

70-71. *they are eternal flues to eternal fire:* The fires of Hell are all within Dis.

80. *spirits purged from Heaven for its glory:* The Rebellious Angels. We have already seen, on the other side of Acheron, the Angels who sinned by refusing to take sides.

95. *time and time again:* A literal translation of the original would read "more than seven times." "Seven" is used here as an indeterminate number indicating simply "quite a number of times." Italian makes rather free use of such numbers.

106. *leaves me:* Dante shifts tenses more freely than English readers are accustomed to.

113. *That Great Soul stood alone:* Virgil's allegorical function as Human Reason is especially important to an interpretation of this passage.

122. *a less secret gate:* The Gate of Hell. According to an early medieval tradition, these demons gathered at the outer gate to oppose the descent of Christ into Limbo at the time of the Harrowing of Hell, but Christ broke the door open and it has remained so ever since. The service of the Mass for Holy Saturday still sings *Hodie portas mortis et seras pariter Salvator noster disrupit.* (On this day our Saviour broke open the door of the dead and its lock as well.)

125. *a Great One:* A Messenger of Heaven. He is described in the next Canto.

– Even Human Reason (Virgil) is stopped (puzzled) by the mystery of evil/sin (The fallen Angels)

Canto IX

CIRCLE SIX *The Heretics*

At the Gate of Dis the Poets wait in dread. Virgil tries to hide his anxiety from Dante, but both realize that without Divine Aid they will surely be lost. To add to their terrors THREE INFERNAL FURIES, symbols of Eternal Remorse, appear on a near-by tower, from which they threaten the Poets and call for MEDUSA to come and change them to stone. Virgil at once commands Dante to turn and shut his eyes. To make doubly sure, Virgil himself places his hands over Dante's eyes, for there is an Evil upon which man must not look if he is to be saved.

But at the moment of greatest anxiety a storm shakes the dirty air of Hell and the sinners in the marsh begin to scatter like frightened Frogs. THE HEAVENLY MESSENGER is approaching. He appears walking majestically through Hell, looking neither to right nor to left. With a touch he throws open the Gate of Dis while his words scatter the Rebellious Angels. Then he returns as he came.

The Poets now enter the gate unopposed and find themselves in the Sixth Circle. Here they find a countryside like a vast cemetery. Tombs of every size stretch out before them, each with its lid lying beside it, and each wrapped in flames. Cries of anguish sound endlessly from the entombed dead.

This is the torment of the HERETICS of every cult. By Heretic, Dante means specifically those who did violence to God by denying immortality. Since they taught that the soul dies with the body, so their punishment is an eternal grave in the fiery morgue of God's wrath.

My face had paled to a mask of cowardice
when I saw my Guide turn back. The sight of it
the sooner brought the color back to his.

He stood apart like one who strains to hear
what he cannot see, for the eye could not reach far
across the vapors of that midnight air.

"Yet surely we were meant to pass these tombs,"
he said aloud. "If not . . . so much was promised . . .
Oh how time hangs and drags till our aid comes!"

I saw too well how the words with which he ended
covered his start, and even perhaps I drew
a worse conclusion from that than he intended.

"Tell me, Master, does anyone ever come
from the first ledge, whose only punishment
is hope cut off, into this dreary bottom?"

I put this question to him, still in fear
of what his broken speech might mean; and he:
"Rarely do any of us enter here.

Once before, it is true, I crossed through Hell
conjured by cruel Erichtho who recalled
the spirits to their bodies. Her dark spell

forced me, newly stripped of my mortal part,
to enter through this gate and summon out
a spirit from Judaïca. Take heart,

that is the last depth and the darkest lair
and the farthest from Heaven which encircles all,
and at that time I came back even from there.

The marsh from which the stinking gasses bubble
lies all about this capital of sorrow
whose gates we may not pass now without
trouble."

All this and more he expounded; but the rest
was lost on me, for suddenly my attention
was drawn to the turret with the fiery crest

where all at once three hellish and inhuman
Furies sprang to view, bloodstained and wild.
Their limbs and gestures hinted they were women.

Belts of greenest hydras wound and wound
about their waists, and snakes and horned serpents
grew from their heads like matted hair and bound

their horrid brows. My Master, who well knew
the handmaids of the Queen of Woe, cried: "Look:
the terrible Erinyes of Hecate's crew.

That is Megaera to the left of the tower.
Alecto is the one who raves on the right.
Tisiphone stands between." And he said no more.

With their palms they beat their brows, with their nails they clawed
their bleeding breasts. And such mad wails broke from them
that I drew close to the Poet, overawed.

And all together screamed, looking down at me:
"Call Medusa that we may change him to stone!
Too lightly we let Theseus go free."

"Turn your back and keep your eyes shut tight;
for should the Gorgon come and you look at her,
never again would you return to the light."

This was my Guide's command. And he turned me about
himself, and would not trust my hands alone,
but, with his placed on mine, held my eyes shut.

Men of sound intellect and probity,
weigh with good understanding what lies hidden
behind the veil of my strange allegory!

Suddenly there broke on the dirty swell
of the dark marsh a squall of terrible sound
that sent a tremor through both shores of Hell;

a sound as if two continents of air,
one frigid and one scorching, clashed head on
in a war of winds that stripped the forests bare,

ripped off whole boughs and blew them helter skelter
along the range of dust it raised before it
making the beasts and shepherds run for shelter.

The Master freed my eyes. "Now turn," he said,
"and fix your nerve of vision on the foam
there where the smoke is thickest and most acrid."

As frogs before the snake that hunts them down
churn up their pond in flight, until the last
squats on the bottom as if turned to stone—

so I saw more than a thousand ruined souls
scatter away from one who crossed dry-shod
the Stygian marsh into Hell's burning bowels.

With his left hand he fanned away the dreary
vapors of that sink as he approached;
and only of that annoyance did he seem weary.

Clearly he was a Messenger from God's Throne,
and I turned to my Guide; but he made me a sign
that I should keep my silence and bow down.

Ah, what scorn breathed from that Angel-presence!
He reached the gate of Dis and with a wand
he waved it open, for there was no resistance.

"Outcasts of Heaven, you twice-loathsome crew,"
he cried upon that terrible sill of Hell,
"how does this insolence still live in you?

Why do you set yourselves against that Throne
whose Will none can deny, and which, times past,
has added to your pain for each rebellion?

Why do you butt against Fate's ordinance?
Your Cerberus, if you recall, still wears
his throat and chin peeled for such arrogance."

Then he turned back through the same filthy tide
by which he had come. He did not speak to us,
but went his way like one preoccupied

by other presences than those before him.
And we moved toward the city, fearing nothing
after his holy words. Straight through the dim

and open gate we entered unopposed.
And I, eager to learn what new estate
of Hell those burning fortress walls enclosed,

began to look about the very moment
we were inside, and I saw on every hand
a countryside of sorrow and new torment.

As at Arles where the Rhone sinks into stagnant marshes,
as at Pola by the Quarnaro Gulf, whose waters
close Italy and wash her farthest reaches,

the uneven tombs cover the even plain—
such fields I saw here, spread in all directions,
except that here the tombs were chests of pain:

for, in a ring around each tomb, great fires
raised every wall to a red heat. No smith
works hotter iron in his forge. The biers

stood with their lids upraised, and from their pits
an anguished moaning rose on the dead air
from the desolation of tormented spirits.

And I: "Master, what shades are these who lie
buried in these chests and fill the air
with such a painful and unending cry?"

"These are the arch-heretics of all cults,
with all their followers," he replied. "Far more
than you would think lie stuffed into these vaults.

Like lies with like in every heresy,
and the monuments are fired, some more, some less;
to each depravity its own degree."

He turned then, and I followed through that night
between the wall and the torments, bearing right.

Notes

1-15. DANTE'S FEAR AND VIRGIL'S ASSURANCE. Allegorically, this highly dramatic scene once more represents the limits of the power of Human Reason. There are occasions, Dante makes clear, in which only Divine Aid will suffice. The anxiety here is the turmoil of the mind that hungers after God and awaits His sign in fear and doubt, knowing that unless that sign is given, the final evil cannot be surmounted.

Aside from the allegorical significance the scene is both powerfully and subtly drawn. Observing Dante's fear, Virgil hides his own. Dante, however, penetrates the dissimulation, and is all the more afraid. To reassure himself (or to know the worst, perhaps) he longs to ask Virgil whether or not he really knows the way. But he cannot ask bluntly; he has too much respect for his Guide's feelings. Therefore, he generalizes the question in such a way as to make it inoffensive.

Having drawn so delicate a play of cross-motives in such brief space, Dante further seizes the scene as an opportunity for reinforcing Virgil's fitness to be his Guide. The economy of means with which Dante brings his several themes to assist one another is in the high tradition of dramatic poetry.

14. *from the first ledge:* Limbo.

20. *Erichtho:* A sorceress drawn from Lucan (*Pharsalia* VI, 508ff).

24. *a spirit from Judaïca . . . :* Judaïca (or Judecca) is the final pit of Hell. Erichtho called up the spirit in order to foretell the outcome of the campaign between Pompey and Caesar. There is no trace of the legend in which Virgil is chosen for the descent; Virgil, in fact, was still alive at the time of the battle of Pharsalia.

34ff. THE THREE FURIES: (or Erinyes) In classical mythology they were especially malignant spirits who pursued and tormented those who had violated fundamental taboos (desecration of temples, murder of kin, etc.). They are apt symbols of the guilty conscience of the damned.

41. *the Queen of Woe:* Proserpine (or Hecate) was the wife of Pluto, and therefore Queen of the Underworld.

50. *Medusa:* The Gorgon. She turned to stone whoever looked at her. Allegorically she may be said to represent Despair of ever winning the Mercy of God. The further allegory is apparent when we remember that she is summoned by the Furies, who represent Remorse.

51. *too lightly we let Theseus go free:* Theseus and Pirithous tried to kidnap Hecate. Pirithous was killed in the attempt and Theseus was punished by being chained to a great rock. He was later set free by Hercules, who descended to his rescue in defiance of all the powers of Hell. The meaning of the Furies' cry is that Dante must be made an example of. Had they punished Theseus properly, men would have acquired more respect for their powers and would not still be attempting to invade the Underworld.

59-60. *my strange allegory:* Most commentators take this to mean the allegory of the Three Furies, but the lines apply as aptly to the allegory that follows. Dante probably meant both. Almost certainly, too, "my strange allegory" refers to the whole *Commedia.*

61ff. *THE APPEARANCE OF THE MESSENGER:* In Hell, God is expressed only as inviolable power. His messenger is preceded by great storms, his presence sends a terror through the damned, his face is the face of scorn.

95. *Cerberus:* When Cerberus opposed the fated entrance of Hercules into Hell, Hercules threw a chain about his neck and dragged him to the upperworld. Cerberus' throat, according to Dante, is still peeled raw from it.

104. THE SIXTH CIRCLE: Once through the gate, the Poets enter the Sixth Circle and the beginning of the Lower Hell.

109ff. *Arles . . . Pola:* Situated as indicated on the Rhone and the Quarnaro Gulf respectively, these cities were the sites of great cemeteries dating back to the time of Rome. The Quarnaro Gulf is the body of water on which Fiume is situated.

114. *The Heretics:* Within the Sixth Circle are punished the Heretics. They lie in chests resembling great tombs, but the tombs are made of iron and are heated red-hot by great fires. The tombs are uncovered, and the great lids lie about on the ground. As we shall learn soon, these lids will be put into place on the Day of Judgment and sealed forever. Thus, once more the sin is refigured in the punishment, for as Heresy results in the death of the soul, so the Heretics will be sealed forever in their death within a death.

It must be noted, however, that Dante means by "heretic" specifically those skeptics who deny the soul's immortality. They stand in relation to the Lower Hell as the Pagans stood in relation to the Upper Hell. The Pagans did not know how to worship God: the Heretics denied His existence. Each group, in its degree, symbolizes a state of blindness. (Other varieties of Heretics are in Bolgia 9 of Circle VIII.) Moreover, in Dante's system, to deny God is the beginning of Violence, Bestiality, and Fraud; and it is these sins which are punished below.

131. *bearing right:* Through all of Hell the Poets bear left in their descent with only two exceptions, the first in their approach to the Heretics, the second in their approach to Geryon, the monster of fraud (see note XVII, 29 below). Note that both these exceptions occur at a major division of the *Inferno*. There is no satisfactory explanation of Dante's allegorical intent in making these exceptions.

Furies: Symbols of eternal remorse
(conscience - I have sinned)

Medusa: symbol of despair
turns heart to "stone"

Intro

Canto X

CIRCLE SIX *The Heretics*

As the Poets pass on, one of the damned hears Dante speaking, recognizes him as a Tuscan, and calls to him from one of the fiery tombs. A moment later he appears. He is FARINATA DEGLI UBERTI, a great war-chief of the Tuscan Ghibellines. The majesty and power of his bearing seem to diminish Hell itself. He asks Dante's lineage and recognizes him as an enemy. They begin to talk politics, but are interrupted by another shade, who rises from the same tomb.

This one is CAVALCANTE DEI CAVALCANTI, father of Guido Cavalcanti, a contemporary poet. If it is genius that leads Dante on his great journey, the shade asks, why is Guido not with him? Can Dante presume to a greater genius than Guido's? Dante replies that he comes this way only with the aid of powers Guido has not sought. His reply is a classic example of many-leveled symbolism as well as an overt criticism of a rival poet. The senior Cavalcanti mistakenly infers from Dante's reply that Guido is dead, and swoons back into the flames.

Farinata, who has not deigned to notice his fellow-sinner, continues from the exact point at which he had been interrupted. It is as if he refuses to recognize the flames in which he is shrouded. He proceeds to prophesy Dante's banishment from Florence, he defends his part in Florentine politics, and then, in answer to Dante's question, he explains how it is that the damned can foresee the future but have no knowledge of the present. He then names others who share his tomb, and Dante takes his leave with considerable respect for his great enemy, pausing only long enough to leave word for Cavalcanti that Guido is still alive.

We go by a secret path along the rim
of the dark city, between the wall and the torments.
My Master leads me and I follow him.

"Supreme Virtue, who through this impious land
wheel me at will down these dark gyres," I said,
"speak to me, for I wish to understand.

Tell me, Master, is it permitted to see
the souls within these tombs? The lids are raised,
and no one stands on guard." And he to me:

"All shall be sealed forever on the day
these souls return here from Jehosaphat
with the bodies they have given once to clay.

In this dark corner of the morgue of wrath
lie Epicurus and his followers,
who make the soul share in the body's death.

And here you shall be granted presently
not only your spoken wish, but that other as well,
which you had thought perhaps to hide from me."

And I: "Except to speak my thoughts in few
and modest words, as I learned from your example,
dear Guide, I do not hide my heart from you."

"O Tuscan, who go living through this place
speaking so decorously, may it please you pause
a moment on your way, for by the grace

of that high speech in which I hear your birth,
I know you for a son of that noble city
which perhaps I vexed too much in my time on earth."

These words broke without warning from inside
one of the burning arks. Caught by surprise,
I turned in fear and drew close to my Guide.

And he: "Turn around. What are you doing? Look there:
it is Farinata rising from the flames.
From the waist up his shade will be made clear."

My eyes were fixed on him already. Erect,
he rose above the flame, great chest, great brow;
he seemed to hold all Hell in disrespect.

My Guide's prompt hands urged me among the dim
and smoking sepulchres to that great figure,
and he said to me: "Mind how you speak to him."

And when I stood alone at the foot of the tomb,
the great soul stared almost contemptuously,
before he asked: "Of what line do you come?"

Because I wished to obey, I did not hide
anything from him: whereupon, as he listened,
he raised his brows a little, then replied:

"Bitter enemies were they to me,
to my fathers, and to my party, so that twice
I sent them scattering from high Italy."

"If they were scattered, still from every part
they formed again and returned both times," I answered,
"but yours have not yet wholly learned that art."

At this another shade rose gradually,
visible to the chin. It had raised itself,
I think, upon its knees, and it looked around me

as if it expected to find through that black air
that blew about me, another traveler.
And weeping when it found no other there,

turned back. "And if," it cried, "you travel through
this dungeon of the blind by power of genius,
where is my son? why is he not with you?"

And I to him: "Not by myself am I borne
this terrible way. I am led by him who waits there,
and whom perhaps your Guido held in scorn."

For by his words and the manner of his torment
I knew his name already, and could, therefore,
answer both what he asked and what he meant.

Instantly he rose to his full height:
"He *held?* What is it you say? Is he dead, then?
Do his eyes no longer fill with that sweet light?"

And when he saw that I delayed a bit
in answering his question, he fell backwards
into the flame, and rose no more from it.

But that majestic spirit at whose call
I had first paused there, did not change expression,
nor so much as turn his face to watch him fall.

"And if," going on from his last words, he said,
"men of my line have yet to learn that art,
that burns me deeper than this flaming bed.

But the face of her who reigns in Hell shall not
be fifty times rekindled in its course
before you learn what griefs attend that art.

And as you hope to find the world again,
tell me: why is that populace so savage
in the edicts they pronounce against my strain?"

And I to him: "The havoc and the carnage
that dyed the Arbia red at Montaperti
have caused these angry cries in our assemblage."

He sighed and shook his head. "I was not alone
in that affair," he said, "nor certainly
would I have joined the rest without good reason.

But I *was* alone at that time when every other
consented to the death of Florence; I
alone with open face defended her."

"Ah, so may your soul sometime have rest,"
I begged him, "solve the riddle that pursues me
through this dark place and leaves my mind perplexed:

you seem to see in advance all time's intent,
if I have heard and understood correctly;
but you seem to lack all knowledge of the present."

"We see asquint, like those whose twisted sight
can make out only the far-off," he said,
"for the King of All still grants us that much light.

When things draw near, or happen, we perceive
nothing of them. Except what others bring us
we have no news of those who are alive.

So may you understand that all we know
will be dead forever from that day and hour
when the Portal of the Future is swung to."

Then, as if stricken by regret, I said:
"Now, therefore, will you tell that fallen one
who asked about his son, that he is not dead,

and that, if I did not reply more quickly,
it was because my mind was occupied
with this confusion you have solved for me."

And now my Guide was calling me. In haste,
therefore, I begged that mighty shade to name
the others who lay with him in that chest.

And he: "More than a thousand cram this tomb.
The second Frederick is here, and the Cardinal
of the Ubaldini. Of the rest let us be dumb."

And he disappeared without more said, and I
turned back and made my way to the ancient Poet,
pondering the words of the dark prophecy.

He moved along, and then, when we had started,
he turned and said to me, "What troubles you?
Why do you look so vacant and downhearted?"

And I told him. And he replied: "Well may you bear
those words in mind." Then, pausing, raised a finger:
"Now pay attention to what I tell you here:

when finally you stand before the ray
of that Sweet Lady whose bright eye sees all,
from her you will learn the turnings of your way."

So saying, he bore left, turning his back
on the flaming walls, and we passed deeper yet
into the city of pain, along a track

that plunged down like a scar into a sink
which sickened us already with its stink.

Notes

11. *Jehosaphat:* A valley outside Jerusalem. The popular belief that it would serve as the scene of the Last Judgment was based on *Joel* iii, 2, 12.

14. *Epicurus:* The Greek philosopher. The central aim of his philosophy was to achieve happiness, which he defined as the absence of pain. For Dante this doctrine meant the denial of the Eternal life, since the whole aim of the Epicurean was temporal happiness.

17. *not only your spoken wish, but that other as well:* "All knowing" Virgil is frequently presented as being able to read Dante's mind. The "other wish" is almost certainly Dante's desire to speak to someone from Florence with whom he could discuss politics. Many prominent Florentines were Epicureans.

22. *Tuscan:* Florence lies in the province of Tuscany. Italian, to an extent unknown in America, is a language of dialects, all of them

readily identifiable even when they are not well understood by the hearer. Dante's native Tuscan has become the main source of modern official Italian. Two very common sayings still current in Italy are: *"Lingua toscana, lingua di Dio"* (the Tuscan tongue is the language of God) and—to express the perfection of Italian speech—*"Lingua toscana in bocca romana* (the Tuscan tongue in a Roman mouth).

32-51. *Farinata:* Farinata degli Uberti (DEH-lyee Oob-EHR-tee) was head of the ancient noble house of the Uberti. He became leader of the Ghibellines of Florence in 1239, and played a large part in expelling the Guelphs in 1248. The Guelphs returned in 1251, but Farinata remained. His arrogant desire to rule singlehanded led to difficulties, however, and he was expelled in 1258. With the aid of the Manfredi of Siena, he gathered a large force and defeated the Guelphs at Montaperti on the River Arbia in 1260. Re-entering Florence in triumph, he again expelled the Guelphs, but at the Diet of Empoli, held by the victors after the battle of Montaperti, he alone rose in open counsel to resist the general sentiment that Florence should be razed. He died in Florence in 1264. In 1266 the Guelphs once more returned and crushed forever the power of the Uberti, destroying their palaces and issuing special decrees against persons of the Uberti line. In 1283 a decree of heresy was published against Farinata.

26. *that noble city:* Florence.

39. *"Mind how you speak to him":* The surface interpretation is clearly that Virgil means Dante to show proper respect to so majestic a soul. (Cf. Canto XVI, 14-15.) But the allegorical level is more interesting here. Virgil (as Human Reason) is urging Dante to go forward on his own. These final words then would be an admonition to Dante to guide his speech according to the highest principles.

52. *another shade:* Cavalcante dei Cavalcanti was a famous Epicurean ("like lies with like"). He was the father of Guido Cavalcanti, a poet and friend of Dante. Guido was also Farinata's son-in-law.

61. *Not by myself:* Cavalcanti assumes that the resources of human genius are all that are necessary for such a journey. (It is an assumption that well fits his character as an Epicurean.) Dante replies as a man of religion that other aid is necessary.

63. *whom perhaps your Guido held in scorn:* This reference has not been satisfactorily explained. Virgil is a symbol on many levels—of Classicism, of religiosity, of Human Reason. Guido might have scorned him on any of these levels, or on all of them. One interpretation might be that Dante wished to present Guido as an example of how skepticism acts as a limitation upon a man of genius. Guido's

skepticism does not permit him to see beyond the temporal. He does not see that Virgil (Human Reason expressed as Poetic Wisdom) exists only to lead one to Divine Love, and therefore he cannot undertake the final journey on which Dante has embarked.

70. *and when he saw that I delayed:* Dante's delay is explained in lines 112-114.

79. *her who reigns in Hell:* Hecate or Proserpine. She is also the moon goddess. The sense of this prophecy, therefore, is that Dante will be exiled within fifty full moons. Dante was banished from Florence in 1302, well within the fifty months of the prophecy.

83. *that populace:* The Florentines.

97-108. THE KNOWLEDGE OF THE DAMNED: Dante notes with surprise that Farinata can foresee the future, but that Cavalcanti does not know whether his son is presently dead or alive. Farinata explains by outlining a most ingenious detail of the Divine Plan: the damned can see far into the future, but nothing of what is present or *of what has happened.* Thus, after Judgment, when there is no longer any Future, the intellects of the damned will be void.

119. *the second Frederick:* The Emperor Frederick II. In Canto XIII Dante has Pier delle Vigne speak of him as one worthy of honor, but he was commonly reputed to be an Epicurean.

119-120. *the Cardinal of the Ubaldini:* In the original Dante refers to him simply as "il Cardinale." Ottaviano degli Ubaldini (born *circa* 1209, died 1273) became a Cardinal in 1245, but his energies seem to have been directed exclusively to money and political intrigue. When he was refused an important loan by the Ghibellines, he is reported by many historians as having remarked: "I may say that if I have a soul, I have lost it in the cause of the Ghibellines, and no one of them will help me now." The words "If I have a soul" would be enough to make him guilty in Dante's eyes of the charge of heresy.

131. *that Sweet Lady:* Beatrice.

Canto XI

CIRCLE SIX *The Heretics*

The Poets reach the inner edge of the SIXTH CIRCLE and find a great jumble of rocks that had once been a cliff, but which has fallen into rubble as the result of the great earthquake that shook Hell when Christ died. Below them lies the SEVENTH CIRCLE, and so fetid is the air that arises from it that the Poets cower for shelter behind a great tomb until their breaths can grow accustomed to the stench.

Dante finds an inscription on the lid of the tomb labeling it as the place in Hell of POPE ANASTASIUS.

Virgil takes advantage of the delay to outline in detail THE DIVISION OF THE LOWER HELL, a theological discourse based on The Ethics *and* The Physics *of Aristotle with subsequent medieval interpretations. Virgil explains also why it is that the Incontinent are not punished within the walls of Dis, and rather ingeniously sets forth the reasons why Usury is an act of Violence against Art, which is the child of Nature and hence the Grandchild of God. (By "Art," Dante means the arts and crafts by which man draws from nature, i.e., Industry.)*

As he concludes he rises and urges Dante on. By means known only to Virgil, he is aware of the motion of the stars and from them he sees that it is about two hours before Sunrise of Holy Saturday.

We came to the edge of an enormous sink
  rimmed by a circle of great broken boulders.
  Here we found ghastlier gangs. And here the stink

thrown up by the abyss so overpowered us
  that we drew back, cowering behind the wall
  of one of the great tombs; and standing thus,

I saw an inscription in the stone, and read:
"I guard Anastasius, once Pope,
he whom Photinus led from the straight road."

"Before we travel on to that blind pit
we must delay until our sense grows used
to its foul breath, and then we will not mind it,"

my Master said. And I then: "Let us find
some compensation for the time of waiting."
And he: "You shall see I have just that in mind.

My son," he began, "there are below this wall
three smaller circles, each in its degree
like those you are about to leave, and all

are crammed with God's accurst. Accordingly,
that you may understand their sins at sight,
I will explain how each is prisoned, and why.

Malice is the sin most hated by God.
And the aim of malice is to injure others
whether by fraud or violence. But since fraud

is the vice of which man alone is capable,
God loathes it most. Therefore, the fraudulent
are placed below, and their torment is more painful.

The first below are the violent. But as violence
sins in three persons, so is that circle formed
of three descending rounds of crueler torments.

Against God, self, and neighbor is violence shown.
Against their persons and their goods, I say,
as you shall hear set forth with open reason.

Murder and mayhem are the violation
of the person of one's neighbor: and of his goods;
harassment, plunder, arson, and extortion.

Therefore, homicides, and those who strike
in malice—destroyers and plunderers—all lie
in that first round, and like suffers with like.

A man may lay violent hands upon his own
person and substance; so in that second round
eternally in vain repentance moan

the suicides and all who gamble away
and waste the good and substance of their lives
and weep in that sweet time when they should be gay.

Violence may be offered the deity
in the heart that blasphemes and refuses Him
and scorns the gifts of Nature, her beauty and bounty.

Therefore, the smallest round brands with its mark
both Sodom and Cahors, and all who rail
at God and His commands in their hearts' dark.

Fraud, which is a canker to every conscience,
may be practiced by a man on those who trust him,
and on those who have reposed no confidence.

The latter mode seems only to deny
the bond of love which all men have from Nature;
therefore within the second circle lie

simoniacs, sycophants, and hypocrites,
falsifiers, thieves, and sorcerers,
grafters, pimps, and all such filthy cheats.

The former mode of fraud not only denies
the bond of Nature, but the special trust
added by bonds of friendship or blood-ties.

Hence, at the center point of all creation,
in the smallest circle, on which Dis is founded,
the traitors lie in endless expiation."

"Master," I said, "the clarity of your mind
impresses all you touch; I see quite clearly
the orders of this dark pit of the blind.

But tell me: those who lie in the swamp's bowels,
those the wind blows about, those the rain beats,
and those who meet and clash with such mad howls—

why are *they* not punished in the rust-red city
  if God's wrath be upon them? and if it is not,
  why must they grieve through all eternity?"

And he: "Why does your understanding stray
  so far from its own habit? or can it be
  your thoughts are turned along some other way?

Have you forgotten that your *Ethics* states
  the three main dispositions of the soul
  that lead to those offenses Heaven hates—

incontinence, malice, and bestiality?
  and how incontinence offends God least
  and earns least blame from Justice and Charity?

Now if you weigh this doctrine and recall
  exactly who they are whose punishment
  lies in that upper Hell outside the wall,

you will understand at once why they are confined
  apart from these fierce wraiths, and why less anger
  beats down on them from the Eternal Mind."

"O sun which clears all mists from troubled sight,
  such joy attends your rising that I feel
  as grateful to the dark as to the light.

Go back a little further," I said, "to where
  you spoke of usury as an offense
  against God's goodness. How is that made clear?"

"Philosophy makes plain by many reasons,"
  he answered me, "to those who heed her teachings,
  how all of Nature,—her laws, her fruits, her seasons,—

springs from the Ultimate Intellect and Its art:
  and if you read your *Physics* with due care,
  you will note, not many pages from the start,

that Art strives after her by imitation,
  as the disciple imitates the master;
  Art, as it were, is the Grandchild of Creation.

By this, recalling the Old Testament
near the beginning of Genesis, you will see
that in the will of Providence, man was meant

to labor and to prosper. But usurers,
by seeking their increase in other ways,
scorn Nature in herself and her followers.

But come, for it is my wish now to go on:
the wheel turns and the Wain lies over Caurus,
the Fish are quivering low on the horizon,

and there beyond us runs the road we go
down the dark scarp into the depths below."

Notes

2. *broken boulders:* These boulders were broken from the earthquake that shook Hell at the death of Christ.

3. *the stink:* The stink is, of course, symbolic of the foulness of Hell and its sins. The action of the poets in drawing back from it, and their meditations on the nature of sin, are therefore subject to allegorical as well as to literal interpretation.

8-9. ANASTASIUS and PHOTINUS: Anastasius II was Pope from 496 to 498. This was the time of schism between the Eastern (Greek) and Western (Roman) churches. Photinus, deacon of Thessalonica, was of the Greek church and held to the Acacian heresy, which denied the divine paternity of Christ. Dante follows the report that Anastasius gave communion to Photinus, thereby countenancing his heresy. Dante's sources, however, had probably confused Anastasius II, the Pope, with Anastasius I, who was Emperor from 491 to 518. It was the Emperor Anastasius who was persuaded by Photinus to accept the Acacian heresy.

17. *three smaller circles:* The Poets are now at the cliff that bounds the Sixth Circle. Below them lie Circles Seven, Eight, and Nine. They are smaller in circumference, being closer to the center, but they are all intricately subdivided, and will be treated at much greater length than were the Circles of Upper Hell.

LOWER HELL: The structure of Dante's Hell is based on Aristotle (as Virgil makes clear in his exposition), but with certain Christian symbolisms, exceptions, and misconstructions of Aristotle's text.

The major symbolisms are the three beasts met in Canto I. The exceptions are the two peculiarly Christian categories of sin: Paganism and Heresy. The misconstructions of Aristotle's text involve the classification of "bestiality." Aristotle classified it as a different thing from vice or malice, but medieval commentators construed the passage to mean "another sort of malice." Dante's intent is clear, however; he understood Aristotle to make three categories of sin: Incontinence, Violence and Bestiality, and Fraud and Malice. Incontinence is punished in the Upper Hell. The following table sets forth the categories of the Lower Hell.

THE CLASSIFICATIONS OF SIN IN LOWER HELL

Heresy..Circle VI

THE VIOLENT AND BESTIAL (Circle VII) (SINS OF THE LION)	Round 1.	Against Neighbors. (Murderers and war-makers)
	Round 2.	Against Self. (Suicides and destroyers of their own substance)
	Round 3.	Against God, Art, and Nature. (Blasphemers, perverts, and usurers)

THE FRAUDULENT AND MALICIOUS (SINS OF THE LEOPARD)	(Circle VIII) (Simple Fraud)	Bolgia 1.	Seducers and panderers.
		Bolgia 2.	Flatterers.
		Bolgia 3.	Simoniacs.
		Bolgia 4.	Fortune tellers and diviners.
		Bolgia 5.	Grafters.
		Bolgia 6.	Hypocrites.
		Bolgia 7.	Thieves.
		Bolgia 8.	Evil counselors.
		Bolgia 9.	Sowers of discord.
		Bolgia 10.	Counterfeiters and alchemists.
	(Circle IX) (Compound Fraud)	Caïna.	Treachery against kin.
		Antenora.	Treachery against country.
		Ptolemea.	Treachery against guests and hosts.
		Judaïca.	Treachery against lords and benefactors.

50. *Sodom and Cahors:* Both these cities are used as symbols for the sins that are said to have flourished within them. Sodom (*Genesis* xix) is, of course, identified with unnatural sex practices. Cahors, a city in southern France, was notorious in the Middle Ages for its usurers.

64. *the center point of all creation:* In the Ptolemaic system the earth was the center of the Universe. In Dante's geography, the bottom of Hell is the center of the earth.

70. *those who lie, etc.:* These are, of course, the sinners of the Upper Hell.

73. *the rust-red city:* Dis. All of Lower Hell is within the city walls.

79. *your* Ethics: *The Ethics* of Aristotle.

101. *your* Physics: *The Physics* of Aristotle.

113. *the Wain lies over Caurus etc.:* The Wain is the constellation of the Great Bear. Caurus was the northwest wind in classical mythology. Hence the constellation of the Great Bear now lies in the northwest. The Fish is the constellation and zodiacal sign of Pisces. It is just appearing over the horizon. The next sign of the zodiac is Aries. We know from Canto I that the sun is in Aries, and since the twelve signs of the zodiac each cover two hours of the day, it must now be about two hours before dawn. It is, therefore, approximately 4:00 A.M. of Holy Saturday.

The stars are not visible in Hell, but throughout the *Inferno* Virgil reads them by some special power which Dante does not explain.

Charon - boatman on river Acheron

Chiron - head of Centaurs

Text.

Canto XII

CIRCLE SEVEN: *Round One* *The Violent Against Neighbors*

The Poets begin the descent of the fallen rock wall, having first to evade the MINOTAUR, who menaces them. Virgil tricks him and the Poets hurry by.

Below them they see the RIVER OF BLOOD, which marks the First Round of the Seventh Circle as detailed in the previous Canto. Here are punished the VIOLENT AGAINST THEIR NEIGHBORS, great war-makers, cruel tyrants, highwaymen—all who shed the blood of their fellowmen. As they wallowed in blood during their lives, so they are immersed in the boiling blood forever, each according to the degree of his guilt, while fierce Centaurs patrol the banks, ready to shoot with their arrows any sinner who raises himself out of the boiling blood beyond the limits permitted him. ALEXANDER THE GREAT is here, up to his lashes in the blood, and with him ATTILA, THE SCOURGE OF GOD. They are immersed in the deepest part of the river, which grows shallower as it circles to the other side of the ledge, then deepens again.

The Poets are challenged by the Centaurs, but Virgil wins a safe conduct from CHIRON, their chief, who assigns NESSUS to guide them and to bear them across the shallows of the boiling blood. Nessus carries them across at the point where it is only ankle deep and immediately leaves them and returns to his patrol.

The scene that opened from the edge of the pit
  was mountainous, and such a desolation
  that every eye would shun the sight of it:

a ruin like the Slides of Mark near Trent
on the bank of the Adige, the result of an earthquake
or of some massive fault in the escarpment—

for, from the point on the peak where the mountain split
to the plain below, the rock is so badly shattered
a man at the top might make a rough stair of it.

Such was the passage down the steep, and there
at the very top, at the edge of the broken cleft,
lay spread the Infamy of Crete, the heir

of bestiality and the lecherous queen
who hid in a wooden cow. And when he saw us,
he gnawed his own flesh in a fit of spleen.

And my Master mocked: "How you do pump your breath!
Do you think, perhaps, it is the Duke of Athens,
who in the world above served up your death?

Off with you, monster; this one does not come
instructed by your sister, but of himself
to observe your punishment in the lost kingdom."

As a bull that breaks its chains just when the knife
has struck its death-blow, cannot stand nor run
but leaps from side to side with its last life—

so danced the Minotaur, and my shrewd Guide
cried out: "Run now! While he is blind with rage!
Into the pass, quick, and get over the side!"

So we went down across the shale and slate
of that ruined rock, which often slid and shifted
under me at the touch of living weight.

I moved on, deep in thought; and my Guide to me:
"You are wondering perhaps about this ruin
which is guarded by that beast upon whose fury

I played just now. I should tell you that when last
I came this dark way to the depths of Hell,
this rock had not yet felt the ruinous blast.

But certainly, if I am not mistaken,
it was just before the coming of Him who took
the souls from Limbo, that all Hell was shaken

so that I thought the universe felt love
and all its elements moved toward harmony,
whereby the world of matter, as some believe,

has often plunged to chaos. It was then,
that here and elsewhere in the pits of Hell,
the ancient rock was stricken and broke open.

But turn your eyes to the valley; there we shall find
the river of boiling blood in which are steeped
all who struck down their fellow men." Oh blind!

Oh ignorant, self-seeking cupidity
which spurs us so in the short mortal life
and steeps us so through all eternity!

I saw an arching fosse that was the bed
of a winding river circling through the plain
exactly as my Guide and Lord had said.

A file of Centaurs galloped in the space
between the bank and the cliff, well armed with arrows,
riding as once on earth they rode to the chase.

And seeing us descend, that straggling band
halted, and three of them moved out toward us,
their long bows and their shafts already in hand.

And one of them cried out while still below:
"To what pain are you sent down that dark coast?
Answer from where you stand, or I draw the bow!"

"Chiron is standing there hard by your side;
our answer will be to him. This wrath of yours
was always your own worst fate," my Guide replied.

And to me he said: "That is Nessus, who died in the wood
for insulting Dejanira. At his death
he plotted his revenge in his own blood.

The one in the middle staring at his chest
is the mighty Chiron, he who nursed Achilles:
the other is Pholus, fiercer than all the rest.

They run by that stream in thousands, snapping their bows
at any wraith who dares to raise himself
out of the blood more than his guilt allows."

We drew near those swift beasts. In a thoughtful pause
Chiron drew an arrow, and with its notch
he pushed his great beard back along his jaws.

And when he had thus uncovered the huge pouches
of his lips, he said to his fellows: "Have you noticed
how the one who walks behind moves what he touches?

That is not how the dead go." My good Guide,
already standing by the monstrous breast
in which the two mixed natures joined, replied:

"It is true he lives; in his necessity
I alone must lead him through this valley.
Fate brings him here, not curiosity.

From singing Alleluia the sublime
spirit who sends me came. He is no bandit.
Nor am I one who ever stooped to crime.

But in the name of the Power by which I go
this sunken way across the floor of Hell,
assign us one of your troop whom we may follow,

that he may guide us to the ford, and there
carry across on his back the one I lead,
for he is not a spirit to move through air."

Chiron turned his head on his right breast
and said to Nessus: "Go with them, and guide them,
and turn back any others that would contest

their passage." So we moved beside our guide
along the bank of the scalding purple river
in which the shrieking wraiths were boiled and dyed.

Some stood up to their lashes in that torrent,
and as we passed them the huge Centaur said:
"These were the kings of bloodshed and despoilment.

Here they pay for their ferocity.
Here is Alexander. And Dionysius,
who brought long years of grief to Sicily.

That brow you see with the hair as black as night
is Azzolino; and that beside him, the blonde,
is Opizzo da Esti, who had his mortal light

blown out by his own stepson." I turned then
to speak to the Poet but he raised a hand:
"Let him be the teacher now, and I will listen."

Further on, the Centaur stopped beside
a group of spirits steeped as far as the throat
in the race of boiling blood, and there our guide

pointed out a sinner who stood alone:
"That one before God's altar pierced a heart
still honored on the Thames." And he passed on.

We came in sight of some who were allowed
to raise the head and all the chest from the river,
and I recognized many there. Thus, as we followed

along the stream of blood, its level fell
until it cooked no more than the feet of the damned.
And here we crossed the ford to deeper Hell.

"Just as you see the boiling stream grow shallow
along this side," the Centaur said to us
when we stood on the other bank, "I would have you know

that on the other, the bottom sinks anew
more and more, until it comes again
full circle to the place where the tyrants stew.

It is there that Holy Justice spends its wrath
on Sextus and Pyrrhus through eternity,
and on Attila, who was a scourge on earth:

and everlastingly milks out the tears
of Rinier da Corneto and Rinier Pazzo,
those two assassins who for many years

stalked the highways, bloody and abhorred."
And with that he started back across the ford.

Notes

4. *the Slides of Mark: Li Slavoni di Marco* are about two miles from Rovereto (between Verona and Trent) on the left bank of the River Adige.

9. *a man at the top might, etc.:* I am defeated in all attempts to convey Dante's emphasis in any sort of a verse line. The sense of the original: "It might provide some sort of a way down for one who started at the top, but (by implication) would not be climbable from below."

12-18. *the Infamy of Crete:* This is the infamous Minotaur of classical mythology. His mother was Pasiphaë, wife of Minos, the King of Crete. She conceived an unnatural passion for a bull, and in order to mate with it, she crept into a wooden cow. From this union the Minotaur was born, half-man, half-beast. King Minos kept him in an ingenious labyrinth from which he could not escape. When Androgeos, the son of King Minos, was killed by the Athenians, Minos exacted an annual tribute of seven maidens and seven youths. These were annually turned into the labyrinth and there were devoured by the Minotaur.

The monster was finally killed by Theseus, Duke of Athens. He was aided by Ariadne, daughter of Minos (and half-sister of the monster). She gave Theseus a ball of cord to unwind as he entered the labyrinth and a sword with which to kill the Minotaur.

The Minotaur was, thus, more beast than human, he was conceived in a sodomitic union, and he was a devourer of human flesh—in all ways a fitting symbol of the souls he guards.

34 ff. THE BROKEN ROCKS OF HELL: According to *Matthew* xxvii, 51, an earthquake shook the earth at the moment of Christ's death. These stones, Dante lets us know, were broken off in that earthquake. We shall find other effects of the same shock in the Eighth Circle. It is worth noting also that both the Upper (See Canto V, 34) and the Lower Hell begin with evidences of this ruin. For details of Virgil's first descent see notes to Canto IX.

38. *the coming of Him, etc.:* For details of Christ's descent into Hell see notes to Canto IV.

40-42. *the universe felt love . . . as some believe:* The Greek philosopher, Empedocles, taught that the universe existed by the counter-balance (discord or mutual repulsion) of its elements. Should the elemental matter feel harmony (love or mutual attraction) all would fly together into chaos.

47. *the river of boiling blood:* This is Phlegethon, the river that circles through the First Round of the Seventh Circle, then sluices through the wood of the suicides (the Second Round) and the burning sands (Third Round) to spew over the Great Cliff into the Eighth Circle, and so, eventually, to the bottom of Hell (Cocytus).

The river is deepest at the point at which the Poets first approach it and grows shallower along both sides of the circle until it reaches the ford, which is at the opposite point of the First Round. The souls of the damned are placed in deeper or shallower parts of the river according to the degree of their guilt.

55. THE CENTAURS: The Centaurs were creatures of classical mythology, half-horse, half-men. They were skilled and savage hunters, creatures of passion and violence. Like the Minotaur, they are symbols of the bestial-human, and as such, they are fittingly chosen as the tormentors of these sinners.

65. *Chiron:* The son of Saturn and of the nymph Philira. He was the wisest and most just of the Centaurs and reputedly was the teacher of Achilles and of other Greek heroes to whom he imparted great skill in bearing arms, medicine, astronomy, music, and augury. Dante places him far down in Hell with the others of his kind, but though he draws Chiron's coarseness, he also grants him a kind of majestic understanding.

67. *Nessus:* Nessus carried travelers across the River Evenus for hire. He was hired to ferry Dejanira, the wife of Hercules, and tried to abduct her, but Hercules killed him with a poisoned arrow. While Nessus was dying, he whispered to Dejanira that a shirt stained with his poisoned blood would act as a love charm should Hercules' affections stray. When Hercules fell in love with Iole, Dejanira sent him

a shirt stained with the Centaur's blood. The shirt poisoned Hercules and he died in agony. Thus Nessus revenged himself with his own blood.

72. *Pholus:* A number of classical poets mention Pholus, but very little else is known of him.

88-89. *the sublime spirit:* Beatrice.

97. *Chiron turned his head on his right breast:* The right is the side of virtue and honor. In Chiron it probably signifies his human side as opposed to his bestial side.

107. *Alexander:* Alexander the Great. *Dionysius:* Dionysius I (died 367 B.C.) and his son, Dionysius II (died 343), were tyrants of Sicily. Both were infamous as prototypes of the bloodthirsty and exorbitant ruler. Dante may intend either or both.

110. *Azzolino (or Ezzelino):* Ezzelino da Romano, Count of Onora (1194-1259). The cruelest of the Ghibelline tyrants. In 1236 Frederick II appointed Ezzelino his vicar in Padua. Ezzelino became especially infamous for his bloody treatment of the Paduans, whom he slaughtered in great numbers.

111. *Opizzo da Esti:* Marquis of Ferrara (1264-1293). The account of his life is confused. One must accept Dante's facts as given.

119-120. *that one . . . a heart still honored on the Thames:* The sinner indicated is Guy de Montfort. His father, Simon de Montfort, was a leader of the barons who rebelled against Henry III and was killed at the battle of Evesham (1265) by Prince Edward (later Edward I).

In 1271, Guy (then Vicar General of Tuscany) avenged his father's death by murdering Henry's nephew (who was also named Henry). The crime was openly committed in a church at Viterbo. The murdered Henry's heart was sealed in a casket and sent to London, where it was accorded various honors.

134. *Sextus:* Probably the younger son of Pompey the Great. His piracy is mentioned in Lucan (*Pharsalia,* VI, 420-422). *Pyrrhus:* Pyrrhus, the son of Achilles, was especially bloodthirsty at the sack of Troy. Pyrrhus, King of Epirus (319-372 B.C.), waged relentless and bloody war against the Greeks and Romans. Either may be intended.

135. *Attila:* King of the Huns from 433 to 453. He was called the Scourge of God.

137. *Rinier da Corneto, Rinier Pazzo:* (Rin-YAIR PAH-tsoe) Both were especially bloodthirsty robber-barons of the thirteenth century.

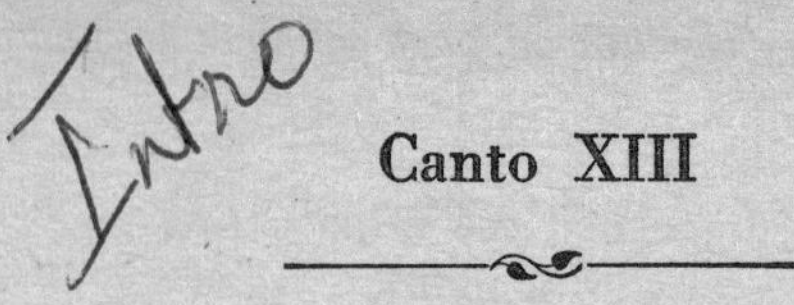

Canto XIII

CIRCLE SEVEN: ***Round Two*** | ***The Violent Against Themselves***

Nessus carries the Poets across the river of boiling blood and leaves them in the Second Round of the Seventh Circle, THE WOOD OF THE SUICIDES. Here are punished those who destroyed their own lives and those who destroyed their substance.

The souls of the Suicides are encased in thorny trees whose leaves are eaten by the odious HARPIES, the overseers of these damned. When the Harpies feed upon them, damaging their leaves and limbs, the wound bleeds. Only as long as the blood flows are the souls of the trees able to speak. Thus, they who destroyed their own bodies are denied a human form; and just as the supreme expression of their lives was self-destruction, so they are permitted to speak only through that which tears and destroys them. Only through their own blood do they find voice. And to add one more dimension to the symbolism, it is the Harpies—defilers of all they touch—who give them their eternally recurring wounds.

The Poets pause before one tree and speak with the soul of PIER DELLE VIGNE. In the same wood they see JACOMO DA SANT' ANDREA, and LANO DA SIENA, two famous SQUANDERERS and DESTROYERS OF GOODS pursued by a pack of savage hounds. The hounds overtake SANT' ANDREA, tear him to pieces and go off carrying his limbs in their teeth, a self-evident symbolic retribution for the violence with which these sinners destroyed their substance in the world. After this scene of horror, Dante speaks to an UNKNOWN FLORENTINE SUICIDE whose soul is inside the bush which was torn by the hound pack when it leaped upon Sant' Andrea.

Nessus had not yet reached the other shore
when we moved on into a pathless wood
that twisted upward from Hell's broken floor.

Its foliage was not verdant, but nearly black.
The unhealthy branches, gnarled and warped and tangled,
bore poison thorns instead of fruit. The track

of those wild beasts that shun the open spaces
men till between Cecina and Corneto
runs through no rougher nor more tangled places.

Here nest the odious Harpies of whom my Master
wrote how they drove Aeneas and his companions
from the Strophades with prophecies of disaster.

Their wings are wide, their feet clawed, their huge bellies
covered with feathers, their necks and faces human.
They croak eternally in the unnatural trees.

"Before going on, I would have you understand,"
my Guide began, "we are in the second round
and shall be till we reach the burning sand.

Therefore look carefully and you will see
things in this wood, which, if I told them to you
would shake the confidence you have placed in me."

I heard cries of lamentation rise and spill
on every hand, but saw no souls in pain
in all that waste; and, puzzled, I stood still.

I think perhaps he thought that I was thinking
those cries rose from among the twisted roots
through which the spirits of the damned were slinking

to hide from us. Therefore my Master said:
"If you break off a twig, what you will learn
will drive what you are thinking from your head."

Puzzled, I raised my hand a bit and slowly
broke off a branchlet from an enormous thorn:
and the great trunk of it cried: "Why do you break me?"

And after blood had darkened all the bowl
of the wound, it cried again: "Why do you tear me?
Is there no pity left in any soul?

Men we were, and now we are changed to sticks;
well might your hand have been more merciful
were we no more than souls of lice and ticks."

As a green branch with one end all aflame
will hiss and sputter sap out of the other
as the air escapes—so from that trunk there came

words and blood together, gout by gout.
Startled, I dropped the branch that I was holding
and stood transfixed by fear, half turned about

to my Master, who replied: "O wounded soul,
could he have believed before what he has seen
in my verses only, you would yet be whole,

for his hand would never have been raised against you.
But knowing this truth could never be believed
till it was seen, I urged him on to do

what grieves me now; and I beg to know your name,
that to make you some amends in the sweet world
when he returns, he may refresh your fame."

And the trunk: "So sweet those words to me that I
cannot be still, and may it not annoy you
if I seem somewhat lengthy in reply.

I am he who held both keys to Frederick's heart,
locking, unlocking with so deft a touch
that scarce another soul had any part

in his most secret thoughts. Through every strife
I was so faithful to my glorious office
that for it I gave up both sleep and life.

That harlot, Envy, who on Caesar's face
keeps fixed forever her adulterous stare,
the common plague and vice of court and palace,

inflamed all minds against me. These inflamed
so inflamed him that all my happy honors
were changed to mourning. Then, unjustly blamed,

my soul, in scorn, and thinking to be free
of scorn in death, made me at last, though just,
unjust to myself. By the new roots of this tree

I swear to you that never in word or spirit
did I break faith to my lord and emperor
who was so worthy of honor in his merit.

If either of you return to the world, speak for me,
to vindicate in the memory of men
one who lies prostrate from the blows of Envy."

The Poet stood. Then turned. "Since he is silent,"
he said to me, "do not you waste this hour,
if you wish to ask about his life or torment."

And I replied: "Question him for my part,
on whatever you think I would do well to hear;
I could not, such compassion chokes my heart."

The Poet began again: "That this man may
with all his heart do for you what your words
entreat him to, imprisoned spirit, I pray,

tell us how the soul is bound and bent
into these knots, and whether any ever
frees itself from such imprisonment."

At that the trunk blew powerfully, and then
the wind became a voice that spoke these words:
"Briefly is the answer given: when

out of the flesh from which it tore itself,
the violent spirit comes to punishment,
Minos assigns it to the seventh shelf.

It falls into the wood, and landing there,
wherever fortune flings it, it strikes root,
and there it sprouts, lusty as any tare,

shoots up a sapling, and becomes a tree.
The Harpies, feeding on its leaves then, give it
pain and pain's outlet simultaneously.

Like the rest, we shall go for our husks on Judgment Day,
but not that we may wear them, for it is not just
that a man be given what he throws away.

Here shall we drag them and in this mournful glade
our bodies will dangle to the end of time,
each on the thorns of its tormented shade."

We waited by the trunk, but it said no more;
and waiting, we were startled by a noise
that grew through all the wood. Just such a roar

and trembling as one feels when the boar and chase
approach his stand, the beasts and branches crashing
and clashing in the heat of the fierce race.

And there on the left, running so violently
they broke off every twig in the dark wood,
two torn and naked wraiths went plunging by me.

The leader cried, "Come now, O Death! Come now!"
And the other, seeing that he was outrun
cried out: "Your legs were not so ready, Lano,

in the jousts at the Toppo." And suddenly in his rush,
perhaps because his breath was failing him,
he hid himself inside a thorny bush

and cowered among its leaves. Then at his back,
the wood leaped with black bitches, swift as greyhounds
escaping from their leash, and all the pack

sprang on him; with their fangs they opened him
and tore him savagely, and then withdrew,
carrying his body with them, limb by limb.

Then, taking me by the hand across the wood,
my Master led me toward the bush. Lamenting,
all its fractures blew out words and blood:

"O Jacomo da Sant' Andrea!" it said,
"what have you gained in making me your screen?
What part had I in the foul life you led?"

And when my Master had drawn up to it
he said: "Who were you, who through all your wounds
blow out your blood with your lament, sad spirit?"

And he to us: "You who have come to see
how the outrageous mangling of these hounds
has torn my boughs and stripped my leaves from me,

O heap them round my ruin! I was born
in the city that tore down Mars and raised the Baptist.
On that account the God of War has sworn

her sorrow shall not end. And were it not
that something of his image still survives
on the bridge across the Arno, some have thought

those citizens who of their love and pain
afterwards rebuilt it from the ashes
left by Attila, would have worked in vain.

I am one who has no tale to tell:
I made myself a gibbet of my own lintel."

Notes

6-10. The reference here is to the Maremma district of Tuscany which lies between the mountains and the sea. The river Cecina is the northern boundary of this district; Corneto is on the river Marta, which forms the southern boundary. It is a wild district of marsh and forest.

10-15. THE HARPIES: These hideous birds with the faces of malign women were often associated with the Erinyes (Furies). Their original function in mythology was to snatch away the souls of men at the command of the Gods. Later, they were portrayed as defilers of food, and, by extension, of everything they touched. The islands of the Strophades were their legendary abode. Aeneas and his men landed there and fought with the Harpies, who drove them back and pronounced a prophecy of unbearable famine upon them.

18. *The burning sand:* The Third Round of this Circle.

25. *I think perhaps he thought that I was thinking:* The original is *"Cred' io ch'ei credette ch'io credesse."* This sort of word play was considered quite elegant by medieval rhetoricians and by the ornate Sicilian School of poetry. Dante's style is based on a rejection of all such devices in favor of a sparse and direct diction. The best explanation of this unusual instance seems to be that Dante is anticipating his talk with Pier delle Vigne, a rhetorician who, as we shall see, delights in this sort of locution. (An analogous stylistic device is common in opera, where the musical phrase identified with a given character may be sounded by the orchestra when the character is about to appear.)

48. *In my verses only:* The *Aeneid,* Book III, describes a similar bleeding plant. There, Aeneas pulls at a myrtle growing on a Thracian hillside. It bleeds where he breaks it and a voice cries out of the ground. It is the voice of Polydorus, son of Priam and friend of Aeneas. He had been treacherously murdered by the Thracian king.

58. *I am he, etc.:* Pier delle Vigne (Pee-YAIR deh-leh VEE-nyeh), 1190-1249. A famous and once-powerful minister of Emperor Frederick II. He enjoyed Frederick's whole confidence until 1247 when he was accused of treachery and was imprisoned and blinded. He committed suicide to escape further torture. (For Frederick see Canto X.) Pier delle Vigne was famous for his eloquence and for his mastery of the ornate Provençal-inspired Sicilian School of Italian Poetry, and Dante styles his speech accordingly. The double balanced construction of line 59, the repetition of key words in lines 67-69, and 70-72 are characteristic of this rhetorical fashion. It is worth noting, however, that the style changes abruptly in the middle of line 72. There, his courtly preamble finished, delle Vigne speaks from the heart, simply and passionately.

58. *who held both keys:* The phrasing unmistakably suggests the Papal keys; delle Vigne may be suggesting that he was to Frederick as the Pope is to God.

64. *Caesar:* Frederick II was of course Caesar of the Roman Empire, but in this generalized context "Caesar" seems to be used as a generic term for any great ruler, *i.e.*, "The harlot, Envy, never turns her attention from those in power."

72. *new roots:* Pier delle Vigne had only been in Hell fifty-one years, a short enough time on the scale of eternity.

98. *wherever fortune flings it:* Just as the soul of the suicide refused to accept divine regulation of its mortal life span, so eternal justice takes no special heed of where the soul falls.

102. *pain and pain's outlet simultaneously:* Suicide also gives pain and its outlet simultaneously.

117 ff. THE VIOLENT AGAINST THEIR SUBSTANCE. They are driven naked through the thorny wood pursued by ravening bitches who tear them to pieces and carry off the limbs. (Obviously the limbs must re-form at some point so that the process can be repeated. For a parallel see Canto XXVIII, the Schismatics. Boccaccio uses an identical device in the Decameron V, vi.) The bitches may be taken as symbolizing conscience, the last besieging creditors of the damned who must satisfy their claims by dividing their wretched bodies, since nothing else is left them. It is not simply prodigality that places them here but the *violence* of their wasting. This fad of violent wasting, scandalously prevalent in Dante's Florence, is hard to imagine today.

120. *Lano:* Lano da Siena, a famous squanderer. He died at the ford of the river Toppo near Arezzo in 1287 in a battle against the

Aretines. Boccaccio writes that he deliberately courted death having squandered all his great wealth and being unwilling to live on in poverty. Thus his companion's jeer probably means: "You were not so ready to run then, Lano: why are you running now?"

133. *Jacomo da Sant' Andrea* (YAH-coe-moe): A Paduan with an infamous lust for laying waste his own goods and those of his neighbors. Arson was his favorite prank. On one occasion, to celebrate the arrival of certain noble guests, he set fire to all the workers' huts and outbuildings of his estate. He was murdered in 1239, probably by assassins hired by Ezzolino (for whom see Canto XII).

131-152. AN ANONYMOUS FLORENTINE SUICIDE: All that is known of him is what he says himself.

143. *the city that tore down Mars and raised the Baptist:* Florence. Mars was the first patron of the city and when the Florentines were converted to Christianity they pulled down his equestrian statue and built a church on the site of his temple. The statue of Mars was placed on a tower beside the Arno. When Totila (see note to line 150) destroyed Florence the tower fell into the Arno and the statue with it. Legend has it that Florence could never have been rebuilt had not the mutilated statue been rescued. It was placed on the Ponte Vecchio but was carried away in the flood of 1333.

150. *Attila:* Dante confuses Attila with Totila, King of the Ostrogoths (died 552). He destroyed Florence in 542. Attila (d. 453), King of the Huns, destroyed many cities of northern Italy, but not Florence.

Canto XIV

CIRCLE SEVEN: ***Round Three*** ***The Violent Against God, Nature, and Art***

Dante, in pity, restores the torn leaves to the soul of his countryman and the Poets move on to the next round, a great PLAIN OF BURNING SAND upon which there descends an eternal slow RAIN OF FIRE. Here, scorched by fire from above and below, are three classes of sinners suffering differing degrees of exposure to the fire. The BLASPHEMERS (The Violent against God) are stretched supine upon the sand, the SODOMITES (The Violent against Nature) run in endless circles, and the USURERS (The Violent against Art, which is the Grandchild of God) huddle on the sands.

The Poets find CAPANEUS stretched out on the sands, the chief sinner of that place. He is still blaspheming God. They continue along the edge of the Wood of the Suicides and come to a blood-red rill which flows boiling from the Wood and crosses the burning plain. Virgil explains the miraculous power of its waters and discourses on the OLD MAN OF CRETE and the origin of all the rivers of Hell.

The symbolism of the burning plain is obviously centered in sterility (the desert image) and wrath (the fire image). Blasphemy, sodomy, and usury are all unnatural and sterile actions: thus the unbearing desert is the eternity of these sinners; and thus the rain, which in nature should be fertile and cool, descends as fire. Capaneus, moreover, is subjected not only to the wrath of nature (the sands below) and the wrath of God (the fire from above), but is tortured most by his own inner violence, which is the root of blasphemy.

Love of that land that was our common source
  moved me to tears; I gathered up the leaves
  and gave them back. He was already hoarse.

We came to the edge of the forest where one goes
  from the second round to the third, and there we saw
  what fearful arts the hand of Justice knows.

To make these new things wholly clear, I say
  we came to a plain whose soil repels all roots.
  The wood of misery rings it the same way

the wood itself is ringed by the red fosse.
  We paused at its edge: the ground was burning sand,
  just such a waste as Cato marched across.

O endless wrath of God: how utterly
  thou shouldst become a terror to all men
  who read the frightful truths revealed to me!

Enormous herds of naked souls I saw,
  lamenting till their eyes were burned of tears;
  they seemed condemned by an unequal law,

for some were stretched supine upon the ground,
  some squatted with their arms about themselves,
  and others without pause roamed round and round.

Most numerous were those that roamed the plain.
  Far fewer were the souls stretched on the sand,
  but moved to louder cries by greater pain.

And over all that sand on which they lay
  or crouched or roamed, great flakes of flame fell slowly
  as snow falls in the Alps on a windless day.

Like those Alexander met in the hot regions
of India, flames raining from the sky
to fall still unextinguished on his legions:

whereat he formed his ranks, and at their head
set the example, trampling the hot ground
for fear the tongues of fire might join and spread—

just so in Hell descended the long rain
upon the damned, kindling the sand like tinder
under a flint and steel, doubling the pain.

In a never-ending fit upon those sands,
the arms of the damned twitched all about their bodies,
now here, now there, brushing away the brands.

"Poet," I said, "master of every dread
we have encountered, other than those fiends
who sallied from the last gate of the dead—

who is that wraith who lies along the rim
and sets his face against the fire in scorn,
so that the rain seems not to mellow him?"

And he himself, hearing what I had said
to my Guide and Lord concerning him, replied:
"What I was living, the same am I now, dead.

Though Jupiter wear out his sooty smith
from whom on my last day he snatched in anger
the jagged thunderbolt he pierced me with;

though he wear out the others one by one
who labor at the forge at Mongibello
crying again 'Help! Help! Help me, good Vulcan!'

as he did at Phlegra; and hurl down endlessly
with all the power of Heaven in his arm,
small satisfaction would he win from me."

At this my Guide spoke with such vehemence
as I had not heard from him in all of Hell:
"O Capaneus, by your insolence

you are made to suffer as much fire inside
as falls upon you. Only your own rage
could be fit torment for your sullen pride."

Then he turned to me more gently. "That," he said,
"was one of the Seven who laid siege to Thebes.
Living, he scorned God, and among the dead

he scorns Him yet. He thinks he may detest
God's power too easily, but as I told him,
his slobber is a fit badge for his breast.

Now follow me; and mind for your own good
you do not step upon the burning sand,
but keep well back along the edge of the wood."

We walked in silence then till we reached a rill
that gushes from the wood; it ran so red
the memory sends a shudder through me still.

As from the Bulicame springs the stream
the sinful women keep to their own use;
so down the sand the rill flowed out in steam.

The bed and both its banks were petrified,
as were its margins; thus I knew at once
our passage through the sand lay by its side.

"Among all other wonders I have shown you
since we came through the gate denied to none,
nothing your eyes have seen is equal to

the marvel of the rill by which we stand,
for it stifles all the flames above its course
as it flows out across the burning sand."

So spoke my Guide across the flickering light,
and I begged him to bestow on me the food
for which he had given me the appetite.

"In the middle of the sea, and gone to waste,
there lies a country known as Crete," he said,
"under whose king the ancient world was chaste.

Once Rhea chose it as the secret crypt
and cradle of her son; and better to hide him,
her Corybantes raised a din when he wept.

An ancient giant stands in the mountain's core.
He keeps his shoulder turned toward Damietta,
and looks toward Rome as if it were his mirror.

His head is made of gold; of silverwork
his breast and both his arms, of polished brass
the rest of his great torso to the fork.

He is of chosen iron from there down,
except that his right foot is terra cotta;
it is this foot he rests more weight upon.

Every part except the gold is split
by a great fissure from which endless tears
drip down and hollow out the mountain's pit.

Their course sinks to this pit from stone to stone,
becoming Acheron, Phlegethon, and Styx.
Then by this narrow sluice they hurtle down

to the end of all descent, and disappear
into Cocytus. You shall see what sink that is
with your own eyes. I pass it in silence here."

And I to him: "But if these waters flow
from the world above, why is this rill met only
along this shelf?" And he to me: "You know

the place is round, and though you have come deep
  into the valley through the many circles,
  always bearing left along the steep,

you have not traveled any circle through
  its total round; hence when new things appear
  from time to time, that hardly should surprise you."

And I: "Where shall we find Phlegethon's course?
  And Lethe's? One you omit, and of the other
  you only say the tear-flood is its source.

"In all you ask of me you please me truly,"
  he answered, "but the red and boiling water
  should answer the first question you put to me,

and you shall stand by Lethe, but far hence:
  there, where the spirits go to wash themselves
  when their guilt has been removed by penitence."

And then he said: "Now it is time to quit
  this edge of shade: follow close after me
  along the rill, and do not stray from it;

for the unburning margins form a lane,
and by them we may cross the burning plain."

Notes

12. *just such a waste as Cato marched across:* In 47 B.C., Cato of Utica led an army across the Libyan desert. Lucan described the march in *Pharsalia* IX, 587 ff.

28-33. *Like those Alexander:* This incident of Alexander the Great's campaign in India is described in *De Meteoris* of Albertus Magnus and was taken by him with considerable alteration from a letter reputedly sent to Aristotle by Alexander.

43. *that wraith who lies along the rim:* Capaneus, one of the seven captains who warred on Thebes. As he scaled the walls of Thebes, Capaneus defied Jove to protect them. Jove replied with a

thunderbolt that killed the blasphemer with his blasphemy still on his lips. (Statius, *Thebiad* x, 845 ff.)

53. *Mongibello:* Mt. Etna. Vulcan was believed to have his smithy inside the volcano.

55. *as he did at Phlegra:* At the battle of Phlegra in Thessaly the Titans tried to storm Olympus. Jove drove them back with the help of the thunderbolts Vulcan forged for him. Capaneus himself is reminiscent of the Titans: like them he is a giant, and he certainly is no less impious.

73. *we reached a rill:* The rill, still blood-red and still boiling, is the overflow of Phlegethon which descends across the Wood of the Suicides and the Burning Plain to plunge over the Great Cliff into the Eighth Circle. It is clearly a water of marvels, for it not only petrifies the sands over which it flows, but its clouds of steam quench all the flames above its course. It is obvious that the Poets' course across the plain will lie along the margins of this rill.

76. *the Bulicame* (Boo-lee-KAH-meh): A hot sulphur spring near Viterbo. The choice is strikingly apt, for the waters of the Bulicame not only boil and steam but have a distinctly reddish tint as a consequence of their mineral content. A part of the Bulicame flows out through what was once a quarter reserved to prostitutes; and they were given special rights to the water, since they were not permitted to use the public baths.

94. *Rhea:* Wife of Saturn (Cronos) and mother of Jove (Zeus). It had been prophesied to Saturn that one of his own children would dethrone him. To nullify the prophecy Saturn devoured each of his children at birth. On the birth of Jove, Rhea duped Saturn by letting him bolt down a stone wrapped in baby clothes. After this tribute to her husband's appetite she hid the infant on Mount Ida in Crete. There she posted her Corybantes (or Bacchantes) as guards and instructed them to set up a great din whenever the baby cried. Thus Saturn would not hear him. The Corybantic dances of the ancient Greeks were based on the frenzied shouting and clashing of swords on shields with which the Corybantes protected the infant Jove.

97. *An ancient giant:* This is the Old Man of Crete. The original of this figure occurs in *Daniel* ii, 32-34, where it is told by Daniel as Nebuchadnezzar's dream. Dante follows the details of the original closely but adds a few of his own and a totally different interpretation. In Dante each metal represents one of the ages of man, each deteriorating from the Golden Age of Innocence. The left foot, terminating the Age of Iron, is the Holy Roman Empire. The right

foot, of terra cotta, is the Roman Catholic Church, a more fragile base than the left, but the one upon which the greater weight descends. The tears of the woes of man are a Dantean detail: they flow down the great fissure that defaces all but the Golden Age. Thus, starting in woe, they flow through man's decline, into the hollow of the mountain and become the waters of all Hell. Dante's other major addition is the site and position of the figure: equidistant from the three continents, the Old Man stands at a sort of center of Time, his back turned to Damietta in Egypt (here symbolizing the East, the past, the birth of religion) and fixes his gaze upon Rome (the West, the future, the Catholic Church). It is certainly the most elaborately worked single symbol in the *Inferno.*

113. *Cocytus:* The frozen lake that lies at the bottom of Hell. (See Cantos XXXII-XXXIV.)

124-125. *Phlegethon . . . Lethe:* Dante asks about Phlegethon and is told that he has already seen it (in the First Round: it is the river of boiling blood) and, in fact, that he is standing beside a branch of it. He asks about Lethe, the river of forgetfulness, and is told it lies ahead.

Canto XV

CIRCLE SEVEN: *Round Three* — *The Violent Against Nature*

Protected by the marvelous powers of the boiling rill, the Poets walk along its banks across the burning plain. The WOOD OF THE SUICIDES is behind them; the GREAT CLIFF at whose foot lies the EIGHTH CIRCLE is before them.

They pass one of the roving bands of SODOMITES. One of the sinners stops Dante, and with great difficulty the Poet recognizes him under his baked features as SER BRUNETTO LATINO. This is a reunion with a dearly-loved man and writer, one who had considerably influenced Dante's own development, and Dante addresses him with great and sorrowful affection, paying him the highest tribute offered to any sinner in the Inferno. *BRUNETTO prophesies Dante's sufferings at the hands of the Florentines, gives an account of the souls that move with him through the fire, and finally, under Divine Compulsion, races off across the plain.*

We go by one of the stone margins now
  and the steam of the rivulet makes a shade above it,
  guarding the stream and banks from the flaming snow.

As the Flemings in the lowland between Bruges
  and Wissant, under constant threat of the sea,
  erect their great dikes to hold back the deluge;

as the Paduans along the shores of the Brent
  build levees to protect their towns and castles
  lest Chiarentana drown in the spring torrent—

to the same plan, though not so wide nor high,
  did the engineer, whoever he may have been,
  design the margin we were crossing by.

Already we were so far from the wood
  that even had I turned to look at it,
  I could not have made it out from where I stood,

when a company of shades came into sight
  walking beside the bank. They stared at us
  as men at evening by the new moon's light

stare at one another when they pass by
  on a dark road, pointing their eyebrows toward us
  as an old tailor squints at his needle's eye.

Stared at so closely by that ghostly crew,
  I was recognized by one who seized the hem
  of my skirt and said: "Wonder of wonders! You?"

And I, when he stretched out his arm to me,
  searched his baked features closely, till at last
  I traced his image from my memory

in spite of the burnt crust, and bending near
  to put my face closer to his, at last
  I answered: "Ser Brunetto, are *you* here?"

"O my son! may it not displease you," he cried,
  "if Brunetto Latino leave his company
  and turn and walk a little by your side."

And I to him: "With all my soul I ask it.
  Or let us sit together, if it please him
  who is my Guide and leads me through this pit."

"My son!" he said, "whoever of this train
  pauses a moment, must lie a hundred years
  forbidden to brush off the burning rain.

Therefore, go on; I will walk at your hem,
and then rejoin my company, which goes
mourning eternal loss in eternal flame."

I did not dare descend to his own level
but kept my head inclined, as one who walks
in reverence meditating good and evil.

"What brings you here before your own last day?
What fortune or what destiny?" he began.
"And who is he that leads you this dark way?"

"Up there in the happy life I went astray
in a valley," I replied, "before I had reached
the fullness of my years. Only yesterday

at dawn I turned from it. This spirit showed
himself to me as I was turning back,
and guides me home again along this road."

And he: "Follow your star, for if in all
of the sweet life I saw one truth shine clearly,
you cannot miss your glorious arrival.

And had I lived to do what I meant to do,
I would have cheered and seconded your work,
observing Heaven so well disposed toward you.

But that ungrateful and malignant stock
that came down from Fiesole of old
and still smacks of the mountain and the rock,

for your good works will be your enemy.
And there is cause: the sweet fig is not meant
to bear its fruit beside the bitter sorb-tree.

Even the old adage calls them blind,
an envious, proud, and avaricious people:
see that you root their customs from your mind.

It is written in your stars, and will come to pass,
that your honours shall make both sides hunger for you:
but the goat shall never reach to crop that grass.

Let the beasts of Fiesole devour their get
like sows, but never let them touch the plant,
if among their rankness any springs up yet,

in which is born again the holy seed
of the Romans who remained among their rabble
when Florence made a new nest for their greed."

"Ah, had I all my wish," I answered then,
"you would not yet be banished from the world
in which you were a radiance among men,

for that sweet image, gentle and paternal,
you were to me in the world when hour by hour
you taught me how man makes himself eternal,

lives in my mind, and now strikes to my heart;
and while I live, the gratitude I owe it
will speak to men out of my life and art.

What you have told me of my course, I write
by another text I save to show a Lady
who will judge these matters, if I reach her height.

This much I would have you know: so long, I say,
as nothing in my conscience troubles me
I am prepared for Fortune, come what may.

Twice already in the eternal shade
I have heard this prophecy; but let Fortune turn
her wheel as she please, and the countryman his spade."

My guiding spirit paused at my last word
and, turning right about, stood eye to eye
to say to me: "Well heeded is well heard."

But I did not reply to him, going on
with Ser Brunetto to ask him who was with him
in the hot sands, the best-born and best known.

And he to me: "Of some who share this walk
it is good to know; of the rest let us say nothing,
for the time would be too short for so much talk.

In brief, we all were clerks and men of worth,
great men of letters, scholars of renown;
all by the one same crime defiled on earth.

Priscian moves there along the wearisome
sad way, and Francesco d'Accorso, and also there,
if you had any longing for such scum,

you might have seen that one the Servant of Servants
sent from the Arno to the Bacchiglione
where he left his unnatural organ wrapped in cerements.

I would say more, but there across the sand
a new smoke rises and new people come,
and I must run to be with my own band.

Remember my *Treasure*, in which I shall live on:
I ask no more." He turned then, and he seemed,
across that plain, like one of those who run

for the green cloth at Verona; and of those,
more like the one who wins, than those who lose.

Notes

The Violent Against Nature. Dante calls them *i sodomiti*, the Sodomites: At root, the moral decedents of the people of biblical Sodom, by which Dante meant homosexuals, though he would probably have classed as sodomy oral and anal sex between heterosexuals, his puritanism classing all such sexuality as "bestial." The connotations of the word "bestial" when so used have led to the more recent sense of *sodomy* as sexual union of a human being and an animal, though this is only one of the word's senses, the original reference to homosexual Sodom remaining firm. In XII, 12–13, Passiphaë is mentioned as having begotten the Minotaur after coupling with a great bull, but she is not among the damned souls there, nor does she appear here on the burning plain whose wretches include a number of known or suspected homosexuals, but none with a reputation as an "animal lover." Passiphaë seems, in fact, to be used as a sort of musical key to this passage on bestial behavior, but sodomy in the recent sense is not otherwise treated, as later in Cantos XXXII–XXXIII cannibalism is not specifically mentioned, though the act of cannibalism rings through all the phrasing as an ambiguous suggestion. It is almost as if Dante thought these sins too grievous to discuss openly.

10. *though not so wide nor high:* Their width is never precisely specified, but we shall see when Dante walks along speaking to Ser Brunetto (line 40) that their height is about that of a man.

23-119. *Ser Brunetto Latino:* or Latini. (Born between 1210 and 1230, died 1294.) A prominent Florentine Guelph who held, among many other posts, that of notary, whence the title *Ser* (sometimes *Sere*). He was not Dante's schoolmaster as many have supposed—he was much too busy and important a man for that. Dante's use of the word "master" is to indicate spiritual indebtedness to Brunetto and his works. It is worth noting that Dante addresses him in Italian as "voi" instead of using the less respectful "tu" form. Farinata is the only other sinner so addressed in the *Inferno.* Brunetto's two principal books, both of which Dante admires, were the prose *Livre dou Tresor (The Book of the Treasure)* and the poetic *Tesoretta (The Little Treasure).* Dante learned a number of his devices from the allegorical journey which forms the *Tesoretto.*

Dante's surprise at finding Brunetto here is worth puzzling about. So too is the fact that he did not ask Ciacco about him (Canto VI) when he mentioned other prominent Florentines. One speculation is that Dante had not intended to place him in Hell, and that he found reason to believe him guilty of this sin only years after Brunetto's death (the *Inferno* was written between 1310 and 1314, in all probability). This answer is not wholly satisfactory.

40. *I will walk at your hem:* See also line 10. Dante is standing on the dike at approximately the level of Brunetto's head and he cannot descend because of the rain of fire and the burning sands.

61-67. *that ungrateful and malignant stock:* The ancient Etruscan city of Fiesole was situated on a hill about three miles north of the present site of Florence. According to legend, Fiesole had taken the side of Catiline in his war with Julius Caesar. Caesar destroyed the town and set up a new city called Florence on the Arno, peopling it with Romans and Fiesolans. The Romans were the aristocracy of the new city, but the Fiesolans were a majority. Dante ascribes the endless bloody conflicts of Florence largely to the internal strife between these two strains. His scorn of the Fiesolans is obvious in this passage. Dante proudly proclaimed his descent from the Roman strain.

66. *sorb-tree:* A species of tart apple.

67. *calls them blind:* The source of this proverbial expression, "Blind as a Florentine," can no longer be traced with any assurance, though many incidents from Florentine history suggest possible sources.

71. *shall make both sides hunger for you:* Brunetto can scarcely mean that both sides will hunger to welcome the support of a man of Dante's distinction. Rather, that both sides will hunger to destroy him. (See also lines 94-95. Dante obviously accepts this as another dark prophecy.)

73. *the beasts of Fiesole:* The Fiesolans themselves.

89. *to show a Lady:* Beatrice.

94-99. *twice already . . . I have heard:* The prophecies of Ciacco (Canto VI) and of Farinata (Canto X) are the other two places at which Dante's exile and suffering are foretold. Dante replies that come what may he will remain true to his purpose through all affliction; and Virgil turns to look proudly at his pupil uttering a proverb: *"Bene ascolta chi la nota," i.e.,* "Well heeded is well heard."

109. *Priscian:* Latin grammarian and poet of the first half of the sixth century.

110. *Francesco d'Accorso:* (Frahn-CHAY-skoe dah-KAWR-soe) A Florentine scholar. He served as a professor at Bologna and, from 1273 to 1280, at Oxford. He died in Bologna in 1294.

112-13. *that one the Servant of Servants . . . Arno to the Bacchiglione etc.:* "The Servant of Servants" was Dante's old enemy, Boniface VIII. *Servus servorum* is technically a correct papal title, but there is certainly a touch of irony in Dante's application of it in this context. In 1295 Boniface transferred Bishop Andrea de' Mozzi from the Bishopric of Florence (on the Arno) to that of Vicenza (on the Bacchiglione). The transference was reputedly brought about at the request of the Bishop's brother, Tommaso de' Mozzi of Florence, who wished to remove from his sight the spectacle of his brother's stupidity and unnatural vices.

114. *unnatural organ:* The original, *mal protesi nervi,* contains an untranslatable word-play. *Nervi* may be taken as "the male organ" and *protesi* for "erected"; thus the organ aroused to passion for unnatural purposes *(mal).* Or *nervi* may be taken as "nerves" and *mal protesi* for "dissolute." Taken in context, the first rendering strikes me as more Dantean.

121. *the green cloth:* On the first Sunday of Lent all the young men of Verona ran a race for the prize of green cloth. The last runner in was given a live rooster and was required to carry it through the town.

Canto XVI

CIRCLE SEVEN: *Round Three* — *The Violent Against Nature and Art*

The Poets arrive within hearing of the waterfall that plunges over the GREAT CLIFF into the EIGHTH CIRCLE. The sound is still a distant throbbing when three wraiths, recognizing Dante's Florentine dress, detach themselves from their band and come running toward him. They are JACOPO RUSTICUCCI, GUIDO GUERRA, and TEGGHIAIO ALDOBRANDI, all of them Florentines whose policies and personalities Dante admired. Rusticucci and Tegghiaio have already been mentioned in a highly complimentary way in Dante's talk with Ciacco (Canto VI).

The sinners ask for news of Florence, and Dante replies with a passionate lament for her present degradation. The three wraiths return to their band and the Poets continue to the top of the falls. Here, at Virgil's command, Dante removes a CORD from about his waist and Virgil drops it over the edge of the abyss. As if in answer to a signal, a great distorted shape comes swimming up through the dirty air of the pit.

We could already hear the rumbling drive
  of the waterfall in its plunge to the next circle,
  a murmur like the throbbing of a hive,

when three shades turned together on the plain,
  breaking toward us from a company
  that went its way to torture in that rain.

They cried with one voice as they ran toward me:
"Wait, oh wait, for by your dress you seem
a voyager from our own tainted country."

Ah! what wounds I saw, some new, some old,
branded upon their bodies! Even now
the pain of it in memory turns me cold.

My Teacher heard their cries, and turning-to,
stood face to face. "Do as they ask," he said,
"for these are souls to whom respect is due;

and were it not for the darting flames that hem
our narrow passage in, I should have said
it were more fitting you ran after them."

We paused, and they began their ancient wail
over again, and when they stood below us
they formed themselves into a moving wheel.

As naked and anointed champions do
in feeling out their grasp and their advantage
before they close in for the thrust or blow—

so circling, each one stared up at my height,
and as their feet moved left around the circle,
their necks kept turning backward to the right.

"If the misery of this place, and our unkempt
and scorched appearance," one of them began,
"bring us and what we pray into contempt,

still may our earthly fame move you to tell
who and what you are, who so securely
set your live feet to the dead dusts of Hell.

This peeled and naked soul who runs before me
around this wheel, was higher than you think
there in the world, in honor and degree.

Guido Guerra was the name he bore,
the good Gualdrada's grandson. In his life
he won great fame in counsel and in war.

The other who behind me treads this sand
was Tegghiaio Aldobrandi, whose good counsels
the world would have done well to understand.

And I who share their torment, in my life
was Jacopo Rusticucci; above all
I owe my sorrows to a savage wife."

I would have thrown myself to the plain below
had I been sheltered from the falling fire;
and I think my Teacher would have let me go.

But seeing I should be burned and cooked, my fear
overcame the first impulse of my heart
to leap down and embrace them then and there.

"Not contempt," I said, "but the compassion
that seizes on my soul and memory
at the thought of you tormented in this fashion—

it was grief that choked my speech when through the scorching
air of this pit my Lord announced to me
that such men as you are might be approaching.

I am of your own land, and I have always
heard with affection and rehearsed with honor
your name and the good deeds of your happier days.

Led by my Guide and his truth, I leave the gall
and go for the sweet apples of delight.
But first I must descend to the center of all."

"So may your soul and body long continue
together on the way you go," he answered,
"and the honor of your days shine after you—

tell me if courtesy and valor raise
their banners in our city as of old,
or has the glory faded from its days?

For Borsiere, who is newly come among us
and yonder goes with our companions in pain,
taunts us with such reports, and his words have stung us."

"O Florence! your sudden wealth and your upstart
rabble, dissolute and overweening,
already set you weeping in your heart!"

I cried with face upraised, and on the sand
those three sad spirits looked at one another
like men who hear the truth and understand.

"If this be your manner of speaking, and if you can
satisfy others with such ease and grace,"
they said as one, "we hail a happy man.

Therefore, if you win through this gloomy pass
and climb again to see the heaven of stars;
when it rejoices you to say 'I was',

speak of us to the living." They parted then,
breaking their turning wheel, and as they vanished
over the plain, their legs seemed wings. "Amen"

could not have been pronounced between their start
and their disappearance over the rim of sand.
And then it pleased my Master to depart.

A little way beyond we felt the quiver
and roar of the cascade, so close that speech
would have been drowned in thunder. As that river—

the first one on the left of the Appennines
to have a path of its own from Monte Veso
to the Adriatic Sea—which, as it twines

is called the Acquacheta from its source
until it nears Forlì, and then is known
as the Montone in its further course—

resounds from the mountain in a single leap
there above San Benedetto dell'Alpe
where a thousand falls might fit into the steep;

so down from a sheer bank, in one enormous
plunge, the tainted water roared so loud
a little longer there would have deafened us.

I had a cord bound round me like a belt
which I had once thought I might put to use
to snare the leopard with the gaudy pelt.

When at my Guide's command I had unbound
its loops from about my habit, I gathered it
and held it out to him all coiled and wound.

He bent far back to his right, and throwing it
out from the edge, sent it in a long arc
into the bottomless darkness of the pit.

"Now surely some unusual event,"
I said to myself, "must follow this new signal
upon which my good Guide is so intent."

Ah, how cautiously a man should breathe
near those who see not only what we do,
but have the sense which reads the mind beneath!

He said to me: "You will soon see arise
what I await, and what you wonder at;
soon you will see the thing before your eyes."

To the truth which will seem falsehood every man
who would not be called a liar while speaking fact
should learn to seal his lips as best he can.

But here I cannot be still: Reader, I swear
by the lines of my Comedy—so may it live—
that I saw swimming up through that foul air

a shape to astonish the most doughty soul,
a shape like one returning through the sea
from working loose an anchor run afoul

of something on the bottom—so it rose,
its arms spread upward and its feet drawn close.

Notes

21 ff. *a moving wheel:* See Ser Brunetto's words (lines 37-39, Canto XV).

37. *Guido Guerra* (GHEE-doe or GWEE-doe GWEH-rah): (around 1220-1272.) A valiant leader of the Guelphs (hence his name which signifies Guido of War) despite his Ghibelline origin as one of the counts of Guidi. It is a curious fact, considering the prominence of Guido, that Dante is the only writer to label him a sodomite.

38. *the good Gualdrada* (Gwahl-DRAH-dah): The legend of "the good Gualdrada," Guido Guerra's grandmother, is a typical example of the medieval talent for embroidery. She was the daughter of Bellincione Berti de' Ravignana. The legend is that Emperor Otto IV saw her in church and, attracted by her beauty, asked who she was. Bellincione replied that she was the daughter of one whose soul would be made glad to have the Emperor salute her with a kiss. The young-lady-of-all-virtues, hearing her father's words, declared that no man might kiss her unless he were her husband. Otto was so impressed by the modesty and propriety of this remark that he married her to one of his noblemen and settled a large estate upon the couple. It was from this marriage that the counts Guidi de Modigliano (among them Guido Guerra) were said to descend.

Unfortunately for the legend, Otto's first visit to Italy was in 1209, and surviving records show that Count Guido had already had two children by his wife Gualdrada as early as 1202.

41. *Tegghiaio Aldobrandi* (Tegh-YEYE-oh Ahl-doe-BRAHN-dee): Date of birth unknown. He died shortly before 1266. A valiant knight of the family degli Adimari of the Guelph nobles. With Guido Guerra he advised the Florentines not to move against the Sienese at the disastrous battle of Montaperti (See Farinata, Canto

X), knowing that the Sienese had been heavily reinforced by mercenaries. It is probably these good counsels that "the world would have done well to understand." This is another case in which Dante is the only writer to bring the charge of sodomy.

44. *Jacopo Rusticucci* (YAH-coe-poe Roo-stee-KOO-tchee): Dates of birth and death unknown, but mention of him exists in Florentine records of 1235, 1236, 1254, and 1266. A rich and respected Florentine knight. Dante's account of his sin and of its cause is the only record and it remains unsupported: no details of his life are known.

70. *Guglielmo Borsiere* (Goo-lyELL-moe Bohrs-YEHR-eh): "Borsiere" in Italian means "pursemaker," and the legend has grown without verification or likelihood that this was his origin. He was a courtier, a peacemaker, and an arranger of marriages. Boccaccio speaks of him in highly honorable terms in the Eighth Tale of the First Day of the *Decameron.*

93ff. *that river:* The water course described by Dante and made up of the Acquacheta (Ah-kwa-KAY-tah) and the Montone flows directly into the sea without draining into the Po. The placement of it as "first on the left of the Appennines" has been shown by Casella to result from the peculiar orientation of the maps of Dante's time. The "river" has its source and course along a line running almost exactly northwest from Florence. San Benedetto dell' Alpe is a small monastery situated on that line about twenty-five miles from Florence.

106. THE CORD: As might be expected many ingenious explanations have been advanced to account for the sudden appearance of this cord. It is frequently claimed, but without proof, that Dante had been a minor friar of the Franciscans but had left without taking vows. The explanation continues that he had clung to the habit of wearing the white cord of the Franciscans, which he now produces with the information that he had once intended to use it to snare the Leopard.

One invention is probably as good as another. What seems obvious is that the narrative required some sort of device for signaling the monster, and that to meet his narrative need, Dante suddenly invented the business of the cord. Dante, as a conscientious and self-analytical craftsman, would certainly have been aware of the technical weakness of this sudden invention; but Dante the Master was sufficiently self-assured to brush aside one such detail, sure as he must have been of the strength of his total structure.

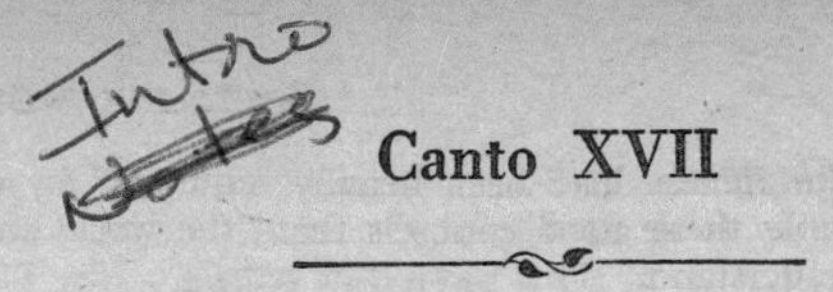

Canto XVII

CIRCLE SEVEN: *Round Three* *The Violent Against Art. Geryon*

The monstrous shape lands on the brink and Virgil salutes it ironically. It is GERYON, the MONSTER OF FRAUD. Virgil announces that they must fly down from the cliff on the back of this monster. While Virgil negotiates for their passage, Dante is sent to examine the USURERS (The Violent against Art).

These sinners sit in a crouch along the edge of the burning plain that approaches the cliff. Each of them has a leather purse around his neck, and each purse is blazoned with a coat of arms. Their eyes, gushing with tears, are forever fixed on these purses. Dante recognizes none of these sinners, but their coats of arms are unmistakably those of well-known Florentine families.

Having understood who they are and the reason for their present condition, Dante cuts short his excursion and returns to find Virgil mounted on the back of Geryon. Dante joins his Master and they fly down from the great cliff.

Their flight carries them from the Hell of the VIOLENT AND THE BESTIAL (The Sins of the Lion) into the Hell of the FRAUDULENT AND MALICIOUS (The Sins of the Leopard).

"Now see the sharp-tailed beast that mounts the brink.
He passes mountains, breaks through walls and weapons.
Behold the beast that makes the whole world stink."

These were the words my Master spoke to me;
then signaled the weird beast to come to ground
close to the sheer end of our rocky levee.

The filthy prototype of Fraud drew near
and settled his head and breast upon the edge
of the dark cliff, but let his tail hang clear.

His face was innocent of every guile,
benign and just in feature and expression;
and under it his body was half reptile.

His two great paws were hairy to the armpits;
all his back and breast and both his flanks
were figured with bright knots and subtle circlets:

never was such a tapestry of bloom
woven on earth by Tartar or by Turk,
nor by Arachne at her flowering loom.

As a ferry sometimes lies along the strand,
part beached and part afloat; and as the beaver,
up yonder in the guzzling Germans' land,

squats halfway up the bank when a fight is on—
just so lay that most ravenous of beasts
on the rim which bounds the burning sand with stone.

His tail twitched in the void beyond that lip,
thrashing, and twisting up the envenomed fork
which, like a scorpion's stinger, armed the tip.

My Guide said: "It is time now we drew near
that monster." And descending on the right
we moved ten paces outward to be clear

of sand and flames. And when we were beside him,
I saw upon the sand a bit beyond us
some people crouching close beside the brim.

The Master paused. "That you may take with you
the full experience of this round," he said,
"go now and see the last state of that crew.

But let your talk be brief, and I will stay
and reason with this beast till you return,
that his strong back may serve us on our way."

So further yet along the outer edge
of the seventh circle I moved on alone.
And came to the sad people of the ledge.

Their eyes burst with their grief; their smoking hands
jerked about their bodies, warding off
now the flames and now the burning sands.

Dogs in summer bit by fleas and gadflies,
jerking their snouts about, twitching their paws
now here, now there, behave no otherwise.

I examined several faces there among
that sooty throng, and I saw none I knew;
but I observed that from each neck there hung

an enormous purse, each marked with its own beast
and its own colors like a coat of arms.
On these their streaming eyes appeared to feast.

Looking about, I saw one purse display
azure on or, a kind of lion; another,
on a blood red field, a goose whiter than whey.

And one that bore a huge and swollen sow
azure on field argent said to me:
"What are you doing in this pit of sorrow?

Leave us alone! And since you have not yet died,
I'll have you know my neighbor Vitaliano
has a place reserved for him here at my side.

A Paduan among Florentines, I sit here
while hour by hour they nearly deafen me
shouting: 'Send us the sovereign cavalier

with the purse of the three goats!' " He half arose,
twisted his mouth, and darted out his tongue
for all the world like an ox licking its nose.

And I, afraid that any longer stay
would anger him who had warned me to be brief,
left those exhausted souls without delay.

Returned, I found my Guide already mounted
upon the rump of that monstrosity.
He said to me: "Now must you be undaunted:

this beast must be our stairway to the pit:
mount it in front, and I will ride between
you and the tail, lest you be poisoned by it."

Like one so close to the quartanary chill
that his nails are already pale and his flesh trembles
at the very sight of shade or a cool rill—

so did I tremble at each frightful word.
But his scolding filled me with that shame that makes
the servant brave in the presence of his lord.

I mounted the great shoulders of that freak
and tried to say "Now help me to hold on!"
But my voice clicked in my throat and I could not speak.

But no sooner had I settled where he placed me
than he, my stay, my comfort, and my courage
in other perils, gathered and embraced me.

Then he called out: "Now, Geryon, we are ready:
bear well in mind that his is living weight
and make your circles wide and your flight steady."

As a small ship slides from a beaching or its pier,
backward, backward—so that monster slipped
back from the rim. And when he had drawn clear

he swung about, and stretching out his tail
he worked it like an eel, and with his paws
he gathered in the air, while I turned pale.

I think there was no greater fear the day
Phaeton let loose the reins and burned the sky
along the great scar of the Milky Way,

nor when Icarus, too close to the sun's track
felt the wax melt, unfeathering his loins,
and heard his father cry "Turn back! Turn back!"—

than I felt when I found myself in air,
afloat in space with nothing visible
but the enormous beast that bore me there.

Slowly, slowly, he swims on through space,
wheels and descends, but I can sense it only
by the way the wind blows upward past my face.

Already on the right I heard the swell
and thunder of the whirlpool. Looking down
I leaned my head out and stared into Hell.

I trembled again at the prospect of dismounting
and cowered in on myself, for I saw fires
on every hand, and I heard a long lamenting.

And then I saw—till then I had but felt it—
the course of our down-spiral to the horrors
that rose to us from all sides of the pit.

As a flight-worn falcon sinks down wearily
though neither bird nor lure has signalled it,
the falconer crying out: "What! spent already!"—

then turns and in a hundred spinning gyres
sulks from her master's call, sullen and proud—
so to that bottom lit by endless fires

the monster Geryon circled and fell,
  setting us down at the foot of the precipice
  of ragged rock on the eighth shelf of Hell.

And once freed of our weight, he shot from there
into the dark like an arrow into air.

Notes

1. *Geryon:* A mythical king of Spain represented as a giant with three heads and three bodies. He was killed by Hercules, who coveted the king's cattle. A later tradition represents him as killing and robbing strangers whom he lured into his realm. It is probably on this account that Dante chose him as the prototype of fraud, though in a radically altered bodily form. Some of the details of Dante's Geryon may be drawn from *Revelations* ix, 9-20, but most of them are almost certainly his own invention: a monster with the general shape of a dragon but with the tail of a scorpion, hairy arms, a gaudily-marked reptilian body, and the face of a just and honest man. The careful reader will note that the gaudily-spotted body suggests the Leopard; the hairy paws, the Lion; and that the human face represents the essentially human nature of Fraud, which thus embodies corruption of the Appetite, of the Will, and of the Intellect.

17. *Tartar . . . Turk:* These were the most skilled weavers of Dante's time.

18. *Arachne:* She was so famous as a spinner and weaver that she challenged Minerva to a weaving contest. There are various accounts of what happened in the contest, but all of them end with the goddess so moved to anger that she changed Arachne into a spider.

20. *the beaver:* Dante's description of the beaver is probably drawn from some old bestiary or natural history. It may be based on the medieval belief that the beaver fished by crouching on the bank, scooping the fish out with its tail.

21. *the guzzling Germans:* The heavy drinking of the Germans was proverbial in the Middle Ages and far back into antiquity.

29. *descending on the right:* The Poets had crossed on the right bank of the rill. In the course of Geryon's flight they will be carried to the other side of the falls, thus continuing their course to the left. It should be noted that inside the walls of Dis, approaching the second great division of Hell (as here the third) they also moved to the right. No satisfactory reason can be given for these exceptions.

33. *some people:* The Usurers. Virgil explains in Canto XI why they sin against Art, which is the Grandchild of God. They are the third and final category of the Violent against God and His works.

56. *azure on or, a kind of lion:* The arms of the Gianfigliazzi (Djahn-fee-LYAH-tsee) of Florence were a lion azure on a field of gold. The sinner bearing this purse must be Catello di Rosso Gianfigliazzi, who set up as a usurer in France and was made a knight on his return to Florence.

57. *on a blood red field, a goose whiter than whey:* A white goose on a red field was the arms of the noble Ghibelline family of the Ubriachi, or Ebriachi, of Florence. The wearer is probably Ciappo Ubriachi (CHAH-poe Oob-ree-AH-kee), a notorious usurer.

58-59. *sow azure on field argent:* These are the arms of the Scrovegni (Skroe-VAY-nyee) of Padua. The bearer is probably Reginaldo Scrovegni.

62. *Vitaliano:* Vitaliano di Iacopo Vitaliani, another Paduan.

66-67. *the sovereign cavalier:* Giovanni di Buiamonte (Djoe-VAHN-ee dee Boo-yah-MON-teh) was esteemed in Florence as "the sovereign cavalier" and was chosen for many high offices. He was a usurer and a gambler who lost great sums at play. Dante's intent is clearly to bewail the decay of standards which permits Florence to honor so highly a man for whom Hell is waiting so dismally. Buiamonte was of the Becchi (BEH-kee) family whose arms were three black goats on a gold field. "Becchi" in Italian is the plural form of the word for "goat."

79. *quartanary chill:* Quartan fever is an ague that runs a four-day cycle with symptoms roughly like those of malaria. At the approach of the chill, Dante intends his figure to say, any thought of coolness strikes terror into the shivering victim.

101. *Phaeton:* Son of Apollo who drove the chariot of the sun. Phaeton begged his father for a chance to drive the chariot himself but he lost control of the horses and Zeus killed him with a thunderbolt for fear the whole earth would catch fire. The scar left in the sky by the runaway horses is marked by the Milky Way.

103. *Icarus:* Daedalus, the father of Icarus, made wings for himself and his son and they flew into the sky, but Icarus, ignoring his father's commands, flew too close to the sun. The heat melted the wax with which the wings were fastened and Icarus fell into the Aegean and was drowned.

121-25. *flight-worn falcon:* Falcons, when sent aloft, were trained to circle until sighting a bird, or until signaled back by the lure (a stuffed bird). Flight-weary, Dante's metaphoric falcon sinks bit by bit, rebelling against his training and sulking away from his master in wide slow circles. The weighed, slow, downward flight of Geryon is powerfully contrasted with his escaping bound into the air once he has deposited his burden.

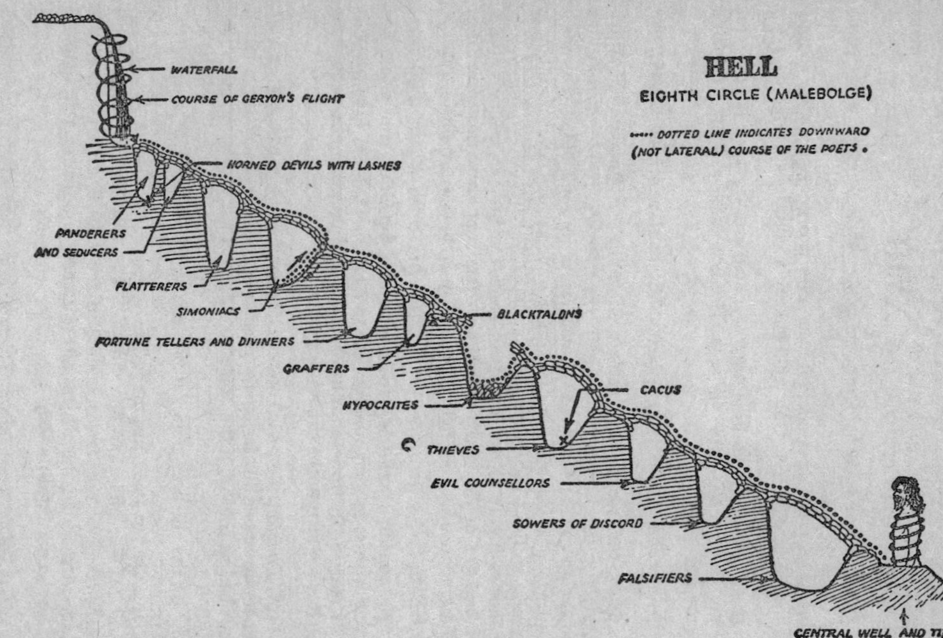
HELL
EIGHTH CIRCLE (MALEBOLGE)
DOTTED LINE INDICATES DOWNWARD (NOT LATERAL) COURSE OF THE POETS.
WATERFALL
COURSE OF GERYON'S FLIGHT
HORNED DEVILS WITH LASHES
PANDERERS AND SEDUCERS
FLATTERERS
SIMONIACS
FORTUNE TELLERS AND DIVINERS
GRAFTERS
BLACKTALONS
HYPOCRITES
CACUS
THIEVES
EVIL COUNSELLORS
SOWERS OF DISCORD
FALSIFIERS
CENTRAL WELL AND TITANS

Canto XVIII

CIRCLE EIGHT *(Malebolge)* — *The Fraudulent and Malicious*

BOLGIA ONE — *The Panderers and Seducers*

BOLGIA TWO — *The Flatterers*

Dismounted from Geryon, the Poets find themselves in the EIGHTH CIRCLE, called MALEBOLGE (The Evil Ditches). This is the upper half of the HELL OF THE FRAUDULENT AND MALICIOUS. Malebolge is a great circle of stone that slopes like an amphitheater. The slopes are divided into ten concentric ditches; and within these ditches, each with his own kind, are punished those guilty of SIMPLE FRAUD.

A series of stone dikes runs like spokes from the edge of the great cliff face to the center of the place, and these serve as bridges.

The Poets bear left toward the first ditch, and Dante observes below him and to his right the sinners of the first bolgia, *The PANDERERS and SEDUCERS. These make two files, one along either bank of the ditch, and are driven at an endless fast walk by horned demons who hurry them along with great lashes. In life these sinners goaded others on to serve their own foul purposes; so in Hell are they driven in their turn. The horned demons who drive them symbolize the sinners' own vicious natures, embodiments of their own guilty consciences. Dante may or may not have intended the horns of the demons to symbolize cuckoldry and adultery.*

The Poets see VENEDICO CACCIANEMICO and JASON in the first pit, and pass on to the second, where they find the souls of the FLATTERERS sunk in excrement, the true equivalent of their false flatteries on earth. They observe ALESSIO INTERMINELLI and THAIS, and pass on.

There is in Hell a vast and sloping ground
called Malebolge, a lost place of stone
as black as the great cliff that seals it round.

Precisely in the center of that space
there yawns a well extremely wide and deep.
I shall discuss it in its proper place.

The border that remains between the well-pit
and the great cliff forms an enormous circle,
and ten descending troughs are cut in it,

offering a general prospect like the ground
that lies around one of those ancient castles
whose walls are girded many times around

by concentric moats. And just as, from the portal,
the castle's bridges run from moat to moat
to the last bank; so from the great rock wall

across the embankments and the ditches, high
and narrow cliffs run to the central well,
which cuts and gathers them like radii.

Here, shaken from the back of Geryon,
we found ourselves. My Guide kept to the left
and I walked after him. So we moved on.

Below, on my right, and filling the first ditch
along both banks, new souls in pain appeared,
new torments, and new devils black as pitch.

All of these sinners were naked; on our side
of the middle they walked toward us; on the other,
in our direction, but with swifter stride.

Just so the Romans, because of the great throng
in the year of the Jubilee, divide the bridge
in order that the crowds may pass along,

so that all face the Castle as they go
on one side toward St. Peter's, while on the other,
all move along facing toward Mount Giordano.

And everywhere along that hideous track
I saw horned demons with enormous lashes
move through those souls, scourging them on the back.

Ah, how the stragglers of that long rout stirred
their legs quick-march at the first crack of the lash!
Certainly no one waited a second, or third!

As we went on, one face in that procession
caught my eye and I said: "That sinner there:
It is certainly not the first time I've seen that one."

I stopped, therefore, to study him, and my Guide
out of his kindness waited, and even allowed me
to walk back a few steps at the sinner's side.

And that flayed spirit, seeing me turn around,
thought to hide his face, but I called to him:
"You there, that walk along with your eyes on the ground—

if those are not false features, then I know you
as Venedico Caccianemico of Bologna:
what brings you here among this pretty crew?"

And he replied: "I speak unwillingly,
but something in your living voice, in which
I hear the world again, stirs and compels me.

It was I who brought the fair Ghisola 'round
to serve the will and lust of the Marquis,
however sordid that old tale may sound.

There are many more from Bologna who weep away
eternity in this ditch; we fill it so
there are not as many tongues that are taught to say

'sipa' in all the land that lies between
the Reno and the Saveno, as you must know
from the many tales of our avarice and spleen."

And as he spoke, one of those lashes fell
across his back, and a demon cried, "Move on,
you pimp, there are no women here to sell."

Turning away then, I rejoined my Guide.
We came in a few steps to a raised ridge
that made a passage to the other side.

This we climbed easily, and turning right
along the jagged crest, we left behind
the eternal circling of those souls in flight.

And when we reached the part at which the stone
was tunneled for the passage of the scourged,
my Guide said, "Stop a minute and look down

on these other misbegotten wraiths of sin.
You have not seen their faces, for they moved
in the same direction we were headed in."

So from that bridge we looked down on the throng
that hurried toward us on the other side.
Here, too, the whiplash hurried them along.

And the good Master, studying that train,
said: "Look there, at that great soul that approaches
and seems to shed no tears for all his pain—

what kingliness moves with him even in Hell!
It is Jason, who by courage and good advice
made off with the Colchian Ram. Later it fell

that he passed Lemnos, where the women of wrath,
enraged by Venus' curse that drove their lovers
out of their arms, put all their males to death.

There with his honeyed tongue and his dishonest
lover's wiles, he gulled Hypsipyle,
who, in the slaughter, had gulled all the rest.

And there he left her, pregnant and forsaken.
Such guilt condemns him to such punishment;
and also for Medea is vengeance taken.

All seducers march here to the whip.
And let us say no more about this valley
and those it closes in its stony grip."

We had already come to where the walk
crosses the second bank, from which it lifts
another arch, spanning from rock to rock.

Here we heard people whine in the next chasm,
and knock and thump themselves with open palms,
and blubber through their snouts as if in a spasm.

Steaming from that pit, a vapour rose
over the banks, crusting them with a slime
that sickened my eyes and hammered at my nose.

That chasm sinks so deep we could not sight
its bottom anywhere until we climbed
along the rock arch to its greatest height.

Once there, I peered down; and I saw long lines
of people in a river of excrement
that seemed the overflow of the world's latrines.

I saw among the felons of that pit
one wraith who might or might not have been tonsured—
one could not tell, he was so smeared with shit.

He bellowed: "You there, why do you stare at me
more than at all the others in this stew?"
And I to him: "Because if memory

serves me, I knew you when your hair was dry.
You are Alessio Interminelli da Lucca.
That's why I pick you from this filthy fry."

And he then, beating himself on his clown's head:
"Down to this have the flatteries I sold
the living sunk me here among the dead."

And my Guide prompted then: "Lean forward a bit
and look beyond him, there—do you see that one
scratching herself with dungy nails, the strumpet

who fidgets to her feet, then to a crouch?
It is the whore Thaïs who told her lover
when he sent to ask her, 'Do you thank me much?'

'Much? Nay, past all believing!' And with this
let us turn from the sight of this abyss."

Notes

2. *Malebolge: Bolgia* (BOWL-djah) in Italian equals "ditch" or "pouch." That combination of meanings is not possible in a single English word, but it is well to bear in mind that Dante intended both meanings: not only a ditch of evil, but a pouch full of it, a filthy treasure of ill-gotten souls.

5. *a well:* This is the final pit of Hell, and in it are punished the Treacherous (those Guilty of Compound Fraud). Cantos XXIX-XXXIV will deal with this part of Hell.

22. *below, on my right:* (See diagram.) The Poets have, as usual, borne left from the point where Geryon left them. They are walking along the outer ridge of the first *bolgia,* and the sinners are below them on the right. The Panderers are walking toward them along the near bank; the seducers are walking the other way (*i.e.,* in the

same direction as the Poets) along the far bank. Dante places the Seducers closer to the center of Hell, thereby indicating that their sin is a shade worse than that of the Panderers. It is difficult to see why Dante should think so, but since both receive exactly the same punishment, the distinction is more or less academic.

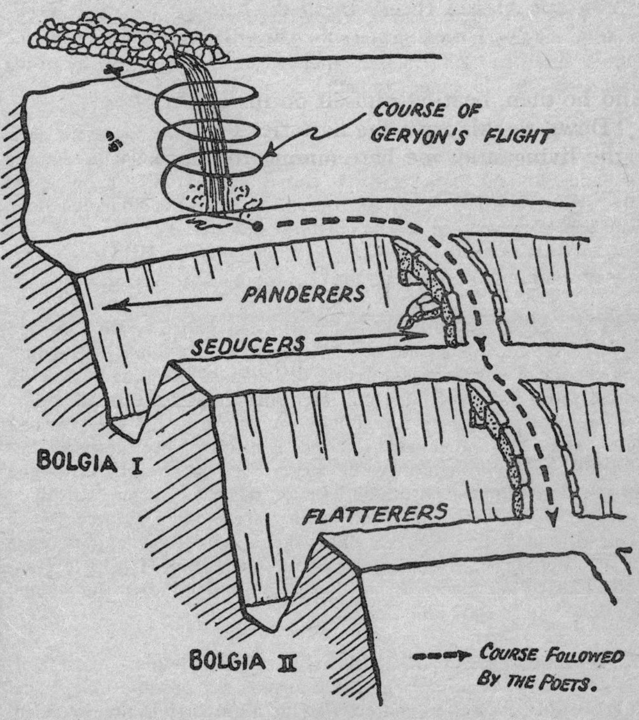

28-33. Boniface VIII had proclaimed 1300 a Jubilee Year, and consequently throngs of pilgrims had come to Rome. Since the date of the vision is also 1300, the Roman throngs are moving back and forth across the Tiber via Ponte Castello Sant' Angelo at the very time Dante is watching the sinners in Hell.

47. *thought to hide his face:* The general rule of the sinners above the great barrier cliff has been a great willingness—in fact, an eagerness—to make themselves known and to be remembered in the world. From this point to the bottom of Hell that rule is reversed, and the

sinners, with a few exceptions, try to conceal their identity, asking only to be forgotten. This change should be noted as one more evidence of Dante's architectural sense of detail: this exploitation of many interrelated themes and their progression from point to point of the great journey give the poem its symphonic and many-leveled richness.

50. *Venedico Caccianemico* (Ven-AID-ee-coe Kah-tchah-neh-MEE-coe): A nobleman of Bologna. To win the favor of the Marquis Obbizo da Este of Ferrara, Caccianemico acted as the procurer of his own sister Ghisola, called "la bella" or "Ghisolabella."

61. *sipa:* Bolognese dialect for "si," *i.e.*, "yes." Bologna lies between the Savena and the Reno. This is a master taunt at Bologna as a city of panderers and seducers, for it clearly means that the Bolognese then living on earth were fewer in number than the Bolognese dead who had been assigned to this *bolgia*.

70. *turning right:* See diagram.

83-96. *Jason:* Leader of the Argonauts. He carried off the Colchian Ram (*i.e.*, The Golden Fleece). "The good advice" that helped him win the fleece was given by Medea, daughter of the King of Colchis, whom Jason took with him and later abandoned for Creusa. ("Also for Medea is vengeance taken.") In the course of his very Grecian life, Jason had previously seduced Hypsipyle and deserted her to continue his voyage after the fleece. She was one of the women of Lemnos whom Aphrodite, because they no longer worshiped her, cursed with a foul smell which made them unbearable to their husbands and lovers. The women took their epic revenge by banding together to kill all their males, but Hypsipyle managed to save her father, King Thoas, by pretending to the women that she had already killed him.

THE FLATTERERS. BOLGIA 2.

It should be noted as characteristic of Dante's style that he deliberately coarsens his language when he wishes to describe certain kinds of coarseness. The device has earned Dante the title of "master of the disgusting." It may well be added that what is disgusting in the Victorian drawing-room may be the essential landscape of Hell. Among the demons who guard the grafters (Cantos XXI-XXII), and among the sowers of discord (Canto XXVIII), Dante reinvokes the same gargoyle quality. It would be ridiculous prudery to refine Dante's diction at these points.

122. *Alessio Interminelli da Lucca* (In-ter-min-ELL-ee): One of the noble family of the Interminelli or Interminei, a prominent White

family of Lucca. About all that is known of Alessio is the fact that he was still alive in 1295.

131. *Thaïs:* The flattery uttered by Thaïs is put into her mouth by Terence in his *Eunuchus* (Act III, 1:1-2). Thaïs' lover had sent her a slave, and later sent a servant to ask if she thanked him much. *Magnas vero agere gratias Thais mihi?* The servant reported her as answering *Ingentes!* Cicero later commented on the passage as an example of immoderate flattery, and Dante's conception of Thaïs probably springs from this source. (*De Amicitia,* 26.)

Canto XIX

CIRCLE EIGHT: ***Bolgia Three*** ***The Simoniacs***

Dante comes upon the SIMONIACS (sellers of ecclesiastic favors and offices) and his heart overflows with the wrath he feels against those who corrupt the things of God. This bolgia *is lined with round tube-like holes and the sinners are placed in them upside down with the soles of their feet ablaze. The heat of the blaze is proportioned to their guilt.*

The holes in which these sinners are placed are debased equivalents of the baptismal fonts common in the cities of Northern Italy and the sinners' confinement in them is temporary: as new sinners arrive, the souls drop through the bottoms of their holes and disappear eternally into the crevices of the rock.

As always, the punishment is a symbolic retribution. Just as the Simoniacs made a mock of holy office, so are they turned upside down in a mockery of the baptismal font. Just as they made a mockery of the holy water of baptism, so is their hellish baptism by fire, after which they are wholly immersed in the crevices below. The oily fire that licks at their soles may also suggest a travesty on the oil used in Extreme Unction (last rites for the dying).

Virgil carries Dante down an almost sheer ledge and lets him speak to one who is the chief sinner of that place, POPE NICHOLAS III. Dante delivers himself of another stirring denunciation of those who have corrupted church office, and Virgil carries him back up the steep ledge toward the FOURTH BOLGIA.

O Simon Magus! O you wretched crew
  who follow him, pandering for silver and gold
  the things of God which should be wedded to

love and righteousness! O thieves for hire,
now must the trump of judgment sound your doom
here in the third fosse of the rim of fire!

We had already made our way across
to the next grave, and to that part of the bridge
which hangs above the mid-point of the fosse.

O Sovereign Wisdom, how Thine art doth shine
in Heaven, on Earth, and in the Evil World!
How justly doth Thy power judge and assign!

I saw along the walls and on the ground
long rows of holes cut in the livid stone;
all were cut to a size, and all were round.

They seemed to be exactly the same size
as those in the font of my beautiful San Giovanni,
built to protect the priests who come to baptize;

(one of which, not so long since, I broke open
to rescue a boy who was wedged and drowning in it.
Be this enough to undeceive all men.)

From every mouth a sinner's legs stuck out
as far as the calf. The soles were all ablaze
and the joints of the legs quivered and writhed about.

Withes and tethers would have snapped in their throes.
As oiled things blaze upon the surface only,
so did they burn from the heels to the points of their toes.

"Master," I said, "who is that one in the fire
who writhes and quivers more than all the others?
From him the ruddy flames seem to leap higher."

And he to me: "If you wish me to carry you down
along that lower bank, you may learn from him
who he is, and the evil he has done."

And I: "What you will, I will. You are my lord
and know I depart in nothing from your wish;
and you know my mind beyond my spoken word."

We moved to the fourth ridge, and turning left
my Guide descended by a jagged path
into the strait and perforated cleft.

Thus the good Master bore me down the dim
and rocky slope, and did not put me down
till we reached the one whose legs did penance for him.

"Whoever you are, sad spirit," I began,
"who lie here with your head below your heels
and planted like a stake—speak if you can."

I stood like a friar who gives the sacrament
to a hired assassin, who, fixed in the hole,
recalls him, and delays his death a moment.

"Are you there already, Boniface? Are you there
already?" he cried. "By several years the writ
has lied. And all that gold, and all that care—

are you already sated with the treasure
for which you dared to turn on the Sweet Lady
and trick and pluck and bleed her at your pleasure?"

I stood like one caught in some raillery,
not understanding what is said to him,
lost for an answer to such mockery.

Then Virgil said. "Say to him: 'I am not he,
I am not who you think.' " And I replied
as my good Master had instructed me.

The sinner's feet jerked madly; then again
his voice rose, this time choked with sighs and tears,
and said at last: "What do you want of me then?

If to know who I am drives you so fearfully
that you descend the bank to ask it, know
that the Great Mantle was once hung upon me.

And in truth I was a son of the She-Bear,
so sly and eager to push my whelps ahead,
that I pursed wealth above, and myself here.

Beneath my head are dragged all who have gone
before me in buying and selling holy office;
there they cower in fissures of the stone.

I too shall be plunged down when that great cheat
for whom I took you comes here in his turn.
Longer already have I baked my feet

and been planted upside-down, than he shall be
before the west sends down a lawless Shepherd
of uglier deeds to cover him and me.

He will be a new Jason of the Maccabees;
and just as that king bent to his high priests' will,
so shall the French king do as this one please."

Maybe—I cannot say—I grew too brash
at this point, for when he had finished speaking
I said: "Indeed! Now tell me how much cash

our Lord required of Peter in guarantee
before he put the keys into his keeping?
Surely he asked nothing but 'Follow me!'

Nor did Peter, nor the others, ask silver or gold
of Matthew when they chose him for the place
the despicable and damned apostle sold.

Therefore stay as you are; this hole well fits you—
and keep a good guard on the ill-won wealth
that once made you so bold toward Charles of Anjou.

And were it not that I am still constrained
  by the reverence I owe to the Great Keys
  you held in life, I should not have refrained

from using other words and sharper still;
  for this avarice of yours grieves all the world,
  tramples the virtuous, and exalts the evil.

Of such as you was the Evangelist's vision
  when he saw She who Sits upon the Waters
  locked with the Kings of earth in fornication.

She was born with seven heads, and ten enormous
  and shining horns strengthened and made her glad
  as long as love and virtue pleased her spouse.

Gold and silver are the gods you adore!
  In what are you different from the idolator,
  save that he worships one, and you a score?

Ah Constantine, what evil marked the hour—
  not of your conversion, but of the fee
  the first rich Father took from you in dower!"

And as I sang him this tune, he began to twitch
  and kick both feet out wildly, as if in rage
  or gnawed by conscience—little matter which.

And I think, indeed, it pleased my Guide: his look
  was all approval as he stood beside me
  intent upon each word of truth I spoke.

He approached, and with both arms he lifted me,
  and when he had gathered me against his breast,
  remounted the rocky path out of the valley,

nor did he tire of holding me clasped to him,
  until we reached the topmost point of the arch
  which crosses from the fourth to the fifth rim

of the pits of woe. Arrived upon the bridge,
  he tenderly set down the heavy burden
  he had been pleased to carry up that ledge

which would have been hard climbing for a goat.
Here I looked down on still another moat.

Notes

1. *Simon Magus*: Simon the Samarian magician (see *Acts* viii, 9-24) from whom the word "Simony" derives. Upon his conversion to Christianity he offered to buy the power to administer the Holy Ghost and was severely rebuked by Peter.

8. *the next grave:* The next *bolgia.*

9. *that part of the bridge:* The center point. The center of each span is obviously the best observation point.

11. *Evil World:* Hell.

17-18. *the font of my beautiful San Giovanni:* It was the custom in Dante's time to baptize only on Holy Saturday and on Pentecost. These occasions were naturally thronged, therefore, and to protect the priests a special font was built in the Baptistry of San Giovanni with marble stands for the priests, who were thus protected from both the crowds and the water in which they immersed those to be baptized. The Baptistry is still standing, but the font is no longer in it. A similar font still exists, however, in the Baptistry at Pisa.

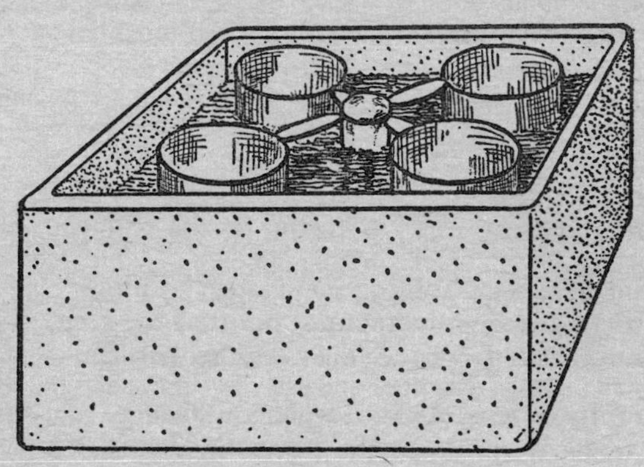

Probable detail of baptismal font.

19-21. In these lines Dante is replying to a charge of sacrilege that had been rumored against him. One day a boy playing in the baptismal font became jammed in the marble tube and could not be extricated. To save the boy from drowning, Dante took it upon himself to smash the tube. This is his answer to all men on the charge of sacrilege.

29. *more than all the others:* The fire is proportioned to the guilt of the sinner. These are obviously the feet of the chief sinner of this *bolgia*. In a moment we shall discover that he is Pope Nicholas III.

46-47. *like a friar, etc.:* Persons convicted of murdering for hire were sometimes executed by being buried alive upside down. If the friar were called back at the last moment, he should have to bend over the hole in which the man is fixed upside down awaiting the first shovelful of earth.

POPE NICHOLAS III: Giovanni Gaetano degli Orsini, Pope from 1277-1280. His presence here is self-explanatory. He is awaiting the arrival of his successor, Boniface VIII, who will take his place in the stone tube and who will in turn be replaced by Clement V, a Pope even more corrupt than Boniface. With the foresight of the damned he had read the date of Boniface's death (1303) in the Book of Fate. Mistaking Dante for Boniface, he thinks his foresight has erred by three years, since it is now 1300.

66. *the Great Mantle:* of the Papacy.

67. *son of the She-Bear:* Nicholas' family name, degli Orsini, means in Italian "of the bear cubs."

69. *pursed:* A play on the second meaning of *bolgia* (*i.e.*, "purse"). "Just as I put wealth in my purse when alive, so am I put in this foul purse now that I am dead."

77-79. *a lawless Shepherd . . . Jason of the Maccabees . . . the French King:* The reference is to Clement V, Pope from 1305 to 1314. He came from Gascony (the West) and was involved in many intrigues with the King of France. It was Clement V who moved the Papal See to Avignon where it remained until 1377. He is compared to Jason (see *Maccabees* iv, 7ff.) who bought an appointment as High Priest of the Jews from King Antiochus and thereupon introduced pagan and venal practices into the office in much the same way as Clement used his influence with Philip of France to secure and corrupt his high office.

Clement will succeed Boniface in Hell because Boniface's successor,

Benedictus XI (1303-1304), was a good and holy man. The terms each guilty Pope must serve in this hellish baptism are:

Nicholas III 1280-1303
(four good Popes intervene)

Boniface VIII 1303-1314
(one good Pope intervenes)

Clement V 1314—not stated

88-89. *nor did Peter . . . of Matthias:* Upon the expulsion of Judas from the band of Apostles, Matthias was chosen in his place.

93. *Charles of Anjou:* The seventh son of Louis VIII of France. Charles became King of Naples and of Sicily largely through the good offices of Pope Urban IV and later of Clement IV. Nicholas III withdrew the high favor his predecessors had shown Charles, but the exact nature and extent of his opposition are open to dispute. Dante probably believed, as did many of his contemporaries, that Nicholas instigated the massacre called the Sicilian Vespers, in which the Sicilians overthrew the rule of Charles and held a general slaughter of the French who had been their masters. The Sicilian Vespers, however, was a popular and spontaneous uprising, and it did not occur until Nicholas had been dead for two years.

Dante may have erred in interpreting the Sicilian question, but his point is indisputably clear when he laments the fact that simoniacally acquired wealth had involved the Papacy in war and political intrigue, thereby perverting it from its spiritual purpose.

95. *the Great Keys:* of the Papacy.

100-105. *the Evangelist . . . She Who Sits upon the Waters:* St. John the Evangelist. His vision of She who sits upon the waters is set forth in *Revelations* xvii. The Evangelist intended it as a vision of Pagan Rome, but Dante interprets it as a vision of the Roman Church in its simoniacal corruption. The seven heads are the seven sacraments; the ten horns, the ten commandments.

109-11. *Ah Constantine, etc.:* The first rich Father was Silvester (Pope from 314 to 355). Before him the Popes possessed nothing, but when Constantine was converted and Catholicism became the official religion of the Empire, the church began to acquire wealth. Dante and the scholars of his time believed, according to a document called "The Donation of Constantine," that the Emperor had moved his Empire to the East in order to leave sovereignty of the West to the Church. The document was not shown to be a forgery until the fifteenth century. Knowledge of the forgery would not, however, have altered Dante's view; he was unwavering in his belief that wealth was the greatest disaster that had befallen the Church, for in wealth lay the root of the corruption which Dante denounced so passionately.

Canto XX

CIRCLE EIGHT: *Bolgia Four* — *The Fortune Tellers and Diviners*

Dante stands in the middle of the bridge over the FOURTH BOLGIA and looks down at the souls of the FORTUNE TELLERS and DIVINERS. Here are the souls of all those who attempted by forbidden arts to look into the future. Among these damned are: AMPHIAREUS, TIRESIAS, ARUNS, MANTO, EURYPYLUS, MICHAEL SCOTT, GUIDO BONATTI, and ASDENTE.

Characteristically, the sin of these wretches is reversed upon them: their punishment is to have their heads turned backwards on their bodies and to be compelled to walk backwards through all eternity, their eyes blinded with tears. Thus, those who sought to penetrate the future cannot even see in front of themselves; they attempted to move themselves forward in time, so must they go backwards through all eternity; and as the arts of sorcery are a distortion of God's law, so are their bodies distorted in Hell.

No more need be said of them: Dante names them, and passes on to fill the Canto with a lengthy account of the founding of Virgil's native city of Mantua.

Now must I sing new griefs, and my verses strain
  to form the matter of the Twentieth Canto
  of Canticle One, the Canticle of Pain.

My vantage point permitted a clear view
  of the depths of the pit below: a desolation
  bathed with the tears of its tormented crew,

who moved about the circle of the pit
at about the pace of a litany procession.
Silent and weeping, they wound round and round it.

And when I looked down from their faces, I saw
that each of them was hideously distorted
between the top of the chest and the lines of the jaw;

for the face was reversed on the neck, and they came on
backwards, staring backwards at their loins,
for to look before them was forbidden. Someone,

sometime, in the grip of a palsy may have been
distorted so, but never to my knowledge;
nor do I believe the like was ever seen.

Reader, so may God grant you to understand
my poem and profit from it, ask yourself
how I could check my tears, when near at hand

I saw the image of our humanity
distorted so that the tears that burst from their eyes
ran down the cleft of their buttocks. Certainly

I wept. I leaned against the jagged face
of a rock and wept so that my Guide said: "Still?
Still like the other fools? There is no place

for pity here. Who is more arrogant
within his soul, who is more impious
than one who dares to sorrow at God's judgment?

Lift up your eyes, lift up your eyes and see
him the earth swallowed before all the Thebans,
at which they cried out: 'Whither do you flee,

Amphiareus? Why do you leave the field?'
And he fell headlong through the gaping earth
to the feet of Minos, where all sin must yield.

Observe how he has made a breast of his back.
In life he wished to see too far before him,
and now he must crab backwards round this track.

And see Tiresias, who by his arts
succeeded in changing himself from man to woman,
transforming all his limbs and all his parts;

later he had to strike the two twined serpents
once again with his conjurer's wand before
he could resume his manly lineaments.

And there is Aruns, his back to that one's belly,
the same who in the mountains of the Luni
tilled by the people of Carrara's valley,

made a white marble cave his den, and there
with unobstructed view observed the sea
and the turning constellations year by year.

And she whose unbound hair flows back to hide
her breasts—which you cannot see—and who also wears
all of her hairy parts on that other side,

was Manto, who searched countries far and near,
then settled where I was born. In that connection
there is a story I would have you hear.

Tiresias was her sire. After his death,
Thebes, the city of Bacchus, became enslaved,
and for many years she roamed about the earth.

High in sweet Italy, under the Alps that shut
the Tyrolean gate of Germany, there lies
a lake known as Benacus roundabout.

Through endless falls, more than a thousand and one,
Mount Appennine from Garda to Val Cammonica
is freshened by the waters that flow down

into that lake. At its center is a place
where the Bishops of Brescia, Trentine, and Verona
might all give benediction with equal grace.

Peschiera, the beautiful fortress, strong in war
against the Brescians and the Bergamese,
sits at the lowest point along that shore.

There, the waters Benacus cannot hold
within its bosom, spill and form a river
that winds away through pastures green and gold.

But once the water gathers its full flow,
it is called Mincius rather than Benacus
from there to Governo, where it joins the Po.

Still near its source, it strikes a plain, and there
it slows and spreads, forming an ancient marsh
which in the summer heats pollutes the air.

The terrible virgin, passing there by chance,
saw dry land at the center of the mire,
untilled, devoid of all inhabitants.

There, shunning all communion with mankind,
she settled with the ministers of her arts,
and there she lived, and there she left behind

her vacant corpse. Later the scattered men
who lived nearby assembled on that spot
since it was well defended by the fen.

Over those whited bones they raised the city,
and for her who had chosen the place before all others
they named it—with no further augury—

Mantua. Far more people lived there once—
before sheer madness prompted Casalodi
to let Pinamonte play him for a dunce.

Therefore, I charge you, should you ever hear
other accounts of this, to let no falsehood
confuse the truth which I have just made clear."

And I to him: "Master, within my soul
your word is certainty, and any other
would seem like the dead lumps of burned out coal.

But tell me of those people moving down
to join the rest. Are any worth my noting?
For my mind keeps coming back to that alone."

And he: "That one whose beard spreads like a fleece
over his swarthy shoulders, was an augur
in the days when so few males remained in Greece

that even the cradles were all but empty of sons.
He chose the time for cutting the cable at Aulis,
and Calchas joined him in those divinations.

He is Eurypylus. I sing him somewhere
in my High Tragedy; you will know the place
who know the whole of it. The other there,

the one beside him with the skinny shanks
was Michael Scott, who mastered every trick
of magic fraud, a prince of mountebanks.

See Guido Bonatti there; and see Asdente,
who now would be wishing he had stuck to his last,
but repents too late, though he repents aplenty.

And see on every hand the wretched hags
who left their spinning and sewing for soothsaying
and casting of spells with herbs, and dolls, and rags.

But come: Cain with his bush of thorns appears
already on the wave below Seville,
above the boundary of the hemispheres;

and the moon was full already yesternight,
as you must well remember from the wood,
for it certainly did not harm you when its light

shone down upon your way before the dawn."
And as he spoke to me, we traveled on.

Notes

A GENERAL NOTE:

The rather long account of the origin of Mantua with which Dante fills up this Canto often prompts students to ask why he does not delete this "irrelevant account" in order to spend more time on the diviners. The answer to that question (it could be asked in connection with many other passages in the *Commedia*) points to the core of Dante's allegorical style. The fact is that once he has placed the diviners in their proper pit and assigned them an appropriate punishment, his essential allegorical function has been fulfilled: nothing more need be said.

Thus, the structure carries all. Once the poem is under way, it is enough simply to name a man as being in a certain place in Hell suffering a certain punishment, and that man is not only located as precisely as an x drawn on a map locates the point it marks, but the sin which that man typifies is located on the scale of value which is constructed into the whole nature of the Universe as Dante saw it.

The Poet is thereby left free to pass on to the discussion of all those matters of theology, history, politics, and "science" which fascinate him. But there is nothing "irrelevant" about these multiple interests. Dante's journey is "to experience all." He is not simply taking a long walk: he is constructing a Universe. As part of that construction, he reaches out to draw data from a variety of sources. These are not "data" in the scientific sense. Rather they are "typical" data: *i.e.,* each of Dante's side discussions considers data that are central to its type: the history of Mantua relates to the history of Troy, to the history of Virgil, to the history of Rome, to the history of Florence. Moreover, the history of Mantua is excerpted as typical from the whole range of history (as if Dante were saying: "Thus are the States of man begun") to advance one of the great themes of the *Commedia*—the backgrounds of civilization as Dante knew it.

3. *Canticle One: The Inferno.* The other Canticles are, of course, *The Purgatorio* and *The Paradiso.*

4. *my vantage point:* Virgil, it will be recalled, had set Dante down on the bridge across the Fourth Bolgia.

8. *at about the pace of a litany procession:* The litanies are chanted not only in church (before the mass), but sometimes in procession, the priest chanting the prayers and the marchers the response. As one might gather from the context, the processions move very slowly.

10. *And when I looked down from their faces:* A typically Dantean conception. Dante often writes as if the eye pin-pointed on one feature of a figure seen at a distance. The pin-point must then be deliberately shifted before the next feature can be observed. As far as I know, this stylistic device is peculiar to Dante.

14. *loins:* General usage seems to have lost sight of the fact that the first meaning of "loin" is "that part of a human being or quadruped on either side of the spinal column between the hipbone and the false ribs." (Webster.)

23-24. *tears . . . ran down the cleft of the buttocks:* Since the heads of these sinners are backwards on their necks, their tears would run down their backs, and this is the obvious track they must follow. But what a debasement of sorrow! This is the sort of detail Dante knew how to use with maximum effect.

26-30. VIRGIL SCOLDS DANTE FOR SHOWING PITY. It is worth noting that Virgil has not scolded Dante for showing pity in earlier cases, though he might easily have done so and for exactly the same reason. One interpretation may be that Dante was not yet ready to recognize the true nature of evil. Another may be that Human Reason (despite Dante's earlier reference to his "all-knowing Master") is essentially fallible. Beatrice, a higher creature, is so made that she is incapable of being moved by the creatures of Hell (see Canto II), as is the Divine Messenger who springs open the Gates of Dis (Canto IX).

34. *Amphiareus:* Another of the seven Captains who fought against Thebes (v. Capaneus, Canto XIV). Statius (*Thebaid* VII, 690 ff. and VIII, 8 ff.) tells how he foresaw his own death in this war, and attempted to run away from it, but was swallowed in his flight by an earthquake. I have Romanized his name from "Amphiaraus."

40. *Tiresias:* A Theban diviner and magician. Ovid (*Metamorphoses* III) tells how he came on two twined serpents, struck them apart with his stick, and was thereupon transformed into a woman. Seven years later he came on two serpents similarly entwined, struck them apart, and was changed back.

46-48. *Aruns:* An Etruscan soothsayer (see Lucan, *Pharsalia,* I, 580 ff.). He foretold the war between Pompey and Julius Caesar, and also that it would end with Caesar's victory and Pompey's death. *Luni:*

Also *Luna*. An ancient Etruscan city. *Carrara's valley:* The Carrarese valley is famous for its white (Carrara) marble.

46. *that one's:* Tiresias.

55. *Manto:* The text is self-explanatory. Dante's version of the founding of Mantua is based on a reference in the *Aeneid* X, 198-200.

63 ff. *Benacus:* The ancient name for the famous Lago di Garda, which lies a short distance north of Mantua. The other places named in this passage lie around Lago di Garda. On an island in the lake the three dioceses mentioned in line 68 conjoined. All three bishops, therefore, had jurisdiction on the island.

95-96. *Casalodi . . . Pinamonte:* Albert, Count of Casalodi and Lord of Mantua, let himself be persuaded by Pinamonte de Buonaccorsi to banish the nobles from Mantua as a source of danger to his rule. Once the nobles had departed, Pinamonte headed a rebellion against the weakened lord and took over the city himself.

106. *That one whose beard:* Eurypylus, Greek augur. According to Greek custom an augur was summoned before each voyage to choose the exact propitious moment for departure (cutting the cables). Dante has Virgil imply that Eurypylus and Calchas were selected to choose the moment for Agamemnon's departure from Aulis to Troy. Actually, according to the *Aeneid,* Eurypylus was not at Aulis. The *Aeneid* (II, 110 ff.) tells how Eurypylus and Calchas were both consulted in choosing the moment for the departure from Troy. Dante seems to have confused the two incidents.

109. *even the cradles were all but empty of sons:* At the time of the Trojan Wars, Greece was said to be so empty of males that scarcely any were to be found even in the cradles.

116. *Michael Scott:* An Irish scholar of the first half of the thirteenth century. His studies were largely in the occult. Sir Walter Scott refers to him in *The Lay of the Last Minstrel.*

118. *Guido Bonatti:* A thirteenth-century astrologer of Forli. He was court astrologer to Guido da Montefeltro (see Canto XXVII) advising him in his wars. *Asdente:* A shoemaker of Parma who turned diviner and won wide fame for his forecastings in the last half of the thirteenth century.

124 ff. *Cain with his bush of thorns:* The Moon. Cain with a bush of thorns was the medieval equivalent of our Man in the Moon. Dante seems to mean by "Seville" the whole area of Spain and the Straits of Gibraltar (Pillars of Hercules), which were believed to be the western limit of the world. The moon is setting (*i.e.,* it appears on the western waves) on the morning of Holy Saturday, 1300.

Canto XXI

CIRCLE EIGHT: *Bolgia Five* *The Grafters*

The Poets move on, talking as they go, and arrive at the FIFTH BOLGIA. Here the GRAFTERS are sunk in boiling pitch and guarded by DEMONS, who tear them to pieces with claws and grappling hooks if they catch them above the surface of the pitch.

The sticky pitch is symbolic of the sticky fingers of the Grafters. It serves also to hide them from sight, as their sinful dealings on earth were hidden from men's eyes. The demons, too, suggest symbolic possibilities, for they are armed with grappling hooks and are forever ready to rend and tear all they can get their hands on.

The Poets watch a demon arrive with a grafting SENATOR of LUCCA and fling him into the pitch where the demons set upon him.

To protect Dante from their wrath, Virgil hides him behind some jagged rocks and goes ahead alone to negotiate with the demons. They set upon him like a pack of mastiffs, but Virgil secures a safe-conduct from their leader, MALACODA. Thereupon Virgil calls Dante from hiding, and they are about to set off when they discover that the BRIDGE ACROSS THE SIXTH BOLGIA lies shattered. Malacoda tells them there is another further on and sends a squad of demons to escort them. Their adventures with the demons continue through the next Canto.

These two Cantos may conveniently be remembered as the GARGOYLE CANTOS. If the total Commedia *is built like a cathedral (as so many critics have suggested), it is here certainly that Dante attaches his grotesqueries. At no other point in the* Commedia *does Dante give such free rein to his coarsest style.*

Thus talking of things which my Comedy does not care
to sing, we passed from one arch to the next
until we stood upon its summit. There

we checked our steps to study the next fosse
and the next vain lamentations of Malebolge;
awesomely dark and desolate it was.

As in the Venetian arsenal, the winter through
there boils the sticky pitch to caulk the seams
of the sea-battered bottoms when no crew

can put to sea—instead of which, one starts
to build its ship anew, one plugs the planks
which have been sprung in many foreign parts;

some hammer at a mast, some at a rib;
some make new oars, some braid and coil new lines;
one patches up the mainsail, one the jib—

so, but by Art Divine and not by fire,
a viscid pitch boiled in the fosse below
and coated all the bank with gluey mire.

I saw the pitch; but I saw nothing in it
except the enormous bubbles of its boiling,
which swelled and sank, like breathing, through all the pit.

And as I stood and stared into that sink,
my Master cried, "Take care!" and drew me back
from my exposed position on the brink.

I turned like one who cannot wait to see
the thing he dreads, and who, in sudden fright,
runs while he looks, his curiosity

competing with his terror—and at my back
I saw a figure that came running toward us
across the ridge, a Demon huge and black.

Ah what a face he had, all hate and wildness!
Galloping so, with his great wings outspread
he seemed the embodiment of all bitterness.

Across each high-hunched shoulder he had thrown
one haunch of a sinner, whom he held in place
with a great talon round each ankle bone.

"Blacktalons of our bridge," he began to roar,
"I bring you one of Santa Zita's Elders!
Scrub him down while I go back for more:

I planted a harvest of them in that city:
everyone there is a grafter except Bonturo.
There 'Yes' is 'No' and 'No' is 'Yes' for a fee."

Down the sinner plunged, and at once the Demon
spun from the cliff; no mastiff ever sprang
more eager from the leash to chase a felon.

Down plunged the sinner and sank to reappear
with his backside arched and his face and both his feet
glued to the pitch, almost as if in prayer.

But the Demons under the bridge, who guard that place
and the sinners who are thrown to them, bawled out:
"You're out of bounds here for the Sacred Face:

this is no dip in the Serchio: take your look
and then get down in the pitch. And stay below
unless you want a taste of a grappling hook."

Then they raked him with more than a hundred hooks
bellowing: "Here you dance below the covers.
Graft all you can there: no one checks your books."

They dipped him down into that pitch exactly
as a chef makes scullery boys dip meat in a boiler,
holding it with their hooks from floating free.

And the Master said: *"You* had best not be seen
by these Fiends till I am ready. Crouch down here.
One of these rocks will serve you as a screen.

And whatever violence you see done to me,
you have no cause to fear. I know these matters:
I have been through this once and come back safely."

With that, he walked on past the end of the bridge;
and it wanted all his courage to look calm
from the moment he arrived on the sixth ridge.

With that same storm and fury that arouses
all the house when the hounds leap at a tramp
who suddenly falls to pleading where he pauses—

so rushed those Fiends from below, and all the pack
pointed their gleaming pitchforks at my Guide.
But he stood fast and cried to them: "Stand back!

Before those hooks and grapples make too free,
send up one of your crew to hear me out,
then ask yourselves if you still care to rip me."

All cried as one: "Let Malacoda go."
So the pack stood and one of them came forward,
saying: "What good does he think *this* will do?"

"Do you think, Malacoda," my good Master said,
"you would see me here, having arrived this far
already, safe from you and every dread,

without Divine Will and propitious Fate?
Let me pass on, for it is willed in Heaven
that I must show another this dread state."

The Demon stood there on the flinty brim,
so taken aback he let his pitchfork drop;
then said to the others: "Take care not to harm him!"

"O you crouched like a cat," my Guide called to me,
"among the jagged rock piles of the bridge,
come down to me, for now you may come safely."

Hearing him, I hurried down the ledge;
and the Demons all pressed forward when I appeared,
so that I feared they might not keep their pledge.

So once I saw the Pisan infantry
march out under truce from the fortress at Caprona,
staring in fright at the ranks of the enemy.

I pressed the whole of my body against my Guide,
and not for an instant did I take my eyes
from those black fiends who scowled on every side.

They swung their forks saying to one another:
"Shall I give him a touch in the rump?" and answering:
"Sure; give him a taste to pay him for his bother."

But the Demon who was talking to my Guide
turned round and cried to him: "At ease there, Snatcher!"
And then to us: "There's no road on this side:

the arch lies all in pieces in the pit.
If you *must* go on, follow along this ridge;
there's another cliff to cross by just beyond it.

In just five hours it will be, since the bridge fell,
a thousand two hundred sixty-six years and a day;
that was the time the big quake shook all Hell.

I'll send a squad of my boys along that way
to see if anyone's airing himself below:
you can go with them: there will be no foul play.

Front and center here, Grizzly and Hellken,"
he began to order them. "You too, Deaddog.
Curlybeard, take charge of a squad of ten.

Take Grafter and Dragontooth along with you.
Pigtusk, Catclaw, Cramper, and Crazyred.
Keep a sharp lookout on the boiling glue

as you move along, and see that these gentlemen
are not molested until they reach the crag
where they can find a way across the den."

"In the name of heaven, Master," I cried, "what sort
of guides are these? Let us go on alone
if you know the way. Who can trust such an escort!

If you are as wary as you used to be
you surely see them grind their teeth at us,
and knot their beetle brows so threateningly."

And he: "I do not like this fear in you.
Let them gnash and knot as they please; they menace only
the sticky wretches simmering in that stew."

They turned along the left bank in a line;
but before they started, all of them together
had stuck their pointed tongues out as a sign

to their Captain that they wished permission to pass,
and he had made a trumpet of his ass.

Notes

A GENERAL NOTE ON DANTE'S TREATMENT OF THE GRAFTERS AND THEIR GUARDS (CANTOS XXI and XXII).

Dante has been called "The Master of the Disgusting" with the stress at times on the mastery and at times on the disgust. The occasional coarseness of details in other Cantos (especially in Cantos XVIII and XXVIII) has offended certain delicate readers. It is worth pointing out that the mention of bodily function is likely to be more shocking in a Protestant than in a Catholic culture. It has often seemed to me that the offensive language of Protestantism is obscenity; the offensive language of Catholicism is profanity or blasphemy: one offends on a scale of unmentionable words for bodily function, the other on a scale of disrespect for the sacred. Dante places the Blasphemous in Hell as the worst of the Violent against God and His Works, but he has no category for punishing those who use four-letter words.

The difference is not, I think, national, but religious. Chaucer, as a man of Catholic England, took exactly Dante's view in the matter of what was and what was not shocking language. In "The Pardoner's Tale," Chaucer sermonized with great feeling against the rioters for their profanity and blasphemy (for the way they rend Christ's body with their oaths) but he is quite free himself with "obscenity." Modern English readers tend to find nothing whatever startling in his profanity, but the schoolboys faithfully continue to underline the marvels of his Anglo-Saxon monosyllables and to make marginal notes on them.

7. *the Venetian arsenal:* The arsenal was not only an arms manufactory but a great center of shipbuilding and repairing.

37. *Blacktàlons:* The original is Malebranche, i.e., "Evil Claws."

38. *Santa Zita:* The patron saint of the city of Lucca. "One of Santa Zita's Elders" would therefore equal "One of Lucca's Senators" (i.e., Aldermen). Commentators have searched the records of Luccan Aldermen who died on Holy Saturday of 1300, and one Martino Bottaio has been suggested as the newcomer, but there is no evidence that Dante had a specific man in mind. More probably he meant simply to underscore the fact that Lucca was a city of grafters, just as Bologna was represented as a city of panderers and seducers.

41. *Bonturo:* Bonturo Dati, a politician of Lucca. The phrase is ironic: Bonturo was the most avid grafter of them all.

51. *Sacred Face: Il volto santo* was an ancient wooden image of Christ venerated by the Luccanese. These ironies and the grotesqueness of the Elder's appearance mark the beginning of the gargoyle dance that swells and rolls through this Canto and the next.

52. *Serchio:* A river near Lucca.

61. You *had best not be seen:* It is only in the passage through this Bolgia, out of the total journey, that Dante presents himself as being in physical danger. Since his dismissal from office and his exile from Florence (on pain of death if he return) was based on a false charge of grafting, the reference is pointedly autobiographical. Such an autobiographical interpretation is certainly consistent with the method of Dante's allegory.

79. *Malacoda:* The name equals "Bad Tail," or "Evil Tail." He is the captain of these grim and semi-military police. I have not translated his name as I have those of the other fiends, since I cannot see that it offers any real difficulty to an English reader.

97-99. *Pisan infantry . . . Caprona, etc.:* A Tuscan army attacked the fortress of Caprona near Pisa in 1289 and after fierce fighting the Pisan defenders were promised a safe-conduct if they would surrender. Dante was probably serving with the Tuscans (the opening lines of the next Canto certainly suggest that he had seen military service). In some accounts it is reported that the Tuscans massacred the Pisans despite their promised safe-conduct—an ominous analogy if true. In any case the emerging Pisans would be sufficently familiar with the treacheries of Italian politics to feel profoundly uneasy at being surrounded by their enemies under such conditions.

110-11. *If you* must *go on, etc.:* Malacoda is lying, as the Poets will discover: all the bridges across the Sixth Bolgia have fallen as a result of the earthquake that shook Hell at the death of Christ. The great rock fall between the Sixth and Seventh Circle (see Canto IX) was caused by the same shock, as was the ruin at the entrance to the Second Circle (see Canto V).

112-14. *in just five hours . . . a thousand two hundred and sixty six years and a day:* Christ died on Good Friday of the year 34, and it is now Holy Saturday of the year 1300, five hours before the hour of his death. Many commentators (and Dante himself in the *Convivio)* place the hours of Christ's death at exactly noon. Accordingly, it would now be 7:00 A.M. of Holy Saturday—exactly eight minutes since the Poets left the bridge over the Fourth Bolgia (at moonset).

In the gospels of Matthew, Mark, and Luke, however, the hour of Christ's death is precisely stated as 3:00 P.M. Dante would certainly be familiar with the Synoptic Gospels, and on that authority it would now be 10:00 A.M.

As far as the action of the poem is concerned the only question of consequence is the time-lapse from the bridge over the Fourth Bolgia to the talk with Malacoda, a matter of eight minutes or of three hours and eight minutes. One certainly seems too short, the other needlessly long, and while either answer can be supported with good arguments, this may be another case of literal worrying of "poetic" accuracy.

138-40. *tongues . . . trumpet:* The fiends obviously constitute a kind of debased military organization and these grotesqueries are their sign and countersign. Dante, himself, in his present satyr-like humor, finds them quite remarkable signals, as he goes on to note in the next Canto.

Canto XXII

CIRCLE EIGHT: ***Bolgia Five*** ***The Grafters***

The poets set off with their escorts of demons. Dante sees the GRAFTERS lying in the pitch like frogs in water with only their muzzles out. They disappear as soon as they sight the demons and only a ripple on the surface betrays their presence.

One of the Grafters, AN UNIDENTIFIED NAVARRESE, ducks too late and is seized by the demons who are about to claw him, but CURLYBEARD holds them back while Virgil questions him. The wretch speaks of his fellow sinners, FRIAR GOMITA and MICHEL ZANCHE, while the uncontrollable demons rake him from time to time with their hooks.

The Navarrese offers to lure some of his fellow sufferers into the hands of the demons, and when his plan is accepted he plunges into the pitch and escapes. HELLKEN and GRIZZLY fly after him, but too late. They start a brawl in mid-air and fall into the pitch themselves. Curlybeard immediately organizes a rescue party and the Poets, fearing the bad temper of the frustrated demons, take advantage of the confusion to slip away.

I have seen horsemen breaking camp. I have seen
the beginning of the assault, the march and muster,
and at times the retreat and riot. I have been

where chargers trampled your land, O Aretines!
I have seen columns of foragers, shocks of tourney,
and running of tilts. I have seen the endless lines

march to bells, drums, trumpets, from far and near.
I have seen them march on signals from a castle.
I have seen them march with native and foreign gear.

But never yet have I seen horse or foot,
nor ship in range of land nor sight of star,
take its direction from so low a toot.

We went with the ten Fiends—ah, savage crew!—
but "In church with saints; with stewpots in the tavern,"
as the old proverb wisely bids us do.

All my attention was fixed upon the pitch:
to observe the people who were boiling in it,
and the customs and the punishments of that ditch.

As dolphins surface and begin to flip
their arched backs from the sea, warning the sailors
to fall-to and begin to secure ship—

So now and then, some soul, to ease his pain,
showed us a glimpse of his back above the pitch
and quick as lightning disappeared again.

And as, at the edge of a ditch, frogs squat about
hiding their feet and bodies in the water,
leaving only their muzzles sticking out—

so stood the sinners in that dismal ditch;
but as Curlybeard approached, only a ripple
showed where they had ducked back into the pitch.

I saw—the dread of it haunts me to this day—
one linger a bit too long, as it sometimes happens
one frog remains when another spurts away;

and Catclaw, who was nearest, ran a hook
through the sinner's pitchy hair and hauled him in.
He looked like an otter dripping from the brook.

I knew the names of all the Fiends by then;
I had made a note of them at the first muster,
and, marching, had listened and checked them over again.

"Hey, Crazyred," the crew of Demons cried
all together, "give him a taste of your claws.
Dig him open a little. Off with his hide."

And I then: "Master, can you find out, please,
the name and history of that luckless one
who has fallen into the hands of his enemies?"

My Guide approached that wraith from the hot tar
and asked him whence he came. The wretch replied:
"I was born and raised in the Kingdom of Navarre.

My mother placed me in service to a knight;
for she had borne me to a squanderer
who killed himself when he ran through his birthright.

Then I became a domestic in the service
of good King Thibault. There I began to graft,
and I account for it in this hot crevice."

And Pigtusk, who at the ends of his lower lip
shot forth two teeth more terrible than a boar's,
made the wretch feel how one of them could rip.

The mouse had come among bad cats, but here
Curlybeard locked arms around him crying:
"While I've got hold of him the rest stand clear!"

And turning his face to my Guide: "If you want to ask him
anything else," he added, "ask away
before the others tear him limb from limb."

And my Guide to the sinner: "I should like to know
if among the other souls beneath the pitch
are any Italians?" And the wretch: "Just now

I left a shade who came from parts near by.
Would I were still in the pitch with him, for then
these hooks would not be giving me cause to cry."

And suddenly Grafter bellowed in great heat:
"We've stood enough!" And he hooked the sinner's arm
and, raking it, ripped off a chunk of meat.

Then Dragontooth wanted to play, too, reaching down
for a catch at the sinner's legs; but Curlybeard
wheeled round and round with a terrifying frown,

and when the Fiends had somewhat given ground
and calmed a little, my Guide, without delay,
asked the wretch, who was staring at his wound:

"Who was the sinner from whom you say you made
your evil-starred departure to come ashore
among these Fiends?" And the wretch: "It was the shade

of Friar Gomita of Gallura, the crooked stem
of every Fraud: when his master's enemies
were in his hands, he won high praise from them.

He took their money without case or docket,
and let them go. He was in all his dealings
no petty bursar, but a kingly pocket.

With him, his endless crony in the fosse,
is Don Michel Zanche of Logodoro;
they babble about Sardinia without pause.

But look! See that fiend grinning at your side!
There is much more that I should like to tell you,
but oh, I think he means to grate my hide!"

But their grim sergeant wheeled, sensing foul play,
and turning on Cramper, who seemed set to strike,
ordered: "Clear off, you buzzard. Clear off, I say!"

"If either of you would like to see and hear
Tuscans or Lombards," the pale sinner said,
"I can lure them out of hiding if you'll stand clear

and let me sit here at the edge of the ditch,
and get all these Blacktalons out of sight;
for while they're here, no one will leave the pitch.

In exchange for myself, I can fish you up as pretty
a mess of souls as you like. I have only to whistle
the way we do when one of us gets free."

Deaddog raised his snout as he listened to him;
then, shaking his head, said, "Listen to the grafter
spinning his tricks so he can jump from the brim!"

And the sticky wretch, who was all treachery:
"Oh I am more than tricky when there's a chance
to see my friends in greater misery."

Hellken, against the will of all the crew,
could hold no longer. "If you jump," he said
to the scheming wretch, "I won't come after you

at a gallop, but like a hawk after a mouse.
We'll clear the edge and hide behind the bank:
let's see if you're trickster enough for all of us."

Reader, here is new game! The Fiends withdrew
from the bank's edge, and Deaddog, who at first
was most against it, led the savage crew.

The Navarrese chose his moment carefully:
and planting both his feet against the ground,
he leaped, and in an instant he was free.

The Fiends were stung with shame, and of the lot
Hellken most, who had been the cause of it.
He leaped out madly bellowing: "You're caught!"

but little good it did him; terror pressed
harder than wings; the sinner dove from sight
and the Fiend in full flight had to raise his breast.

A duck, when the falcon dives, will disappear
exactly so, all in a flash, while he
returns defeated and weary up the air.

Grizzly, in a rage at the sinner's flight,
flew after Hellken, hoping the wraith would escape,
so he might find an excuse to start a fight.

And as soon as the grafter sank below the pitch,
Grizzly turned his talons against Hellken,
locked with him claw to claw above the ditch.

But Hellken was sparrowhawk enough for two
and clawed him well; and ripping one another,
they plunged together into the hot stew.

The heat broke up the brawl immediately,
but their wings were smeared with pitch and they could not rise.
Curlybeard, upset as his company,

commanded four to fly to the other coast
at once with all their grapples. At top speed
the Fiends divided, each one to his post.

Some on the near edge, some along the far,
they stretched their hooks out to the clotted pair
who were already cooked deep through the scar

of their first burn. And turning to one side
we slipped off, leaving them thus occupied.

Notes

4. *Aretines:* The people of Arezzo. In 1289 the Guelphs of Florence and Lucca defeated the Ghibellines of Arrezo at Campaldino. Dante was present with the Guelphs, though probably as an observer and not as a warrior.

5-6. *tourney . . . tilts:* A tourney was contested by groups of knights in a field; a tilt by individuals who tried to unhorse one another across a barrier.

7. *bells:* The army of each town was equipped with a chariot on which bells were mounted. Signals could be given by the bells and special decorations made the chariot stand out in battle. It served therefore as a rallying point.

8. *signals from a castle:* When troops were in sight of their castle their movements could be directed from the towers—by banners in daytime and by fires at night, much as some naval signals are still given today.

19-21. *dolphins, etc.:* It was a common belief that when dolphins began to leap around a ship they were warning the sailors of an approaching storm.

31 ff. *The Navarrese grafter:* His own speech tells all that is known about him. The recital could serve as a description of many a courtier. Thibault II was King of Navarre, a realm that lay in what is now northern Spain.

54. *and I account:* Dante's irony is certainly intentional: the accounts of the Grafters can not be concealed from God's Justice.

66. *Italians:* Dante uses the term *Latino* strictly speaking, a person from the area of ancient Latium, now (roughly) Lazio, the province in which Rome is located. It was against the Latians that Aeneas fought on coming to Italy. More generally, Dante uses the term for any southern Italian. Here, however, the usage seems precise, since the sinner refers to "points near by" and means Sardinia. Rome is the point in Italy closest to Sardinia.

82. *Friar Gomita of Gallura* (GHAW-mee-ta): In 1300 Sardinia was a Pisan possession, and was divided into four districts, of which Galluria was the northeast. Friar Gomita administered Gallura for his own considerable profit. He was hanged by the Pisan governor when he was found guilty of taking bribes to let prisoners escape.

89. *Michel Zanche de Logodoro* (Mee-KELL ZAHN-keh): He was made Vicar of Logodoro when the King of Sardinia went off to war. The King was captured and did not return. Michel maneuvered a divorce for the Queen and married her himself. About 1290 he was murdered by his son-in-law, Branca d'Oria (see Canto XXXIII).

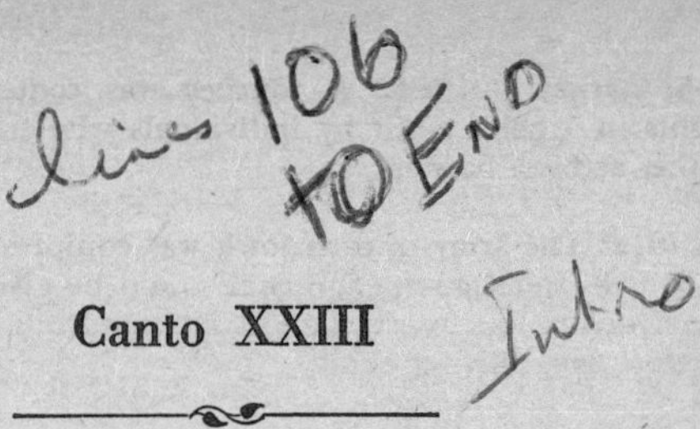

Canto XXIII

CIRCLE EIGHT: *Bolgia Six* *The Hypocrites*

The Poets are pursued by the Fiends and escape them by sliding down the sloping bank of the next pit. They are now in the SIXTH BOLGIA. Here the HYPOCRITES, weighted down by great leaden robes, walk eternally round and round a narrow track. The robes are brilliantly gilded on the outside and are shaped like a monk's habit, for the hypocrite's outward appearance shines brightly and passes for holiness, but under that show lies the terrible weight of his deceit which the soul must bear through all eternity.

The Poets talk to TWO JOVIAL FRIARS and come upon CAIAPHAS, the chief sinner of that place. Caiaphas was the High Priest of the Jews who counseled the Pharisees to crucify Jesus in the name of public expedience. He is punished by being himself crucified to the floor of Hell by three great stakes, and in such a position that every passing sinner must walk upon him. Thus he must suffer upon his own body the weight of all the world's hypocrisy, as Christ suffered upon his body the pain of all the world's sins.

The Jovial Friars tell Virgil how he may climb from the pit, and Virgil discovers that Malacoda lied to him about the bridges over the Sixth Bolgia.

Silent, apart, and unattended we went
as Minor Friars go when they walk abroad,
one following the other. The incident

recalled the fable of the Mouse and the Frog
that Aesop tells. For compared attentively
point by point, "pig" is no closer to "hog"

than the one case to the other. And as one thought
springs from another, so the comparison
gave birth to a new concern, at which I caught

my breath in fear. This thought ran through my mind:
"These Fiends, through us, have been made ridiculous,
and have suffered insult and injury of a kind

to make them smart. Unless we take good care—
now rage is added to their natural spleen—
they will hunt us down as greyhounds hunt the hare."

Already I felt my scalp grow tight with fear.
I was staring back in terror as I said:
"Master, unless we find concealment here

and soon, I dread the rage of the Fiends: already
they are yelping on our trail: I imagine them
so vividly I can hear them now." And he:

"Were I a pane of leaded glass, I could not
summon your outward look more instantly
into myself, than I do your inner thought.

Your fears were mixed already with my own
with the same suggestion and the same dark look;
so that of both I form one resolution:

the right bank may be sloping: in that case
we may find some way down to the next pit
and so escape from the imagined chase."

He had not finished answering me thus
when, not far off, their giant wings outspread,
I saw the Fiends come charging after us.

Seizing me instantly in his arms, my Guide—
like a mother wakened by a midnight noise
to find a wall of flame at her bedside

(who takes her child and runs, and more concerned
for him than for herself, does not pause even
to throw a wrap about her) raised me, turned,

and down the rugged bank from the high summit
flung himself down supine onto the slope
which walls the upper side of the next pit.

Water that turns the great wheel of a land-mill
never ran faster through the end of a sluice
at the point nearest the paddles—as down that hill

my Guide and Master bore me on his breast,
as if I were not a companion, but a son.
And the soles of his feet had hardly come to rest

on the bed of the depth below, when on the height
we had just left, the Fiends beat their great wings.
But now they gave my Guide no cause for fright;

for the Providence that gave them the fifth pit
to govern as the ministers of Its will,
takes from their souls the power of leaving it,

About us now in the depth of the pit we found
a painted people, weary and defeated.
Slowly, in pain, they paced it round and round.

All wore great cloaks cut to as ample a size
as those worn by the Benedictines of Cluny.
The enormous hoods were drawn over their eyes.

The outside is all dazzle, golden and fair;
the inside, lead, so heavy that Frederick's capes,
compared to these, would seem as light as air.

O weary mantle for eternity!
We turned to the left again along their course,
listening to their moans of misery,

but they moved so slowly down that barren strip,
tired by their burden, that our company
was changed at every movement of the hip.

And walking thus, I said: "As we go on,
may it please you to look about among these people
for any whose name or history may be known."

And one who understood Tuscan cried to us there
as we hurried past: "I pray you check your speed.
you who run so fast through the sick air:

it may be I am one who will fit your case."
And at his words my Master turned and said:
"Wait now, then go with him at his own pace."

I waited there, and saw along that track
two souls who seemed in haste to be with me;
but the narrow way and their burden held them back.

When they had reached me down that narrow way
they stared at me in silence and amazement,
then turned to one another. I heard one say:

"This one seems, by the motion of his throat,
to be alive; and if they are dead, how is it
they are allowed to shed the leaden coat?"

And then to me "O Tuscan, come so far
to the college of the sorry hypocrites,
do not disdain to tell us who you are."

And I: "I was born and raised a Florentine
on the green and lovely banks of Arno's waters,
I go with the body that was always mine.

But who are *you,* who sighing as you go
distill in floods of tears that drown your cheeks?
What punishment is this that glitters so?"

"These burnished robes are of thick lead," said one,
"and are hung on us like counterweights, so heavy
that we, their weary fulcrums, creak and groan.

Jovial Friars and Bolognese were we.
We were chosen jointly by your Florentines
to keep the peace, an office usually

held by a single man; near the Gardingo
one still may see the sort of peace we kept.
I was called Catalano, he, Loderingo."

I began: "O Friars, your evil . . ."—and then I saw
a figure crucified upon the ground
by three great stakes, and I fell still in awe.

When he saw me there, he began to puff great sighs
into his beard, convulsing all his body;
and Friar Catalano, following my eyes,

said to me: "That one nailed across the road
counselled the Pharisees that it was fitting
one man be tortured for the public good.

Naked he lies fixed there, as you see,
in the path of all who pass; there he must feel
the weight of all through all eternity.

His father-in-law and the others of the Council
which was a seed of wrath to all the Jews,
are similarly staked for the same evil."

Then I saw Virgil marvel for a while
over that soul so ignominiously
stretched on the cross in Hell's eternal exile.

Then, turning, he asked the Friar: "If your law permit,
can you tell us if somewhere along the right
there is some gap in the stone wall of the pit

through which we two may climb to the next brink
without the need of summoning the Black Angels
and forcing them to raise us from this sink?"

He: "Nearer than you hope, there is a bridge
that runs from the great circle of the scarp
and crosses every ditch from ridge to ridge,

except that in this it is broken; but with care
you can mount the ruins which lie along the slope
and make a heap on the bottom." My Guide stood there

motionless for a while with a dark look.
At last he said: "He lied about this business,
who spears the sinners yonder with his hook."

And the Friar: "Once at Bologna I heard the wise
discussing the Devil's sins; among them I heard
that he is a liar and the father of lies."

When the sinner had finished speaking, I saw the face
of my sweet Master darken a bit with anger:
he set off at a great stride from that place,

and I turned from that weighted hypocrite
to follow in the prints of his dear feet.

Notes

4. *the fable of the Mouse and the Frog:* The fable was not by Aesop, but was attributed to him in Dante's time: A mouse comes to a body of water and wonders how to cross. A frog, thinking to drown the mouse, offers to ferry him, but the mouse is afraid he will fall off. The frog thereupon suggests that the mouse tie himself to one of the frog's feet. In this way they start across, but in the middle

the frog dives from under the mouse, who struggles desperately to stay afloat while the frog tries to pull him under. A hawk sees the mouse struggling and swoops down and seizes him; but since the frog is tied to the mouse, it too is carried away, and so both of them are devoured.

6. *point by point:* The mouse would be the Navarrese Grafter. The frog would be the two fiends, Grizzly and Hellken. By seeking to harm the Navarrese they came to grief themselves.

22. *a pane of leaded glass:* A mirror. Mirrors were backed with lead in Dante's time.

43. *land-mill:* As distinguished from the floating mills common in Dante's time and up to the advent of the steam engine. These were built on rafts that were anchored in the swift-flowing rivers of Northern Italy.

44-45. *ran faster . . . at the point nearest the paddles:* The sharp drop of the sluice makes the water run fastest at the point at which it hits the wheel.

59. *the Benedictines of Cluny:* The habit of these monks was especially ample and elegant. St. Bernard once wrote ironically to a nephew who had entered this monastery: "If length of sleeves and amplitude of hood made for holiness, what could hold me back from following [your lead]."

62. *Frederick's capes:* Frederick II executed persons found guilty of treason by fastening them into a sort of leaden shell. The doomed man was then placed in a cauldron over a fire and the lead was melted around him.

68-9. *our company was changed, etc.:* Another tremendous Dantean figure. Sense: "They moved so slowly that at every step (movement of the hip) we found ourselves beside new sinners."

100. *Jovial Friars:* A nickname given to the military monks of the order of the Glorious Virgin Mary founded at Bologna in 1261. Their original aim was to serve as peacemakers, enforcers of order, and protectors of the weak, but their observance of their rules became so scandalously lax, and their management of worldly affairs so self-seeking, that the order was disbanded by Papal decree.

101-2. *We were chosen jointly . . . to keep the peace:* Catalano dei Malavolti (c. 1210-1285), a Guelph, and Loderingo degli Andolo (c. 1210-1293), a Ghibelline, were both Bolognese and, as brothers of the Jovial Friars, both had served as *podestà* (the chief officer charged with keeping the peace) of many cities for varying terms. In 1266 they were jointly appointed to the office of *podestà* of Florence on the theory that a bipartisan administration by men of God would bring peace to the city. Their tenure of office was marked by great violence, however; and they were forced to leave in a matter of months. Modern scholarship has established the fact that they served as instruments of Clement IV's policy in Florence, working at his orders to overthrow the Ghibellines under the guise of an impartial administration.

103. *Gardingo:* The site of the palace of the Ghibelline family degli Uberti. In the riots resulting from the maladministration of the two Jovial Friars, the Ghibellines were forced out of the city and the Uberti palace was razed.

107 ff. *a figure crucified upon the ground:* Caiaphas. His words were: "It is expedient that one man shall die for the people and that the whole nation perish not." (*John* xi, 50).

118. *his father-in-law and the others:* Annas, father-in-law of Caiaphas, was the first before whom Jesus was led upon his arrest. (*John* xviii, 13). He had Jesus bound and delivered to Caiaphas.

121. *I saw Virgil marvel:* Caiaphas had not been there on Virgil's first descent into Hell.

137-38. *he lied . . . who spears the sinners yonder:* Malacoda.

143. *darken a bit:* The original is *turbato un poco d'ira.* A bit of anger befits the righteous indignation of Human Reason, but immoderate anger would be out of character. One of the sublimities of Dante's writing is the way in which even the smallest details reinforce the great concepts.

Canto XXIV

CIRCLE EIGHT: *Bolgia Seven* *The Thieves*

The Poets climb the right bank laboriously, cross the bridge of the SEVENTH BOLGIA and descend the far bank to observe the THIEVES. They find the pit full of monstrous reptiles who curl themselves about the sinners like living coils of rope, binding each sinner's hands behind his back, and knotting themselves through the loins. Other reptiles dart about the place, and the Poets see one of them fly through the air and pierce the jugular vein of one sinner who immediately bursts into flames until only ashes remain. From the ashes the sinner reforms painfully.

These are Dante's first observations of the Thieves and will be carried further in the next Canto, but the first allegorical retribution is immediately apparent. Thievery is reptilian in its secrecy; therefore it is punished by reptiles. The hands of the thieves are the agents of their crimes; therefore they are bound forever. And as the thief destroys his fellowmen by making their substance disappear, so is he painfully destroyed and made to disappear, not once but over and over again.

The sinner who has risen from his own ashes reluctantly identifies himself as VANNI FUCCI. He tells his story, and to revenge himself for having been forced to reveal his identity he utters a dark prophecy against Dante.

In the turning season of the youthful year,
  when the sun is warming his rays beneath Aquarius
  and the days and nights already begin to near

their perfect balance; the hoar-frost copies then
  the image of his white sister on the ground,
  but the first sun wipes away the work of his pen.

The peasants who lack fodder then arise
  and look about and see the fields all white,
  and hear their lambs bleat; then they smite their thighs,

go back into the house, walk here and there,
  pacing, fretting, wondering what to do,
  then come out doors again, and there, despair

falls from them when they see how the earth's face
  has changed in so little time, and they take their staffs
  and drive their lambs to feed—so in that place

when I saw my Guide and Master's eyebrows lower,
  my spirits fell and I was sorely vexed;
  and as quickly came the plaster to the sore:

for when he had reached the ruined bridge, he stood
  and turned on me that sweet and open look
  with which he had greeted me in the dark wood.

When he had paused and studied carefully
  the heap of stones, he seemed to reach some plan,
  for he turned and opened his arms and lifted me.

Like one who works and calculates ahead,
  and is always ready for what happens next—
  so, raising me above that dismal bed

to the top of one great slab of the fallen slate,
  he chose another saying: "Climb here, but first
  test it to see if it will hold your weight."

It was no climb for a lead-hung hypocrite:
for scarcely we—he light and I assisted—
could crawl handhold by handhold from the pit;

and were it not that the bank along this side
was lower than the one down which we had slid,
I at least—I will not speak for my Guide—

would have turned back. But as all of the vast rim
of Malebolge leans toward the lowest well,
so each succeeding valley and each brim

is lower than the last. We climbed the face
and arrived by great exertion to the point
where the last rock had fallen from its place.

My lungs were pumping as if they could not stop;
I thought I could not go on, and I sat exhausted
the instant I had clambered to the top.

"Up on your feet! This is no time to tire!"
my Master cried. "The man who lies asleep
will never waken fame, and his desire

and all his life drift past him like a dream,
and the traces of his memory fade from time
like smoke in air, or ripples on a stream.

Now, therefore, rise. Control your breath, and call
upon the strength of soul that wins all battles
unless it sink in the gross body's fall.

There is a longer ladder yet to climb:
this much is not enough. If you understand me,
show that you mean to profit from your time."

I rose and made my breath appear more steady
than it really was, and I replied: "Lead on
as it pleases you to go: I am strong and ready."

We picked our way up the cliff, a painful climb,
for it was narrower, steeper, and more jagged
than any we had crossed up to that time.

I moved along, talking to hide my faintness,
when a voice that seemed unable to form words
rose from the depths of the next chasm's darkness.

I do not know what it said, though by then the Sage
had led me to the top of the next arch;
but the speaker seemed in a tremendous rage.

I was bending over the brim, but living eyes
could not plumb to the bottom of that dark;
therefore I said, "Master, let me advise

that we cross over and climb down the wall:
for just as I hear the voice without understanding,
so I look down and make out nothing at all."

"I make no other answer than the act,"
the Master said: "the only fit reply
to a fit request is silence and the fact."

So we moved down the bridge to the stone pier
that shores the end of the arch on the eighth bank,
and there I saw the chasm's depths made clear;

and there great coils of serpents met my sight,
so hideous a mass that even now
the memory makes my blood run cold with fright.

Let Libya boast no longer, for though its sands
breed chelidrids, jaculi, and phareans,
cenchriads, and two-headed amphisbands,

it never bred such a variety
of vipers, no, not with all Ethiopia
and all the lands that lie by the Red Sea.

Amid that swarm, naked and without hope,
people ran terrified, not even dreaming
of a hole to hide in, or of heliotrope.

Their hands were bound behind by coils of serpents
which thrust their heads and tails between the loins
and bunched in front, a mass of knotted torments.

One of the damned came racing round a boulder,
and as he passed us, a great snake shot up
and bit him where the neck joins with the shoulder.

No mortal pen—however fast it flash
over the page—could write down *o* or *i*
as quickly as he flamed and fell in ash;

and when he was dissolved into a heap
upon the ground, the dust rose of itself
and immediately resumed its former shape.

Precisely so, philosophers declare,
the Phoenix dies and then is born again
when it approaches its five hundredth year.

It lives on tears of balsam and of incense;
in all its life it eats no herb or grain,
and nard and precious myrrh sweeten its cerements.

And as a person fallen in a fit,
possessed by a Demon or some other seizure
that fetters him without his knowing it,

struggles up to his feet and blinks his eyes
(still stupefied by the great agony
he has just passed), and, looking round him, sighs—

such was the sinner when at last he rose.
O Power of God! How dreadful is Thy will
which in its vengeance rains such fearful blows.

Then my Guide asked him who he was. And he
answered reluctantly: "Not long ago
I rained into this gullet from Tuscany.

I am Vanni Fucci, the beast. A mule among men,
I chose the bestial life above the human.
Savage Pistoia was my fitting den."

And I to my Guide: "Detain him a bit longer
and ask what crime it was that sent him here;
I knew him as a man of blood and anger."

The sinner, hearing me, seemed discomforted,
but he turned and fixed his eyes upon my face
with a look of dismal shame; at length he said:

"That you have found me out among the strife
and misery of this place, grieves my heart more
than did the day that cut me from my life.

But I am forced to answer truthfully:
I am put down so low because it was I
who stole the treasure from the Sacristy,

for which others once were blamed. But that you may
find less to gloat about if you escape here,
prick up your ears and listen to what I say:

First Pistoia is emptied of the Black,
then Florence changes her party and her laws.
From Valdimagra the God of War brings back

a fiery vapor wrapped in turbid air:
then in a storm of battle at Piceno
the vapor breaks apart the mist, and there

every White shall feel his wounds anew.
And I have told you this that it may grieve you."

Notes

2. *Aquarius:* The zodiacal sign for the period from January 21 to February 21. The sun is moving north then to approach the vernal equinox (March 21), at which point the days and the nights are equal. The Italian spring comes early, and the first warm days would normally occur under Aquarius.

4. *hoar-frost copies then:* The hoar-frost looks like snow but melts away as soon as the sun strikes it.

7-15. *the peasants, etc.:* A fine example of Dante's ability to build dramatic equivalents for the emotion he wishes to convey.

9. *they smite their thighs:* A common Italian gesture of vexation, about equivalent to smiting the forehead with the palm of the hand.

34-5. *the bank along this side was lower:* See diagram, Canto XIX.

55. *there is a longer ladder yet to climb:* Many allegorical possibilities are obvious here. The whole ascent of Purgatory lies ahead, Virgil points out, and here Dante seems exhausted simply in climbing away from (renouncing) hypocrisy. Further, the descent into Hell is symbolic of the recognition of sin, and the ascent of purgatory of the purification from sin. The ascent is by far the more arduous task.

61. *a painful climb:* The "top" Dante mentions in line 45 must obviously have been the top of the fallen stone that was once the bridge. There remains the difficult climb up the remainder of the cliff.

85-90. *Libya . . . Ethiopia . . . lands that lie by the Red Sea:* The desert areas of the Mediterranean shores. Lucan's *Pharsalia* describes the assortment of monsters listed here by Dante. I have rendered their names from Latin to English jabberwocky to avoid problems of pronunciation. In Lucan *chelydri* make their trails smoke and burn, they are amphibious; *jaculi* fly through the air like darts piercing what they hit; *pharese* plow the ground with their tails; *cenchri* waver from side to side when they move; and *amphisboenae* have a head at each end.

93. *heliotrope:* Not the flower, but the bloodstone, a spotted chalcedony. It was believed to make the wearer invisible.

107. *the Phoenix:* The fabulous Phoenix of Arabia was the only one of its kind in the world. Every five hundred years it built a nest of spices and incense which took fire from the heat of the sun and the beating of the Phoenix's wings. The Phoenix was thereupon cremated and was then re-born from its ashes.

123. *this gullet:* Dante often gives an animate force to the ledges of Hell. The place in which the sinner is punished possesses him as if it were a living force. It should be remembered that, on one level of the allegory, Hell is every sinner's own guilty conscience.

124. *Vanni Fucci* (VAH-nee FOO-tchee): The bastard son of Fuccio de Lazzeri, a nobleman (Black) of Pistoia. In 1293 with two accomplices he stole the treasure of San Jacopo in the Duomo of San Zeno. Others were accused, and one man spent a year in jail on this charge before the guilty persons were discovered. Vanni Fucci had escaped from Pistoia by then, but his accomplices were convicted.

129. *a man of blood and anger:* Dante (the traveler within the narrative rather than Dante the author) claims that he did not know Fucci was a thief, but only that he was a man of blood and violence. He should therefore be punished in the Seventh Circle.

142 ff. *Vanni Fucci's prophecy:* In May of 1301 the Whites of Florence joined with the Whites of Pistoia to expel the Pistoian Blacks and destroy their houses. The ejected Blacks fled to Florence and joined forces with the Florentine Blacks. On November 1st of the same year, Charles of Valois took Florence and helped the Blacks drive out the Whites. Piceno was the scene of a battle in which the Blacks of Florence and Lucca combined in 1302 to capture Serravalle, a White strong point near Pistoia.

Dante's meteorological figure is based on the contemporary belief that electric storms were caused by a conflict between "fiery vapors" and the preponderant "watery vapors." By their contraries the watery vapors (mist) surround the fiery vapors, seeking to extinguish them, and the fiery vapors combat to shatter the mist. Here the fiery vapor is the Blacks and the shattered mist is the Whites.

Canto XXV

A11

CIRCLE EIGHT: *Bolgia Seven* ***The Thieves***

Vanni's rage mounts to the point where he hurls an ultimate obscenity at God, and the serpents immediately swarm over him, driving him off in great pain. The Centaur, CACUS, his back covered with serpents and a fire-eating dragon, also gives chase to punish the wretch.

Dante then meets FIVE NOBLE THIEVES OF FLORENCE and sees the further retribution visited upon the sinners. Some of the thieves appear first in human form, others as reptiles. All but one of them suffer a painful transformation before Dante's eyes. AGNELLO appears in human form and is merged with CIANFA, who appears as a six-legged lizard. BUOSO appears as a man and changes form with FRANCESCO, who first appears as a tiny reptile. Only PUCCIO SCIANCATO remains unchanged, though we are made to understand that his turn will come.

For endless and painful transformation is the final state of the thieves. In life they took the substance of others, transforming it into their own. So in Hell their very bodies are constantly being taken from them, and they are left to steal back a human form from some other sinner. Thus they waver constantly between man and reptile, and no sinner knows what to call his own.

When he had finished, the thief—to his disgrace—
  raised his hands with both fists making figs,
  and cried: "Here, God! I throw them in your face!"

Thereat the snakes became my friends, for one
  coiled itself about the wretch's neck
  as if it were saying: "You shall not go on!"

and another tied his arms behind him again,
knotting its head and tail between his loins
so tight he could not move a finger in pain.

Pistoia! Pistoia! why have you not decreed
to turn yourself to ashes and end your days,
rather than spread the evil of your seed!

In all of Hell's corrupt and sunken halls
I found no shade so arrogant toward God,
not even him who fell from the Theban walls!

Without another word, he fled; and there
I saw a furious Centaur race up, roaring:
"Where is the insolent blasphemer? Where?"

I do not think as many serpents swarm
in all the Maremma as he bore on his back
from the haunch to the first sign of our human form.

Upon his shoulders, just behind his head
a snorting dragon whose hot breath set fire
to all it touched, lay with its wings outspread.

My Guide said: "That is Cacus. Time and again
in the shadow of Mount Aventine he made
a lake of blood upon the Roman plain.

He does not go with his kin by the blood-red fosse
because of the cunning fraud with which he stole
the cattle of Hercules. And thus it was

his thieving stopped, for Hercules found his den
and gave him perhaps a hundred blows with his club,
and of them he did not feel the first ten."

Meanwhile, the Centaur passed along his way,
and three wraiths came. Neither my Guide nor I
knew they were there until we heard them say:

"You there—who are you?" There our talk fell still
and we turned to stare at them. I did not know them,
but by chance it happened, as it often will,

one named another. "Where is Cianfa?" he cried;
"Why has he fallen back?" I placed a finger
across my lips as a signal to my Guide.

Reader, should you doubt what next I tell,
it will be no wonder, for though I saw it happen,
I can scarce believe it possible, even in Hell.

For suddenly, as I watched, I saw a lizard
come darting forward on six great taloned feet
and fasten itself to a sinner from crotch to gizzard.

Its middle feet sank in the sweat and grime
of the wretch's paunch, its forefeet clamped his arms,
its teeth bit through both cheeks. At the same time

its hind feet fastened on the sinner's thighs:
its tail thrust through his legs and closed its coil
over his loins. I saw it with my own eyes!

No ivy ever grew about a tree
as tightly as that monster wove itself
limb by limb about the sinner's body;

they fused like hot wax, and their colors ran
together until neither wretch nor monster
appeared what he had been when he began:

just so, before the running edge of the heat
on a burning page, a brown discoloration
changes to black as the white dies from the sheet.

The other two cried out as they looked on:
"Alas! Alas! Agnello, how you change!
Already you are neither two nor one!"

The two heads had already blurred and blended;
now two new semblances appeared and faded,
one face where neither face began nor ended.

From the four upper limbs of man and beast
two arms were made, then members never seen
grew from the thighs and legs, belly and breast.

Their former likenesses mottled and sank
to something that was both of them and neither;
and so transformed, it slowly left our bank.

As lizards at high noon of a hot day
dart out from hedge to hedge, from shade to shade,
and flash like lightning when they cross the way,

so toward the bowels of the other two,
shot a small monster; livid, furious,
and black as a pepper corn. Its lunge bit through

that part of one of them from which man receives
his earliest nourishment; then it fell back
and lay sprawled out in front of the two thieves.

Its victim stared at it but did not speak:
indeed, he stood there like a post, and yawned
as if lack of sleep, or a fever, had left him weak.

The reptile stared at him, he at the reptile;
from the wound of one and from the other's mouth
two smokes poured out and mingled, dark and vile.

Now let Lucan be still with his history
of poor Sabellus and Nassidius,
and wait to hear what next appeared to me.

Of Cadmus and Arethusa be Ovid silent.
I have no need to envy him those verses
where he makes one a fountain, and one a serpent:

for he never transformed two beings face to face
in such a way that both their natures yielded
their elements each to each, as in this case.

Responding sympathetically to each other,
the reptile cleft his tail into a fork,
and the wounded sinner drew his feet together.

The sinner's legs and thighs began to join:
they grew together so, that soon no trace
of juncture could be seen from toe to loin.

Point by point the reptile's cloven tail
grew to the form of what the sinner lost;
one skin began to soften, one to scale.

The armpits swallowed the arms, and the short shank
of the reptile's forefeet simultaneously
lengthened by as much as the man's arms shrank.

Its hind feet twisted round themselves and grew
the member man conceals; meanwhile the wretch
from his one member generated two.

The smoke swelled up about them all the while:
it tanned one skin and bleached the other; it stripped
the hair from the man and grew it on the reptile.

While one fell to his belly, the other rose
without once shifting the locked evil eyes
below which they changed snouts as they changed pose.

The face of the standing one drew up and in
toward the temples, and from the excess matter
that gathered there, ears grew from the smooth skin;

while of the matter left below the eyes
the excess became a nose, at the same time
forming the lips to an appropriate size.

Here the face of the prostrate felon slips,
  sharpens into a snout, and withdraws its ears
  as a snail pulls in its horns. Between its lips

the tongue, once formed for speech, thrusts out a fork;
  the forked tongue of the other heals and draws
  into his mouth. The smoke has done its work.

The soul that had become a beast went flitting
  and hissing over the stones, and after it
  the other walked along talking and spitting.

Then turning his new shoulders, said to the one
  that still remained: "It is Buoso's turn to go
  crawling along this road as I have done."

Thus did the ballast of the seventh hold
  shift and reshift; and may the strangeness of it
  excuse my pen if the tale is strangely told.

And though all this confused me, they did not flee
  so cunningly but what I was aware
  that it was Puccio Sciancato alone of the three

that first appeared, who kept his old form still.
The other was he for whom you weep, Gaville.

Notes

THE FIVE NOBLE THIEVES OF FLORENCE:
Dante's concise treatment and the various transformations which the thieves undergo may lead to some confusion. It is worth noting that none of these thieves is important as an individual, and, in fact, that very little is known of the lives of these sinners beyond the sufficient fact that they were thieves.

The first three appear in line 35 and hail the Poets rather insolently. They are Agnello Brunelleschi (Ah-NYELL-oh Broo-nell-AY-skee), Buoso (BWOE-soe) degli Abati, and Puccio Sciancato. They have been walking along with Cianfa de' Donati (TCHAHN-fa day Don-AH-tee), but they suddenly miss him and ask about him with some concern. The careful reader will sense that a sudden disappearance is cause for very special concern in this *bolgia,* and sure enough, Cianfa suddenly reappears in the form of a six-legged lizard.

His body has been taken from him and he is driven by a consuming desire to be rid of his reptilian form as fast as possible. He immediately fixes himself upon Agnello and merges his lizard body with Agnello's human form. (A possible symbolic interpretation is that Cianfa is dividing the pains of Hell with a fellow thief, as on earth he might have divided the loot.)

Immediately after Cianfa and Agnello go off together, a tiny reptile bites Buoso degli Abati and exchanges forms with him. The reptile is Francesco dei Cavalcanti. (Here the symbolism is obvious: the thieves must steal from one another the very shapes in which they appear.)

Thus only Puccio Sciancato (POO-tchoe Shahn-KAH-toe) is left unchanged for the time being.

2. *figs:* An obscene gesture made by closing the hand into a fist with the thumb protruding between the first and second fingers. The fig is an ancient symbol for the vulva, and the protruding thumb is an obvious phallic symbol. The gesture is still current in Italy and has lost none of its obscene significance since Dante's time.

25. *Cacus:* The son of Vulcan. He lived in a cave at the foot of Mount Aventine, from which he raided the herds of the cattle of Hercules, which pastured on the Roman plain. Hercules clubbed him to death for his thievery, beating him in rage long after he was dead. Cacus is condemned to the lower pit for his greater crime, instead of guarding Phlegethon with his brother centaurs. Virgil, however, did not describe him as a Centaur (V. *Aeneid* VIII, 193-267). Dante's interpretation of him is probably based on the fact that Virgil referred to him as "half-human."

82. *that part:* The navel.

91 ff. *let Lucan be still, etc.:* In *Pharsalia* (IX, 761 ff.) Lucan relates how Sabellus and Nassidius, two soldiers of the army Cato led across the Libyan desert, were bitten by monsters. Sabellus melted into a puddle and Nassidius swelled until he popped his coat of mail. In his *Metamorphoses,* Ovid wrote how Cadmus was changed into a serpent (IV, 562-603) and how Arethusa was changed into a fountain (V, 572-661).

Dante cites these cases, obviously, that he may boast of how much better he is going to handle the whole matter of transformation. The master knows his own mastery and sees no real point in being modest about it.

146. *he for whom you weep, Gaville:* Francesco dei Cavalcanti. He was killed by the people of Gaville (a village in the Valley of the Arno). His kinsmen rallied immediately to avenge his death, and many of the townsmen of Gaville were killed in the resulting feud.

Canto XXVI

CIRCLE EIGHT: *Bolgia Eight* — *The Evil Counselors*

Dante turns from the Thieves toward the Evil Counselors of the next Bolgia, and between the two he addresses a passionate lament to Florence prophesying the griefs that will befall her from these two sins. At the purported time of the Vision, it will be recalled, Dante was a Chief Magistrate of Florence and was forced into exile by men he had reason to consider both thieves and evil counselors. He seems prompted, in fact, to say much more on this score, but he restrains himself when he comes in sight of the sinners of the next Bolgia, for they are a moral symbolism, all men of gift who abused their genius, perverting it to wiles and stratagems. Seeing them in Hell he knows his must be another road: his way shall not be by deception.

So the Poets move on and Dante observes the EIGHTH BOLGIA in detail. Here the EVIL COUNSELORS move about endlessly, hidden from view inside great flames. Their sin was to abuse the gifts of the Almighty, to steal his virtues for low purposes. And as they stole from God in their lives and worked by hidden ways, so are they stolen from sight and hidden in the great flames which are their own guilty consciences. And as, in most instances at least, they sinned by glibness of tongue, so are the flames made into a fiery travesty of tongues.

Among the others, the Poets see a great doubleheaded flame, and discover that ULYSSES and DIOMEDE are punished together within it. Virgil addresses the flame, and through its wavering tongue Ulysses narrates an unforgettable tale of his last voyage and death.

Joy to you, Florence, that your banners swell,
  beating their proud wings over land and sea,
  and that your name expands through all of Hell!

Among the thieves I found five who had been
your citizens, to my shame; nor yet shall you
mount to great honor peopling such a den!

But if the truth is dreamed of toward the morning,
you soon shall feel what Prato and the others
wish for you. And were that day of mourning

already come it would not be too soon.
So may it come, since it must! for it will weigh
more heavily on me as I pass my noon.

We left that place. My Guide climbed stone by stone
the natural stair by which we had descended
and drew me after him. So we passed on,

and going our lonely way through that dead land
among the crags and crevices of the cliff,
the foot could make no way without the hand.

I mourned among those rocks, and I mourn again
when memory returns to what I saw:
and more than usually I curb the strain

of my genius, lest it stray from Virtue's course;
so if some star, or a better thing, grant me merit,
may I not find the gift cause for remorse.

As many fireflies as the peasant sees
when he rests on a hill and looks into the valley
(where he tills or gathers grapes or prunes his trees)

in that sweet season when the face of him
who lights the world rides north, and at the hour
when the fly yields to the gnat and the air grows
dim—

such myriads of flames I saw shine through
the gloom of the eighth abyss when I arrived
at the rim from which its bed comes into view.

As he the bears avenged so fearfully
beheld Elijah's chariot depart—
the horses rise toward heaven—but could not see

more than the flame, a cloudlet in the sky,
once it had risen—so within the fosse
only those flames, forever passing by

were visible, ahead, to right, to left;
for though each steals a sinner's soul from view
not one among them leaves a trace of the theft.

I stood on the bridge, and leaned out from the edge;
so far, that but for a jut of rock I held to
I should have been sent hurtling from the ledge

without being pushed. And seeing me so intent,
my Guide said: "There are souls within those flames;
each sinner swathes himself in his own torment."

"Master," I said, "your words make me more sure,
but I had seen already that it was so
and meant to ask what spirit must endure

the pains of that great flame which splits away
in two great horns, as if it rose from the pyre
where Eteocles and Polynices lay?"

He answered me: "Forever round this path
Ulysses and Diomede move in such dress,
united in pain as once they were in wrath;

there they lament the ambush of the Horse
which was the door through which the noble seed
of the Romans issued from its holy source;

there they mourn that for Achilles slain
sweet Deidamia weeps even in death;
there they recall the Palladium in their pain."

"Master," I cried, "I pray you and repray
till my prayer becomes a thousand—if these souls
can still speak from the fire, oh let me stay

until the flame draws near! Do not deny me:
You see how fervently I long for it!"
And he to me: "Since what you ask is worthy,

it shall be. But be still and let me speak;
for I know your mind already, and they perhaps
might scorn your manner of speaking, since they were Greek."

And when the flame had come where time and place
seemed fitting to my Guide, I heard him say
these words to it: "O you two souls who pace

together in one flame!—if my days above
won favor in your eyes, if I have earned
however much or little of your love

in writing my High Verses, do not pass by,
but let one of you be pleased to tell where he,
having disappeared from the known world, went to die."

As if it fought the wind, the greater prong
of the ancient flame began to quiver and hum;
then moving its tip as if it were the tongue

that spoke, gave out a voice above the roar.
"When I left Circe," it said, "who more than a year
detained me near Gaëta long before

Aeneas came and gave the place that name,
not fondness for my son, nor reverence
for my aged father, nor Penelope's claim

to the joys of love, could drive out of my mind
the lust to experience the far-flung world
and the failings and felicities of mankind.

I put out on the high and open sea
with a single ship and only those few souls
who stayed true when the rest deserted me.

As far as Morocco and as far as Spain
I saw both shores; and I saw Sardinia
and the other islands of the open main.

I and my men were stiff and slow with age
when we sailed at last into the narrow pass
where, warning all men back from further voyage,

Hercules' Pillars rose upon our sight.
Already I had left Ceuta on the left;
Seville now sank behind me on the right.

'Shipmates,' I said, 'who through a hundred thousand
perils have reached the West, do not deny
to the brief remaining watch our senses stand

experience of the world beyond the sun.
Greeks! You were not born to live like brutes,
but to press on toward manhood and recognition!

With this brief exhortation I made my crew
so eager for the voyage I could hardly
have held them back from it when I was through;

and turning our stern toward morning, our bow toward night,
we bore southwest out of the world of man;
we made wings of our oars for our fool's flight.

That night we raised the other pole ahead
with all its stars, and ours had so declined
it did not rise out of its ocean bed.

Five times since we had dipped our bending oars
beyond the world, the light beneath the moon
had waxed and waned, when dead upon our course

we sighted, dark in space, a peak so tall
I doubted any man had seen the like.
Our cheers were hardly sounded, when a squall

broke hard upon our bow from the new land:
three times it sucked the ship and the sea about
as it pleased Another to order and command.

At the fourth, the poop rose and the bow went down
till the sea closed over us and the light was gone."

Notes

7. *if the truth is dreamed of toward the morning:* A semi-proverbial expression. It was a common belief that those dreams that occur just before waking foretell the future. "Morning" here would

equal both " the rude awakening" and the potential "dawn of a new day."

8. *Prato:* Not the neighboring town (which was on good terms with Florence) but Cardinal Niccolò da Prato, papal legate from Benedict XI to Florence. In 1304 he tried to reconcile the warring factions, but found that neither side would accept mediation. Since none would be blessed, he cursed all impartially and laid the city under an interdict (i.e., forbade the offering of the sacraments). Shortly after this rejection by the Church, a bridge collapsed in Florence, and later a great fire broke out. Both disasters cost many lives, and both were promptly attributed to the Papal curse.

34. *he the bears avenged:* Elisha saw Elijah translated to Heaven in a fiery chariot. Later he was mocked by some children, who called out tauntingly that he should "Go up" as Elijah had. Elisha cursed the children in the name of the Lord, and bears came suddenly upon the children and devoured them. (2 *Kings* ii, 11-24.)

53-54. *the pyre where Eteocles and Polynices lay:* Eteocles and Polynices, sons of Oedipus, succeeded jointly to the throne of Thebes, and came to an agreement whereby each one would rule separately for a year at a time. Eteocles ruled the first year and when he refused to surrender the throne at the appointed time, Polynices led the Seven against Thebes in a bloody war. In single combat the two brothers killed one another. Statius (*Thebaid* XII, 429 ff.) wrote that their mutual hatred was so great that when they were placed on the same funeral pyre the very flame of their burning drew apart in two great raging horns.

56-63. *Ulysses and Diomede, etc.:* They suffer here for their joint guilt in counseling and carrying out many stratagems which Dante considered evil, though a narrator who was less passionately a partisan of the Trojans might have thought their actions justifiable methods of warfare. They are in one flame for their joint guilt, but the flame is divided, perhaps to symbolize the moral that men of evil must sooner or later come to a falling out, for there can be no lasting union except by virtue.

Their first sin was the stratagem of the Wooden Horse, as a result of which Troy fell and Aeneas went forth to found the Roman line. The second evil occurred at Scyros. There Ulysses discovered Achilles in female disguise, hidden by his mother, Thetis, so that he would not be taken off to the war. Deidamia was in love with Achilles and had borne him a son. When Ulysses persuaded her lover to sail for Troy, she died of grief. The third count is Ulysses' theft of the sacred statue of Pallas from the Palladium. Upon the statue, it was believed, depended the fate of Troy. Its theft, therefore, would result in Troy's downfall.

72. *since they were Greek:* Dante knew no Greek, and these sinners

might scorn him, first, because he spoke what to them would seem a barbarous tongue, and second, because as an Italian he would seem a descendant of Aeneas and the defeated Trojans. Virgil, on the other hand, appeals to them as a man of virtuous life (who therefore has a power over sin) and as a poet who celebrated their earthly fame. (Prof. MacAllister suggests another meaning as well: that Dante [and his world] had no direct knowledge of the Greeks, knowing their works through Latin intermediaries. Thus Virgil stood between Homer and Dante.)

80-81. *one of you:* Ulysses. He is the figure in the larger horn of the flame (which symbolizes that his guilt, as leader, is greater than that of Diomede). His memorable account of his last voyage and death is purely Dante's invention.

86. *Circe:* Changed Ulysses' men to swine and kept him a prisoner, though with rather exceptional accommodations.

87. *Gaëta:* Southeastern Italian coastal town. According to Virgil (*Aeneid,* VII, 1 ff.) it was earlier named Caieta by Aeneas in honor of his aged nurse.

90. *Penelope:* Ulysses' wife.

98. *both shores:* Of the Mediterranean.

101. *narrow pass:* The Straits of Gilbraltar, formerly called the Pillars of Hercules. They were presumed to be the Western limit beyond which no man could navigate.

104. *Ceuta:* In Africa, opposite Gibraltar.

105. *Seville:* In Dante's time this was the name given to the general region of Spain. Having passed through the Straits, the men are now in the Atlantic.

115. *morning . . . night:* East and West.

118. *we raised the other pole ahead:* i.e., They drove south across the equator, observed the southern stars, and found that the North Star had sunk below the horizon. The altitude of the North Star is the easiest approximation of latitude. Except for a small correction, it is directly overhead at the North Pole, shows an altitude of 45° at North latitude 45, and is on the horizon at the equator.

124. *a peak:* Purgatory. They sight it after five months of passage. According to Dante's geography, the Northern hemisphere is land and the Southern is all water except for the Mountain of Purgatory which rises above the surface at a point directly opposite Jerusalem.

Canto XXVII

CIRCLE EIGHT: *Bolgia Eight* — *The Evil Counselors*

The double flame departs at a word from Virgil and behind it appears another which contains the soul of COUNT GUIDO DA MONTEFELTRO, a Lord of Romagna. He had overheard Virgil speaking Italian, and the entire flame in which his soul is wrapped quivers with his eagerness to hear recent news of his wartorn country. (As Farinata has already explained, the spirits of the damned have prophetic powers, but lose all track of events as they approach.)

Dante replies with a stately and tragic summary of how things stand in the cities of Romagna. When he has finished, he asks Guido for his story, and Guido recounts his life, and how Boniface VIII persuaded him to sin.

When it had finished speaking, the great flame
stood tall and shook no more. Now, as it left us
with the sweet Poet's license, another came

along that track and our attention turned
to the new flame: a strange and muffled roar
rose from the single tip to which it burned.

As the Sicilian bull—that brazen spit
which bellowed first (and properly enough)
with the lament of him whose file had tuned it—

was made to bellow by its victim's cries
in such a way, that though it was of brass,
it seemed itself to howl and agonize:

so lacking any way through or around
  the fire that sealed them in, the mournful words
  were changed into its language. When they found

their way up to the tip, imparting to it
  the same vibration given them in their passage
  over the tongue of the concealed sad spirit,

we heard it say: "O you at whom I aim
  my voice, and who were speaking Lombard, saying:
  'Go now, I ask no more,' just as I came—

though I may come a bit late to my turn,
  may it not annoy you to pause and speak a while:
  you see it does not annoy me—and I burn.

If you have fallen only recently
  to this blind world from that sweet Italy
  where I acquired my guilt, I pray you, tell me:

is there peace or war in Romagna? for on earth
  I too was of those hills between Urbino
  and the fold from which the Tiber springs to birth."

I was still staring at it from the dim
  edge of the pit when my Guide nudged me, saying:
  "This one is Italian; *you* speak to him."

My answer was framed already; without pause
  I spoke these words to it: "O hidden soul,
  your sad Romagna is not and never was

without war in her tyrants' raging blood;
  but none flared openly when I left just now.
  Ravenna's fortunes stand as they have stood

these many years: Polenta's eagles brood
  over her walls, and their pinions cover Cervia.
  The city that so valiantly withstood

the French, and raised a mountain of their dead,
  feels the Green Claws again. Still in Verrucchio
  the Aged Mastiff and his Pup, who shed

Montagna's blood, raven in their old ranges.
The cities of Lamone and Santerno
are led by the white den's Lion, he who changes

his politics with the compass. And as the city
the Savio washes lies between plain and mountain,
so it lives between freedom and tyranny.

Now, I beg you, let us know your name;
do not be harder than one has been to you;
so, too, you will preserve your earthly fame."

And when the flame had roared a while beneath
the ledge on which we stood, it swayed its tip
to and fro, and then gave forth this breath:

"If I believed that my reply were made
to one who could ever climb to the world again,
this flame would shake no more. But since no shade

ever returned—if what I am told is true—
from this blind world into the living light,
without fear of dishonor I answer you.

I was a man of arms: then took the rope
of the Franciscans, hoping to make amends:
and surely I should have won to all my hope

but for the Great Priest—may he rot in Hell!—
who brought me back to all my earlier sins;
and how and why it happened I wish to tell

in my own words: while I was still encased
in the pulp and bone my mother bore, my deeds
were not of the lion but of the fox: I raced

through tangled ways; all wiles were mine from birth,
and I won to such advantage with my arts
that rumor of me reached the ends of the earth.

But when I saw before me all the signs
of the time of life that cautions every man
to lower his sail and gather in his lines,

that which had pleased me once, troubled my spirit,
  and penitent and confessed, I became a monk.
  Alas! What joy I might have had of it!

It was then the Prince of the New Pharisees drew
  his sword and marched upon the Lateran—
  and not against the Saracen or the Jew,

for every man that stood against his hand
  was a Christian soul: not one had warred on Acre,
  nor been a trader in the Sultan's land.

It was he abused his sacred vows and mine:
  his Office and the Cord I wore, which once
  made those it girded leaner. As Constantine

sent for Silvestro to cure his leprosy,
  seeking him out among Soracte's cells;
  so this one from his great throne sent for me

to cure the fever of pride that burned his blood.
  He demanded my advice, and I kept silent
  for his words seemed drunken to me. So it stood

until he said: "Your soul need fear no wound;
  I absolve your guilt beforehand; and now teach me
  how to smash Penestrino to the ground.

The Gates of Heaven, as you know, are mine
  to open and shut, for I hold the two Great Keys
  so easily let go by Celestine."

His weighty arguments led me to fear
  silence was worse than sin. Therefore, I said:
  "Holy Father, since you clean me here

of the guilt into which I fall, let it be done:
  long promise and short observance is the road
  that leads to the sure triumph of your throne."

Later, when I was dead, St. Francis came
  to claim my soul, but one of the Black Angels
  said: 'Leave him. Do not wrong me. This one's name

went into my book the moment he resolved
to give false counsel. Since then he has been mine,
for who does not repent cannot be absolved;

nor can we admit the possibility
of repenting a thing at the same time it is willed,
for the two acts are contradictory.'

Miserable me! with what contrition
I shuddered when he lifted me, saying: 'Perhaps
you hadn't heard that I was a logician.'

He carried me to Minos: eight times round
his scabby back the monster coiled his tail,
then biting it in rage he pawed the ground

and cried: 'This one is for the thievish fire!'
And, as you see, I am lost accordingly,
grieving in heart as I go in this attire."

His story told, the flame began to toss
and writhe its horn. And so it left, and we
crossed over to the arch of the next fosse

where from the iron treasury of the Lord
the fee of wrath is paid the Sowers of Discord.

Notes

3. *by the sweet Poet's license:* The legend of Virgil as a magician and sorcerer was widespread through the Middle Ages and was probably based on the common belief that his Fourth Eclogue was a specific prophecy of the birth of Christ and of the Christian Era. Some commentators have argued as an extension of this legend that Dante assigns Virgil a magical power of conjuration over the damned, a power of white rather than black magic—that distinction being necessary to save him from damnation. Despite the fact that Dante nowhere makes that distinction himself, this interpretation can be made plausible, but only in the most incidental way. The whole idea of Virgil as a magician is trivial beside Dante's total concept. Virgil's power is divinely given him by Beatrice. That is, it represents Human Reason informed and commanded by Divine Love, a reassertion of a fundamental medieval theme that reason is the handmaiden of faith. His power is God's will and is most clearly expressed

in his words to Minos: "This has been willed where what is willed must be." Only with this light within it, can reason exert its power over evil.

3. *another came:* Guido da Montefeltro (1223-1298). As head of the Ghibellines of Romagna, he was reputed the wisest and cunningest man in Italy.

7. *the Sicilian bull:* In the sixth century B.C. Perillus of Athens constructed for Phalaris, Tyrant of Sicily, a metal bull to be used as an instrument of torture. When victims were placed inside it and roasted to death, their screams passed through certain tuned pipes and emerged as a burlesque bellowing of the bull. Phalaris accepted delivery and showed his gratitude by appointing the inventor the bull's first victim. Later Phalaris was overthrown, and he, too, took his turn inside the bull.

21. *Go now, I ask no more:* These are the words with which Virgil dismisses Ulysses and Diomede, his "license."

29-30. *Urbino and the fold from which the Tiber, etc.:* Romagna is the district that runs south from the Po along the east side of the Apennines. Urbino is due east of Florence and roughly south of Rimini. Between Urbino and Florence rise the Coronaro Mountains which contain the headwaters of the Tiber.

39-41. *Ravenna . . . Polenta's eagles . . . Cervia:* In 1300 Ravenna was ruled by Guido Vecchio da Polenta, father of Francesca da Rimini. His arms bore an eagle and his domain included the small city of Cervia about twelve miles south of Ravenna.

42-44. *The city . . . the Green Claws:* The city is Forlì. In 1282 Guido da Montefeltro defended Forlì from the French, but in 1300 it was under the despotic rule of Sinibaldo degli Ordelaffi, whose arms were a green lion.

44-45. *Verrucchio . . . the Aged Mastiff and his Pup . . . Montagna:* Verrucchio (Vehr-OO-Kyoe) was the castle of Malatesta and his son Malatestino, Lords of Rimini, whom Dante calls dogs for their cruelty. Montagna de' Parcitati (Mon-TAH-nyah day Pahr-tchit-AH-tee), the leader of Rimini's Ghibellines, was captured by Malatesta in 1295 and murdered in captivity by Malatestino.

47-48. *Lamone and Santerno . . . the white den's Lion:* Maginardo (Mah-djin-AHR-doe) de' Pagani (died 1302) ruled Faenza, on the River Lamone, and Imola, close by the River Santerno. His arms were a blue lion on a white field (hence "the Lion from the white den"). He supported the Ghibellines in the north, but the Guelfs in the south (Florence), changing his politics according to the direction in which he was facing.

49-50. *the city the Savio washes:* Cesena. It ruled itself for a number of years, but was taken over by Malatestino in 1314. It lies between Forlì and Rimini.

67. *the Great Priest:* Boniface VIII, so called as Pope.

82. *the Prince of the New Pharisees:* Also Boniface.

83. *marched upon the Lateran:* Boniface had had a long-standing feud with the Colonna family. In 1297 the Colonna walled themselves in a castle twenty-five miles east of Rome at Penestrino (now called Palestrina) in the Lateran. On Guido's advice the Pope offered a fair-sounding amnesty which he had no intention of observing. When the Colonna accepted the terms and left the castle, the Pope destroyed it, leaving the Colonna without a refuge.

86-87. *Acre . . . trader in the Sultan's land:* It was the Saracens who opposed the crusaders at Acre, the Jews who traded in the Sultan's land.

90-92. *Constantine . . . Silvestro . . . Soracte:* In the persecutions of the Christians by the Emperor Constantine, Pope Sylvester I took refuge in the caves of Mount Soracte near Rome. (It is now called Santo Oreste.) Later, according to legend, Constantine was stricken by leprosy and sent for Sylvester, who cured him and converted him to Christianity, in return for which the Emperor was believed to have made the famous "Donation of Constantine." (See Canto XIX.)

102. *so easily let go by Celestine:* Celestine V under the persuasion of Boniface abdicated the Papacy. (See Canto III notes.)

107. *long promise and short observance:* This is the advice upon which Boniface acted in trapping the Colonna with his hypocritical amnesty.

109. *St. Francis came:* To gather in the soul of one of his monks.

110. *Black Angel:* A devil.

130-31. I have taken liberties with these lines in the hope of achieving a reasonably tonic final couplet. The literal reading is: "In which the fee is paid to those who, sowing discord, acquire weight (of guilt and pain)."

Canto XXVIII

CIRCLE EIGHT: *Bolgia Nine* *The Sowers of Discord*

The Poets come to the edge of the NINTH BOLGIA and look down at a parade of hideously mutilated souls. These are the SOWERS OF DISCORD, and just as their sin was to rend asunder what God had meant to be united, so are they hacked and torn through all eternity by a great demon with a bloody sword. After each mutilation the souls are compelled to drag their broken bodies around the pit and to return to the demon, for in the course of the circuit their wounds knit in time to be inflicted anew. Thus is the law of retribution observed, each sinner suffering according to his degree.

Among them Dante distinguishes three classes with varying degrees of guilt within each class. First come the SOWERS OF RELIGIOUS DISCORD. Mahomet is chief among them, and appears first, cleft from crotch to chin, with his internal organs dangling between his legs. His son-in-law, Ali, drags on ahead of him, cleft from topknot to chin. These reciprocal wounds symbolize Dante's judgment that, between them, these two sum up the total schism between Christianity and Mohammedanism. The revolting details of Mahomet's condition clearly imply Dante's opinion of that doctrine. Mahomet issues an ironic warning to another schismatic, FRA DOLCINO.

Next come the SOWERS OF POLITICAL DISCORD, among them PIER DA MEDICINA, the Tribune CURIO, and MOSCA DEI LAMBERTI, each mutilated according to the nature of his sin.

Last of all is BERTRAND DE BORN, SOWER OF DISCORD BETWEEN KINSMEN. He separated father from son, and for that offense carries his head separated from his body, holding it with one hand by the hair, and swinging it as if it were a lantern to light his dark and endless way. The image of Bertrand raising his head at arm's length in order that it might speak more clearly to the Poets on the ridge is one of the most memorable in the Inferno. *For some reason that cannot be ascertained, Dante makes these sinners quite eager to be remembered in the world, despite the fact that many who lie above them in Hell were unwilling to be recognized.*

Who could describe, even in words set free
of metric and rhyme and a thousand times retold,
the blood and wounds that now were shown to me!

At grief so deep the tongue must wag in vain;
the language of our sense and memory
lacks the vocabulary of such pain.

If one could gather all those who have stood
through all of time on Puglia's fateful soil
and wept for the red running of their blood

in the war of the Trojans; and in that long war
which left so vast a spoil of golden rings,
as we find written in Livy, who does not err;

along with those whose bodies felt the wet
and gaping wounds of Robert Guiscard's lances;
with all the rest whose bones are gathered yet

at Ceperano where every last Pugliese
turned traitor; and with those from Tagliacozzo
where Alardo won without weapons—if all these

were gathered, and one showed his limbs run through,
another his lopped off, that could not equal
the mutilations of the ninth pit's crew.

A wine tun when a stave or cant-bar starts
  does not split open as wide as one I saw
  split from his chin to the mouth with which man farts.

Between his legs all of his red guts hung
  with the heart, the lungs, the liver, the gall bladder,
  and the shriveled sac that passes shit to the bung.

I stood and stared at him from the stone shelf;
  he noticed me and opening his own breast
  with both hands cried: "See how I rip myself!

See how Mahomet's mangled and split open!
  Ahead of me walks Ali in his tears,
  his head cleft from the top-knot to the chin.

And all the other souls that bleed and mourn
  along this ditch were sowers of scandal and schism:
  as they tore others apart, so are they torn.

Behind us, warden of our mangled horde,
  the devil who butchers us and sends us marching
  waits to renew our wounds with his long sword

when we have made the circuit of the pit;
  for by the time we stand again before him
  all the wounds he gave us last have knit.

But who are you that gawk down from that sill—
  probably to put off your own descent
  to the pit you are sentenced to for your own evil?"

"Death has not come for him, guilt does not drive
  his soul to torment," my sweet Guide replied.
  "That he may experience all while yet alive

I, who am dead, must lead him through the drear
  and darkened halls of Hell, from round to round:
  and this is true as my own standing here."

More than a hundred wraiths who were marching under
the sill on which we stood, paused at his words
and stared at me, forgetting pain in wonder.

"And if you do indeed return to see
the sun again, and soon, tell Fra Dolcino
unless he longs to come and march with me

he would do well to check his groceries
before the winter drives him from the hills
and gives the victory to the Novarese."

Mahomet, one foot raised, had paused to say
these words to me. When he had finished speaking
he stretched it out and down, and moved away.

Another–he had his throat slit, and his nose
slashed off as far as the eyebrows, and a wound
where one of his ears had been–standing with those

who stared at me in wonder from the pit,
opened the grinning wound of his red gullet
as if it were a mouth, and said through it:

"O soul unforfeited to misery
and whom–unless I take you for another–
I have seen above in our sweet Italy;

if ever again you see the gentle plain
that slopes down from Vercelli to Marcabò,
remember Pier da Medicina in pain,

and announce this warning to the noblest two
of Fano, Messers Guido and Angiolello:
that unless our foresight sees what is not true

they shall be thrown from their ships into the sea
and drown in the raging tides near La Cattolica
to satisfy a tyrant's treachery.

Neptune never saw so gross a crime
  in all the seas from Cyprus to Majorca,
  not even in pirate raids, nor the Argive time.

The one-eyed traitor, lord of the demesne
  whose hill and streams one who walks here beside me
  will wish eternally he had never seen,

will call them to a parley, but behind
  sweet invitations he will work it so
  they need not pray against Focara's wind."

And I to him: "If you would have me bear
  your name to time, show me the one who found
  the sight of that land so harsh, and let me hear

his story and his name." He touched the cheek
  of one nearby, forcing the jaws apart,
  and said: "This is the one; he cannot speak.

This outcast settled Caesar's doubts that day
  beside the Rubicon by telling him:
  'A man prepared is a man hurt by delay.' "

Ah, how wretched Curio seemed to me
  with a bloody stump in his throat in place of the tongue
  which once had dared to speak so recklessly!

And one among them with both arms hacked through
  cried out, raising his stumps on the foul air
  while the blood bedaubed his face: "Remember, too,

Mosca dei Lamberti, alas, who said
  'A thing done has an end!' and with those words
  planted the fields of war with Tuscan dead."

"And brought about the death of all your clan!"
  I said, and he, stung by new pain on pain,
  ran off; and in his grief he seemed a madman.

I stayed to watch those broken instruments,
and I saw a thing so strange I should not dare
to mention it without more evidence

but that my own clear conscience strengthens me,
that good companion that upholds a man
within the armor of his purity.

I saw it there; I seem to see it still—
a body without a head, that moved along
like all the others in that spew and spill.

It held the severed head by its own hair,
swinging it like a lantern in its hand;
and the head looked at us and wept in its despair.

It made itself a lamp of its own head,
and they were two in one and one in two;
how this can be, He knows who so commanded.

And when it stood directly under us
it raised the head at arm's length toward our bridge
the better to be heard, and swaying thus

it cried: "O living soul in this abyss,
see what a sentence has been passed upon me,
and search all Hell for one to equal this!

When you return to the world, remember me:
I am Bertrand de Born, and it was I
who set the young king on to mutiny,

son against father, father against son
as Achitophel set Absalom and David;
and since I parted those who should be one

in duty and in love, I bear my brain
divided from its source within this trunk;
and walk here where my evil turns to pain,

an eye for an eye to all eternity:
thus is the law of Hell observed in me."

8. *Puglia* (POO-lyah): I have used the modern name but some of the events Dante narrates took place in the ancient province of Apulia. The southeastern area of Italy is the scene of all the fighting Dante mentions in the following passage. It is certainly a bloody total of slaughter that Dante calls upon to illustrate his scene.

10. *the war of the Trojans:* The Romans (descended from the Trojans) fought the native Samnites in a long series of raids and skirmishes from 343-290 B.C.

10-12. *and in that long war . . . Livy:* The Punic Wars (264-146 B.C.). Livy writes that in the battle of Cannae (216 B.C.) so many Romans fell that Hannibal gathered three bushels of gold rings from the fingers of the dead and produced them before the Senate at Carthage.

14. *Robert Guiscard:* Dante places Guiscard (1015-1085) in the *Paradiso* among the Warriors of God. He fought the Greeks and Saracens in their attempted invasion of Italy.

16. *Ceperano* (Tcheh-peh-RAH-noe): In 1266 the Pugliese under Manfred, King of Sicily, were charged with holding the pass at Ceperano against Charles of Anjou. The Pugliese, probably under Papal pressure, allowed the French free passage, and Charles went on to defeat Manfred at Benevento. Manfred himself was killed in that battle.

17-18. *Tagliacozzo . . . Alardo:* At Tagliacozzo (Tah-lyah-KAW-tsoe) (1268) in a continuation of the same strife, Charles of Anjou used a stratagem suggested to him by Alard de Valéry and defeated Conradin, nephew of Manfred. "Won without weapons" is certainly an overstatement: what Alardo suggested was a simple but effective concealment of reserve troops. When Conradin seemed to have carried the day and was driving his foes before him, the reserve troops broke on his flank and rear, and defeated Conradin's out-positioned forces.

32. *Ali:* Ali succeeded Mahomet to the Caliphate, but not until three of the disciples had preceded him. Mahomet died in 632, and Ali did not assume the Caliphate until 656.

56. *Fra Dolcino:* (Dohl-TCHEE-noe) In 1300 Fra Dolcino took over the reformist order called the Apostolic Brothers, who preached, among other things, the community of property and of women. Clement V declared them heretical and ordered a crusade against them. The brotherhood retired with its women to an impregnable

position in the hills between Novara and Vercelli, but their supplies gave out in the course of a year-long siege, and they were finally starved out in March of 1307. Dolcino and Margaret of Trent, his "Sister in Christ," were burned at the stake at Vercelli the following June.

74. *Vercelli . . . Marcabò:* Vercelli is the most western town in Lombardy. Marcabò stands near the mouth of the Po.

76-90. *this warning:* Malatestino da Rimini (see preceding Canto), in a move to annex the city of Fano, invited Guido del Cassero and Angioletto da Carignano (Ahn-djoe-LEH-toe dah Kahr-ee-NYAH-noe), leading citizens of Fano, to a conference at La Cattolica, a point on the Adriatic midway between Fano and Rimini. At Malatestino's orders the two were thrown overboard off Focara, a headland swept by such dangerous currents that approaching sailors used to offer prayers for a safe crossing.

83. *Cyprus . . . Majorca:* These islands are at opposite ends of the Mediterranean.

84. *nor the Argive time:* The Greeks were raiders and pirates.

85. *the one-eyed traitor:* Malatestino.

86. *one who walks here beside me:* This is the Roman Tribune Curio, who was banished from Rome by Pompey and joined Caesar's forces, advising him to cross the Rubicon, which was then the boundary between Gaul and the Roman Republic. The crossing constituted invasion, and thus began the Roman Civil War. The Rubicon flows near Rimini.

106. *Mosca dei Lamberti:* Dante had asked Ciacco (Canto VI) for news of Mosca as a man of good works. Now he finds him, his merit canceled by his greater sin. Buondelmonte dei Buondelmonti had insulted the honor of the Amidei by breaking off his engagement to a daughter of that line in favor of a girl of the Donati. When the Amidei met to discuss what should be done, Mosca spoke for the death of Buondelmonte. The Amidei acted upon his advice and from that murder sprang the bloody feud between the Guelphs and Ghibellines of Florence.

119. *a body without a head:* Bertrand de Born (1140-1215), a great knight and master of the troubadours of Provence. He is said to have instigated a quarrel between Henry II of England and his son Prince Henry, called "The Young King" because he was crowned within his father's lifetime.

137. *Achitophel:* One of David's counselors, who deserted him to assist the rebellious Absalom. (II *Samuel,* xv-xvii.)

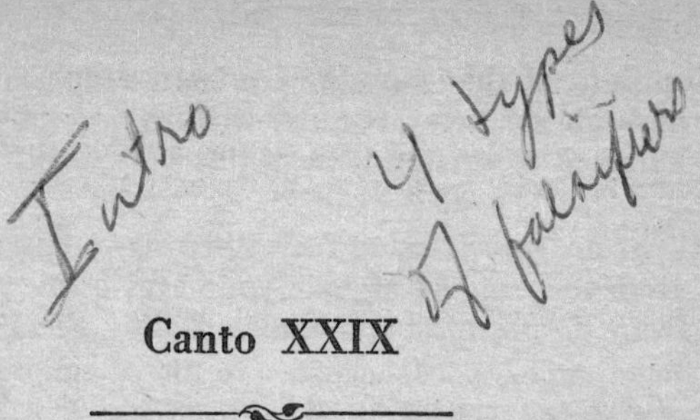

Canto XXIX

CIRCLE EIGHT: *Bolgia Ten* — *The Falsifiers (Class I, Alchemists)*

Dante lingers on the edge of the Ninth Bolgia expecting to see one of his kinsmen, GERI DEL BELLO, among the Sowers of Discord. Virgil, however, hurries him on, since time is short, and as they cross the bridge over the TENTH BOLGIA, Virgil explains that he had a glimpse of Geri among the crowd near the bridge and that he had been making threatening gestures at Dante.

The Poets now look into the last Bolgia *of the Eighth Circle and see THE FALSIFIERS. They are punished by afflictions of every sense: by darkness, stench, thirst, filth, loathsome diseases, and a shrieking din. Some of them, moreover, run ravening through the pit, tearing others to pieces. Just as in life they corrupted society by their falsifications, so in death these sinners are subjected to a sum of corruptions. In one sense they figure forth what society would be if all falsifiers succeeded—a place where the senses are an affliction (since falsification deceives the senses) rather than a guide, where even the body has no honesty, and where some lie prostrate while others run ravening to prey upon them.*

Not all of these details are made clear until the next Canto, for Dante distinguishes four classes of Falsifiers, and in the present Canto we meet only the first class, THE ALCHEMISTS, the Falsifiers of Things. Of this class are GRIFFOLINO D'AREZZO and CAPOCCHIO, with both of whom Dante speaks.

The sight of that parade of broken dead
had left my eyes so sotted with their tears
I longed to stay and weep, but Virgil said:

"What are you waiting for? Why do you stare
as if you could not tear your eyes away
from the mutilated shadows passing there?

You did not act so in the other pits.
Consider—if you mean perhaps to count them—
this valley and its train of dismal spirits

winds twenty-two miles round. The moon already
is under our feet; the time we have is short,
and there is much that you have yet to see."

"Had you known what I was seeking," I replied,
"you might perhaps have given me permission
to stay on longer." (As I spoke, my Guide

had started off already, and I in turn
had moved along behind him; thus, I answered
as we moved along the cliff.) "Within that cavern

upon whose brim I stood so long to stare,
I think a spirit of my own blood mourns
the guilt that sinners find so costly there."

And the Master then: "Hereafter let your mind
turn its attention to more worthy matters
and leave him to his fate among the blind;

for by the bridge and among that shapeless crew
I saw him point to you with threatening gestures,
and I heard him called Geri del Bello. You

were occupied at the time with that headless one
who in his life was master of Altaforte,
and did not look that way; so he moved on."

"O my sweet Guide," I answered. "his death came
by violence and is not yet avenged
by those who share his blood, and, thus, his shame.

For this he surely hates his kin, and, therefore,
as I suppose, he would not speak to me;
and in that he makes me pity him the more."

We spoke of this until we reached the edge
from which, had there been light, we could have seen
the floor of the next pit. Out from that ledge

Malebolge's final cloister lay outspread,
and all of its lay brethren might have been
in sight but for the murk; and from those dead

such shrieks and strangled agonies shrilled through me
like shafts, but barbed with pity, that my hands
flew to my ears. If all the misery

that crams the hospitals of pestilence
in Maremma, Valdichiano, and Sardinia
in the summer months when death sits like a presence

on the marsh air, were dumped into one trench—
that might suggest their pain. And through the screams,
putrid flesh spread up its sickening stench.

Still bearing left we passed from the long sill
to the last bridge of Malebolge. There
the reeking bottom was more visible.

There, High Justice, sacred ministress
of the First Father, reigns eternally
over the falsifiers in their distress.

I doubt it could have been such pain to bear
the sight of the Aeginian people dying
that time when such malignance rode the air

that every beast down to the smallest worm
shriveled and died (it was after that great plague
that the Ancient People, as the poets affirm,

were reborn from the ants)—as it was to see
the spirits lying heaped on one another
in the dank bottom of that fetid valley.

One lay gasping on another's shoulder,
one on another's belly; and some were crawling
on hands and knees among the broken boulders.

Silent, slow step by step, we moved ahead
looking at and listening to those souls
too weak to raise themselves from their stone bed.

I saw two there like two pans that are put
one against the other to hold their warmth.
They were covered with great scabs from head to foot.

No stable boy in a hurry to go home,
or for whom his master waits impatiently,
ever scrubbed harder with his currycomb

than those two spirits of the stinking ditch
scrubbed at themselves with their own bloody claws
to ease the furious burning of the itch.

And as they scrubbed and clawed themselves, their nails
drew down the scabs the way a knife scrapes bream
or some other fish with even larger scales.

"O you," my Guide called out to one, "you there
who rip your scabby mail as if your fingers
were claws and pincers; tell us if this lair

counts any Italians among those who lurk
in its dark depths; so may your busy nails
eternally suffice you for your work."

"We both are Italian whose unending loss
you see before you," he replied in tears.
"But who are you who come to question us?"

"I am a shade," my Guide and Master said,
"who leads this living man from pit to pit
to show him Hell as I have been commanded."

The sinners broke apart as he replied
and turned convulsively to look at me,
as others did who overheard my Guide.

My Master, then, ever concerned for me,
turned and said: "Ask them whatever you wish."
And I said to those two wraiths of misery:

"So may the memory of your names and actions
not die forever from the minds of men
in that first world, but live for many suns,

tell me who you are and of what city;
do not be shamed by your nauseous punishment
into concealing your identity."

"I was a man of Arezzo," one replied,
"and Albert of Siena had me burned;
but I am not here for the deed for which I died.

It is true that jokingly I said to him once:
'I know how to raise myself and fly through air';
and he—with all the eagerness of a dunce—

wanted to learn. Because I could not make
a Daedalus of him—for no other reason—
he had his father burn me at the stake.

But Minos, the infallible, had me hurled
here to the final bolgia of the ten
for the alchemy I practiced in the world."

And I to the Poet: "Was there ever a race
more vain than the Sienese? Even the French,
compared to them, seem full of modest grace."

And the other leper answered mockingly:
"Excepting Stricca, who by careful planning
managed to live and spend so moderately;

and Niccolò, who in his time above
was first of all the shoots in that rank garden
to discover the costly uses of the clove;

and excepting the brilliant company of talents
in which Caccia squandered his vineyards and his woods,
and Abbagliato displayed his intelligence.

But if you wish to know who joins your cry
against the Sienese, study my face
with care and let it make its own reply.

So you will see I am the suffering shadow
of Capocchio, who, by practicing alchemy,
falsified the metals, and you must know,

unless my mortal recollection strays
how good an ape I was of Nature's ways."

Notes

10. *twenty-two miles:* Another instance of "poetic" rather than "literal" detail. Dante's measurements cannot be made to fit together on any scale map.

10-11. *the moon . . . is under our feet:* If the moon, nearly at full, is under their feet, the sun must be overhead. It is therefore approximately noon of Holy Saturday.

18. *cavern:* Dante's use of this word is not literally accurate, but its intent and its poetic force are obvious.

27. *Geri del Bello* (DJEH-ree): A cousin of Dante's father. He became embroiled in a quarrel with the Sacchetti of Florence and was murdered. At the time of the writing he had not been avenged by his kinsmen in accord with the clan code of a life for a life.

29. *Altaforte:* (Ahl-tah-FAWR-teh) Bertrand de Born was Lord of Hautefort.

40-41. *cloister . . . lay brethren:* A Dantean irony. This is the first suggestion of a sardonic mood reminiscent of the Gargoyle Cantos that will grow and swell in this Canto until even Virgil resorts to mocking irony.

47. *Maremma, Valdichiano, and Sardinia:* Malarial plague areas. Valdichiano and Maremma were swamp areas of eastern and western Tuscany.

59. *the Aeginian people dying:* Juno, incensed that the nymph Aegina let Jove possess her, set a plague upon the island that bore her name. Every animal and every human died until only Aeacus, the son born to Aegina of Jove, was left. He prayed to his father for aid and Jove repopulated the island by transforming the ants at his son's feet into men. The Aeginians have since been called Myrmidons, from the Greek word for ant. Ovid (*Metamorphoses* VII, 523-660).

76. *in a hurry to go home:* The literal text would be confusing here. I have translated one possible interpretation of it as offered by Giuseppe Vandelli. The original line is *"ne da colui che mal volentier vegghia"* ("nor by one who unwillingly stays awake," or less literally, but with better force: "nor by one who fights off sleep").

85. *my Guide called out to one:* The sinner spoken to is Griffolino D'arezzo (Ah-RAY-tsoe), an alchemist who extracted large sums of money from Alberto da Siena on the promise of teaching him to fly like Daedalus. When the Sienese oaf finally discovered he had been tricked, he had his "uncle," the Bishop of Siena, burn Griffolino as a sorcerer. Griffolino, however, is not punished for sorcery, but for falsification of silver and gold through alchemy.

125-132. *Stricca . . . Niccolò . . . Caccia . . . Abbagliato:* (STREE-kah, Nee-koe-LAW, KAH-tchah, Ahb-ah-LYAH-toe) All of these Sienese noblemen were members of the Spendthrift Brigade and wasted their substance in competitions of riotous living. Lano (Canto XIII) was also of this company. Niccolò dei Salimbeni discovered some recipe (details unknown) prepared with fabulously expensive spices. "Excepting" is ironical. (cf. the similar usage in XXI, 41.)

137. *Capocchio:* (Kah-PAW-kyoe) Reputedly a Florentine friend of Dante's student days. For practicing alchemy he was burned at the stake at Siena in 1293.

Canto XXX

CIRCLE EIGHT: *Bolgia Ten* — *The Falsifiers (The Remaining Three Classes: Evil Impersonators, Counterfeiters, False Witnesses)*

Just as Capocchio finishes speaking, two ravenous spirits come racing through the pit; and one of them, sinking his tusks into Capocchio's neck, drags him away like prey. Capocchio's companion, Griffolino, identifies the two as GIANNI SCHICCHI and MYRRHA, who run ravening through the pit through all eternity, snatching at other souls and rending them. These are the EVIL IMPERSONATORS, Falsifiers of Persons. In life they seized upon the appearance of others, and in death they must run with never a pause, seizing upon the infernal apparition of these souls, while they in turn are preyed upon by their own furies.

Next the Poets encounter MASTER ADAM, a sinner of the third class, a Falsifier of Money, i.e., a COUNTERFEITER. Like the alchemists, he is punished by a loathsome disease and he cannot move from where he lies, but his disease is compounded by other afflictions, including an eternity of unbearable thirst. Master Adam identifies two spirits lying beside him as POTIPHAR'S WIFE and SINON THE GREEK, sinners of the fourth class, THE FALSE WITNESS, i.e., Falsifiers of Words.

Sinon, angered by Master Adam's identification of him, strikes him across the belly with the one arm he is able to move. Master Adam replies in kind, and Dante, fascinated by their continuing exchange of abuse, stands staring at them until Virgil turns on him in great anger, for "The wish to hear such baseness is degrading." Dante burns with shame, and Virgil immediately forgives him because of his great and genuine repentance.

At the time when Juno took her furious
revenge for Semele, striking in rage
again and again at the Theban royal house,

King Athamas, by her contrivance, grew
so mad, that seeing his wife out for an airing
with his two sons, he cried to his retinue:

"Out with the nets there! Nets across the pass!
for I will take this lioness and her cubs!"
And spread his talons, mad and merciless,

and seizing his son Learchus, whirled him round
and brained him on a rock; at which the mother
leaped into the sea with her other son and drowned.

And when the Wheel of Fortune spun about
to humble the all-daring Trojan's pride
so that both king and kingdom were wiped out;

Hecuba—mourning, wretched, and a slave—
having seen Polyxena sacrificed,
and Polydorus dead without a grave;

lost and alone, beside an alien sea,
began to bark and growl like a dog
in the mad seizure of her misery.

But never in Thebes nor Troy were Furies seen
to strike at man or beast in such mad rage
as two I saw, pale, naked, and unclean,

who suddenly came running toward us then,
snapping their teeth as they ran, like hungry swine
let out to feed after a night in the pen.

One of them sank his tusks so savagely
into Capocchio's neck, that when he dragged him,
the ditch's rocky bottom tore his belly.

And the Aretine, left trembling by me, said:
"That incubus, in life, was Gianni Schicchi;
here he runs rabid, mangling the other dead."

"So!" I answered, "and so may the other one
not sink its teeth in you, be pleased to tell us
what shade it is before it races on."

And he: "That ancient shade in time above
was Myrrha, vicious daughter of Cinyras
who loved her father with more than rightful love.

She falsified another's form and came
disguised to sin with him just as that other
who runs with her, in order that he might claim

the fabulous lead-mare, lay under disguise
on Buoso Donati's death bed and dictated
a spurious testament to the notaries."

And when the rabid pair had passed from sight,
I turned to observe the other misbegotten
spirits that lay about to left and right.

And there I saw another husk of sin,
who, had his legs been trimmed away at the groin,
would have looked for all the world like a mandolin.

The dropsy's heavy humors, which so bunch
and spread the limbs, had disproportioned him
till his face seemed much too small for his swollen paunch.

He strained his lips apart and thrust them forward
the way a sick man, feverish with thirst,
curls one lip toward the chin and the other upward.

"O you exempt from every punishment
of this grim world (I know not why)," he cried,
"look well upon the misery and debasement

of him who was Master Adam. In my first
life's time, I had enough to please me: here,
I lack a drop of water for my thirst.

The rivulets that run from the green flanks
of Casentino to the Arno's flood,
spreading their cool sweet moisture through their banks,

run constantly before me, and their plash
and ripple in imagination dries me
more than the disease that eats my flesh.

Inflexible Justice that has forked and spread
my soul like hay, to search it the more closely,
finds in the country where my guilt was bred

this increase of my grief; for there I learned,
there in Romena, to stamp the Baptist's image
on alloyed gold—till I was bound and burned.

But could I see the soul of Guido here,
or of Alessandro, or of their filthy brother,
I would not trade that sight for all the clear

cool flow of Branda's fountain. One of the three—
if those wild wraiths who run here are not lying—
is here already. But small good it does me

when my legs are useless! Were I light enough
to move as much as an inch in a hundred years,
long before this I would have started off

to cull him from the freaks that fill this fosse,
although it winds on for eleven miles
and is no less than half a mile across.

Because of them I lie here in this pig-pen;
it was they persuaded me to stamp the florins
with three carats of alloy." And I then:

"Who are those wretched two sprawled alongside
your right-hand borders, and who seem to smoke
as a washed hand smokes in winter?" He replied:

"They were here when I first rained into this gully,
and have not changed position since, nor may they,
as I believe, to all eternity.

One is the liar who charged young Joseph wrongly:
the other, Sinon, the false Greek from Troy.
A burning fever makes them reek so strongly."

And one of the false pair, perhaps offended
by the manner of Master Adam's presentation,
punched him in the rigid and distended

belly—it thundered like a drum—and he
retorted with an arm blow to the face
that seemed delivered no whit less politely,

saying to him: "Although I cannot stir
my swollen legs, I still have a free arm
to use at times when nothing else will answer."

And the other wretch said: "It was not so free
on your last walk to the stake, free as it was
when you were coining." And he of the dropsy:

"That's true enough, but there was less truth in you
when they questioned you at Troy." And Sinon then:
"For every word I uttered that was not true

you uttered enough false coins to fill a bushel:
I am put down here for a single crime,
but you for more than any Fiend in Hell."

"Think of the Horse," replied the swollen shade,
"and may it torture you, perjurer, to recall
that all the world knows the foul part you played."

"And to you the torture of the thirst that fries
and cracks your tongue," said the Greek, "and of the water
that swells your gut like a hedge before your eyes."

And the coiner: "So is your own mouth clogged
with the filth that stuffs and sickens it as always;
if I am parched while my paunch is waterlogged,

you have the fever and your cankered brain;
and were you asked to lap Narcissus' mirror
you would not wait to be invited again."

I was still standing, fixed upon those two
when the Master said to me: "Now keep on looking
a little longer and I quarrel with you."

When I heard my Master raise his voice to me,
I wheeled about with such a start of shame
that I grow pale yet at the memory.

As one trapped in a nightmare that has caught
his sleeping mind, wishes within the dream
that it were all a dream, as if it were not—

such I became: my voice could not win through
my shame to ask his pardon; while my shame
already won more pardon than I knew.

"Less shame," my Guide said, ever just and kind,
"would wash away a greater fault than yours.
Therefore, put back all sorrow from your mind;

and never forget that I am always by you
should it occur again, as we walk on,
that we find ourselves where others of this crew

fall to such petty wrangling and upbraiding.
The wish to hear such baseness is degrading."

Notes

1-2. *Juno took her furious revenge:* As in the case of the Aeginians, Jove begot a son (Bacchus) upon a mortal (Semele, daughter of the King Cadmus of Thebes); and Juno, who obviously could not cope with her husband's excursions directly, turned her fury upon the mortals in a number of godlike ways, among them inducing the madness of King Athamas (Semele's brother-in-law) which Ovid recounts in *Metamorphoses* IV, 512 ff.

16. *Hecuba:* Wife of King Priam. When Troy fell she was taken to Greece as a slave. En route she was forced to witness the sacrifice of her daughter and to look upon her son lying murdered and unburied. She went mad in her affliction and fell to howling like a dog. Ovid (*Metamorphoses* XIII, 568 ff.) describes her anguish but does not say she was changed into a dog.

31. *the Aretine:* Capocchio's companion, Griffolino.

32. *Gianni Schicchi:* (DJAHN-ee SKEE-kee) Of the Cavalcanti of Florence. When Buoso di Donati (see Canto XXV) died, his son, Simone, persuaded Schicchi to impersonate the dead man and to dictate a will in Simone's favor. Buoso was removed from the death bed, Schicchi took his place in disguise, and the will was dictated to a notary as if Buoso were still alive. Schicchi took advantage of the occasion to make several bequests to himself, including one of a famous and highly-prized mare.

38. *Myrrha:* The second figure that runs rabid through the pit was the daughter of Cinyras, King of Cyprus. Moved by an incestuous passion for her father, she disguised herself and slipped into his bed. After he had mated with her, the king discovered who she was and threatened to kill her but she ran away and was changed into a myrtle. Adonis was born from her trunk. (Ovid, *Metamorphoses* X, 298 ff.)

61. *Master Adam:* Of Brescia. Under the orders of the Counts Guidi of Romena, he counterfeited Florentine florins of twenty-one

rather than twenty-four carat gold, and on such a scale that a currency crisis arose in Northern Italy. He was burned at the stake by the Florentines in 1281.

65. *Casentino:* A mountainous district in which the Arno rises.

74. *the Baptist's image:* John the Baptist's. As patron of Florence, his image was stamped on the florins.

76-77. *Guido . . . Alessandro . . . their filthy brother:* The Counts Guidi.

79. *Branda:* A spring near Romena. The famous fountain of Branda is in Siena, but Adam is speaking of his home country and must mean the spring.

79-81. *One of the three . . . is here already:* Guido died before 1300.

92. *your right-hand borders:* Master Adam's right side. Dante uses *confini* (borders) for "side," suggesting ironically that Master Adam in his swollen state is more like a territory than a man.

97. *the liar who charged young Joseph:* Potiphar's wife bore false witness against Joseph. (*Genesis* xxxix, 6-23.)

98. *Sinon:* The Greek who glibly talked the Trojans into taking the Horse inside the city walls. (*Aeneid* II, 57-194.)

115-117. *a single crime:* Dante must reckon each false florin as a separate sin.

128. *Narcissus' mirror:* A pool of water. Ovid (*Metamorpheses* III, 407-510) tells how the young Narcissus fell in love with his own reflection in a pool. He remained bent over the reflection till he wasted away and was changed into a flower.

Canto XXXI

THE CENTRAL PIT OF MALEBOLGE *The Giants*

Dante's spirits rise again as the Poets approach the Central Pit, a great well, at the bottom of which lies Cocytus, the Ninth and final circle of Hell. Through the darkness Dante sees what appears to be a city of great towers, but as he draws near he discovers that the great shapes he has seen are the Giants and Titans who stand perpetual guard inside the well-pit with the upper halves of their bodies rising above the rim.

Among the Giants, Virgil identifies NIMROD, builder of the Tower of Babel; EPHIALTES and BRIAREUS, who warred against the Gods; and TITYOS and TYPHON, who insulted Jupiter. Also here, but for no specific offense, is ANTAEUS, and his presence makes it clear that the Giants are placed here less for their particular sins than for their general natures.

These are the sons of earth, embodiments of elemental forces unbalanced by love, desire without restraint and without acknowledgment of moral and theological law. They are symbols of the earth-trace that every devout man must clear from his soul, the unchecked passions of the beast. Raised from the earth, they make the very gods tremble. Now they are returned to the darkness of their origins, guardians of earth's last depth.

At Virgil's persuasion, Antaeus takes the Poets in his huge palm and lowers them gently to the final floor of Hell.

One and the same tongue had first wounded me
  so that the blood came rushing to my cheeks,
  and then supplied the soothing remedy.

Just so, as I have heard, the magic steel
of the lance that was Achilles' and his father's
could wound at a touch, and, at another, heal.

We turned our backs on the valley and climbed from it
to the top of the stony bank that walls it round,
crossing in silence to the central pit.

Here it was less than night and less than day;
my eyes could make out little through the gloom,
but I heard the shrill note of a trumpet bray

louder than any thunder. As if by force,
it drew my eyes; I stared into the gloom
along the path of the sound back to its source.

After the bloody rout when Charlemagne
had lost the band of Holy Knights, Roland
blew no more terribly for all his pain.

And as I stared through that obscurity,
I saw what seemed a cluster of great towers,
whereat I cried: "Master, what is this city?"

And he: "You are still too far back in the dark
to make out clearly what you think you see;
it is natural that you should miss the mark:

You will see clearly when you reach that place
how much your eyes mislead you at a distance;
I urge you, therefore, to increase your pace."

Then taking my hand in his, my Master said:
"The better to prepare you for strange truth,
let me explain those shapes you see ahead:

they are not towers but giants. They stand in the well
from the navel down; and stationed round its bank
they mount guard on the final pit of Hell."

Just as a man in a fog that starts to clear
begins little by little to piece together
the shapes the vapor crowded from the air—

so, when those shapes grew clearer as I drew
across the darkness to the central brink,
error fled from me; and my terror grew.

For just as at Montereggione the great towers
crown the encircling wall; so the grim giants
whom Jove still threatens when the thunder roars

raised from the rim of stone about that well
the upper halves of their bodies, which loomed up
like turrets through the murky air of Hell.

I had drawn close enough to one already
to make out the great arms along his sides,
the face, the shoulders, the breast, and most of the belly.

Nature, when she destroyed the last exemplars
on which she formed those beasts, surely did well
to take such executioners from Mars.

And if she has not repented the creation
of whales and elephants, the thinking man
will see in that her justice and discretion:

for where the instrument of intelligence
is added to brute power and evil will,
mankind is powerless in its own defense.

His face, it seemed to me, was quite as high
and wide as the bronze pine cone in St. Peter's
with the rest of him proportioned accordingly:

so that the bank, which made an apron for him
from the waist down, still left so much exposed
that three Frieslanders standing on the rim,

one on another, could not have reached his hair;
for to that point at which men's capes are buckled,
thirty good hand-spans of brute bulk rose clear.

"Rafel mahee amek zabi almit,"
began a bellowed chant from the brute mouth
for which no sweeter psalmody was fit.

And my Guide in his direction: "Babbling fool,
stick to your horn and vent yourself with it
when rage or passion stir your stupid soul.

Feel there around your neck, you muddle-head,
and find the cord; and there's the horn itself,
there on your overgrown chest." To me he said:

"His very babbling testifies the wrong
he did on earth: he is Nimrod, through whose evil
mankind no longer speaks a common tongue.

Waste no words on him: it would be foolish.
To him all speech is meaningless; as his own,
which no one understands, is simply gibberish."

We moved on, bearing left along the pit,
and a crossbow-shot away we found the next one,
an even huger and more savage spirit.

What master could have bound so gross a beast
I cannot say, but he had his right arm pinned
behind his back, and the left across his breast

by an enormous chain that wound about him
from the neck down, completing five great turns
before it spiraled down below the rim.

"This piece of arrogance," said my Guide to me,
"dared try his strength against the power of Jove;
for which he is rewarded as you see.

He is Ephialtes, who made the great endeavour
with the other giants who alarmed the Gods;
the arms he raised then, now are bound forever."

"Were it possible, I should like to take with me,"
I said to him, "the memory of seeing
the immeasurable Briareus." And he:

"Nearer to hand, you may observe Antaeus
who is able to speak to us, and is not bound.
It is he will set us down in Cocytus,

the bottom of all guilt. The other hulk
stands far beyond our road. He too, is bound
and looks like this one, but with a fiercer sulk."

No earthquake in the fury of its shock
ever seized a tower more violently,
than Ephialtes, hearing, began to rock.

Then I dreaded death as never before;
and I think I could have died for very fear
had I not seen what manacles he wore.

We left the monster, and not far from him
we reached Antaeus, who to his shoulders alone
soared up a good five ells above the rim.

"O soul who once in Zama's fateful vale—
where Scipio became the heir of glory
when Hannibal and all his troops turned tail—

took more than a thousand lions for your prey;
and in whose memory many still believe
the sons of earth would yet have won the day

had you joined with them against High Olympus—
do not disdain to do us a small service,
but set us down where the cold grips Cocytus.

Would you have us go to Tityos or Typhon?—
this man can give you what is longed for here:
therefore do not refuse him, but bend down.

For he can still make new your memory:
he lives, and awaits long life, unless Grace call him
before his time to his felicity."

Thus my Master to that Tower of Pride;
and the giant without delay reached out the hands
which Hercules had felt, and raised my Guide.

Virgil, when he felt himself so grasped,
called to me: "Come, and I will hold you safe."
And he took me in his arms and held me clasped.

The way the Carisenda seems to one
who looks up from the leaning side when clouds
are going over it from that direction,

making the whole tower seem to topple—so
Antaeus seemed to me in the fraught moment
when I stood clinging, watching from below

as he bent down; while I with heart and soul
wished we had gone some other way, but gently
he set us down inside the final hole

whose ice holds Judas and Lucifer in its grip.
Then straightened like a mast above a ship.

Notes

5. *Achilles' lance:* Peleus, father of Achilles, left this magic lance to his son. (Ovid, *Metamorphoses* XIII, 171 ff.) Sonneteers of Dante's time made frequent metaphoric use of this lance: just as the lance could cure and then heal, so could the lady's look destroy with love and her kiss make whole.

14-15. *stared . . . along the path of the sound:* Another of Dante's peculiar reports of how the senses work. He treats his eyes here as if they were radio-compasses tracking a beam. There is not another man in literature who would anatomize this reaction in this way. Compare with this the opening of Canto XX and the note on Dante's peculiar treatment of his vision.

17. *Roland:* Nephew of Charlemagne, hero of the French epic poem, the *Chanson de Roland.* He protected the rear of Charlemagne's column on the return march through the Pyrenees from a war against the Saracens. When he was attacked he was too proud to blow his horn as a signal for help, but as he was dying he blew so prodigious a blast that it was heard by Charlemagne eight miles away. *Band of Holy Knights:* The original is *"la santa gesta,"* which may be interpreted as "the holy undertaking." *"Gesta,"* however, can also mean "a sworn band or fellowship of men at arms" (such as the Knights of the Round Table), and since it was his Knights, rather than his undertaking, that Charlemagne lost, the second rendering seems more apt in context.

40. *Montereggione:* (Mon-teh-reh-DJOE-neh) A castle in Val d'Elsa near Siena built in 1213. Its walls had a circumference of more than half a kilometer and were crowned by fourteen great towers, most of which are now destroyed.

59. *the bronze pine cone in St. Peter's:* Originally a part of a fountain. In Dante's time it stood in front of the Basilica of St. Peter. It is now inside the Vatican. It stands about thirteen feet high (Scartazzini-Vandelli give the height as four meters) but shows signs of mutilation that indicate it was once higher. Many translations incorrectly render the original "la pina" as pine tree. In Italian "pino" is "pine tree" and "pina" is "pine cone." Like most of Dante's measurements it is a poetical rather than a literal assistance in determining the height of the giants. How tall is a man whose face is thirteen feet long? If the face represents one-sixth of a man's height, a minimum figure will be seventy-eight feet; but other interpretations of Dante's details will yield figures ranging from forty to one hundred feet. Lines 65-66, for example, would yield a figure between 300 and 474 inches for the measurement from the waist to (roughly) the collarbone.

63. *Frieslanders:* The men of Friesland were reputed to be the tallest in Europe.

66. *thirty good hand-spans:* Dante uses the word "palma," which in Italian signifies the spread of the open hand, a considerably larger measure than the English "hand" which equals four inches. The Dante Society edition of the *Comedy* equates ten palms to four meters or 158 inches, but 15.8 inches seems excessive. Ten inches would seem closer to a "good hand-span."

67. *Rafel mahee, etc.:* This line, as Virgil explains below, is Nimrod's gibberish.

77. *Nimrod:* The first king of Babylon, supposed to have built the Tower of Babel, for which he is punished, in part, by the confusion of his own tongue and understanding. Nothing in the Biblical reference portrays him as one of the earth-giants.

94. *Ephialtes:* Son of Neptune (the sea) and Iphimedia. With his brother, Otus, he warred against the Gods striving to pile Mt. Ossa on Mt. Olympus, and Mt. Pelion on Mt. Ossa. Apollo restored good order by killing the two brothers.

99. *Briareus:* Another of the giants who rose against the Olympian Gods. Virgil speaks of him as having a hundred arms and fifty hands (*Aeneid* X, 565-568), but Dante has need only of his size, and of his sin, which he seems to view as a kind of revolt of the angels, just as the action of Ephialtes and Otus may be read as a pagan distortion of the Tower of Babel legend. He was the son of Uranus and Tellus.

100. *Antaeus:* The son of Neptune and Tellus (the earth). In battle, his strength grew every time he touched the earth, his mother. He was accordingly invincible until Hercules killed him by lifting him over his head and strangling him in mid-air. Lucan (*Pharsalia* IV, 595-660) describes Antaeus' great lion-hunting feat in the valley of Zama where, in a later era, Scipio defeated Hannibal. Antaeus did not join in the rebellion against the Gods and therefore he is not chained.

123. *Cocytus:* The final pit of Hell. See the remaining Cantos.

124. *Tityos or Typhon:* Also sons of Tellus. They offended Jupiter, who had them hurled into the crater of Etna, below which the Lake Tartarus was supposed to lie.

136. *the Carisenda:* A leaning tower of Bologna.

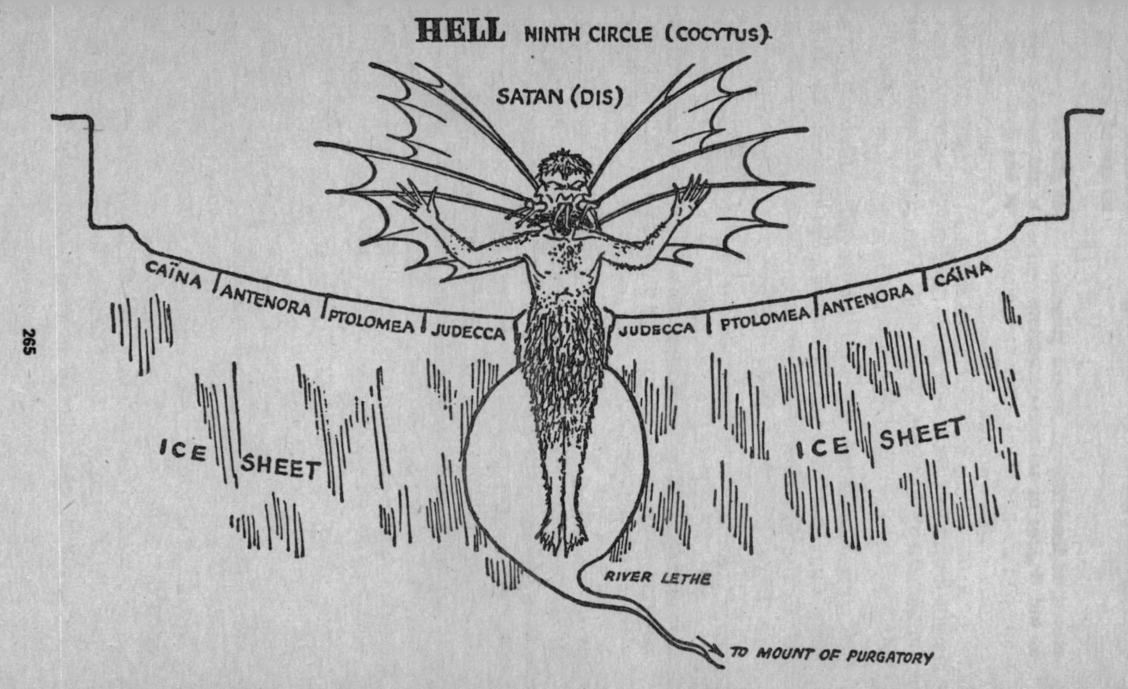
HELL NINTH CIRCLE (COCYTUS).
SATAN (DIS)
CAÏNA
ANTENORA
PTOLOMEA
JUDECCA
JUDECCA
PTOLOMEA
ANTENORA
CAÏNA
ICE SHEET
ICE SHEET
RIVER LETHE
TO MOUNT OF PURGATORY

ALL

Canto XXXII

CIRCLE NINE: *Cocytus* — *Compound Fraud*

ROUND ONE: *Caïna* — *The Treacherous to Kin*

ROUND TWO: *Antenora* — *The Treacherous to Country*

At the bottom of the well Dante finds himself on a huge frozen lake. This is COCYTUS, the NINTH CIRCLE, the fourth and last great water of Hell, and here, fixed in the ice, each according to his guilt, are punished sinners guilty of TREACHERY AGAINST THOSE TO WHOM THEY WERE BOUND BY SPECIAL TIES. The ice is divided into four concentric rings marked only by the different positions of the damned within the ice.

This is Dante's symbolic equivalent of the final guilt. The treacheries of these souls were denials of love (which is God) and of all human warmth. Only the remorseless dead center of the ice will serve to express their natures. As they denied God's love, so are they furthest removed from the light and warmth of His Sun. As they denied all human ties, so are they bound only by the unyielding ice.

The first round is CAINA, named for Cain. Here lie those who were treacherous against blood ties. They have their necks and heads out of the ice and are permitted to bow their heads—a double boon since it allows them some protection from the freezing gale and, further, allows their tears to fall without freezing their eyes shut. Here Dante sees ALESSANDRO and NAPOLEONE DEGLI ALBERTI, and he speaks to CAMICION, who identifies other sinners of this round.

The second round is ANTENORA, named for Antenor, the Trojan who was believed to have betrayed his city to the Greeks. Here lie those guilty of TREACHERY

TO COUNTRY. They, too, have their heads above the ice, but they cannot bend their necks, which are gripped by the ice. Here Dante accidentally kicks the head of BOCCA DEGLI ABBATI and then proceeds to treat him with a savagery he has shown to no other soul in Hell. Bocca names some of his fellow traitors, and the Poets pass on to discover two heads frozen together in one hole. One of them is gnawing the nape of the other's neck.

If I had rhymes as harsh and horrible
as the hard fact of that final dismal hole
which bears the weight of all the steeps of Hell,

I might more fully press the sap and substance
from my conception; but since I must do
without them, I begin with some reluctance.

For it is no easy undertaking, I say,
to describe the bottom of the Universe;
nor is it for tongues that only babble child's play.

But may those Ladies of the Heavenly Spring
who helped Amphion wall Thebes, assist my verse,
that the word may be the mirror of the thing.

O most miscreant rabble, you who keep
the stations of that place whose name is pain,
better had you been born as goats or sheep!

We stood now in the dark pit of the well,
far down the slope below the Giant's feet,
and while I still stared up at the great wall,

I heard a voice cry: "Watch which way you turn:
take care you do not trample on the heads
of the forworn and miserable brethren."

Whereat I turned and saw beneath my feet
and stretching out ahead, a lake so frozen
it seemed to be made of glass. So thick a sheet

never yet hid the Danube's winter course,
nor, far away beneath the frigid sky,
locked the Don up in its frozen source:

for were Tanbernick and the enormous peak
of Pietrapana to crash down on it,
not even the edges would so much as creak.

The way frogs sit to croak, their muzzles leaning
out of the water, at the time and season
when the peasant woman dreams of her day's gleaning—

Just so the livid dead are sealed in place
up to the part at which they blushed for shame,
and they beat their teeth like storks. Each holds his face

bowed toward the ice, each of them testifies
to the cold with his chattering mouth, to his heart's grief
with tears that flood forever from his eyes.

When I had stared about me, I looked down
and at my feet I saw two clamped together
so tightly that the hair of their heads had grown

together. "Who are you," I said, "who lie
so tightly breast to breast?" They strained their necks,
and when they had raised their heads as if to reply,

the tears their eyes had managed to contain
up to that time gushed out, and the cold froze them
between the lids, sealing them shut again

tighter than any clamp grips wood to wood,
and mad with pain, they fell to butting heads
like billy-goats in a sudden savage mood.

And a wraith who lay to one side and below,
and who had lost both ears to frostbite, said,
his head still bowed: "Why do you watch us so?

If you wish to know who they are who share one doom,
they owned the Bisenzio's valley with their father,
whose name was Albert. They sprang from one womb,

and you may search through all Caïna's crew
without discovering in all this waste
a squab more fit for the aspic than these two;

not him whose breast and shadow a single blow
of the great lance of King Arthur pierced with light;
nor yet Focaccia; nor this one fastened so

into the ice that his head is all I see,
and whom, if you are Tuscan, you know well—
his name on the earth was Sassol Mascheroni.

And I—to tell you all and so be through—
was Camicion de' Pazzi. I wait for Carlin
beside whose guilt my sins will shine like virtue."

And leaving him, I saw a thousand faces
discolored so by cold, I shudder yet
and always will when I think of those frozen places.

As we approached the center of all weight,
where I went shivering in eternal shade,
whether it was my will, or chance, or fate,

I cannot say, but as I trailed my Guide
among those heads, my foot struck violently
against the face of one. Weeping, it cried:

"Why do you kick me? If you were not sent
to wreak a further vengeance for Montaperti,
why do you add this to my other torment?"

"Master," I said, "grant me a moment's pause
to rid myself of a doubt concerning this one;
then you may hurry me at your own pace."

The Master stopped at once, and through the volley
of foul abuse the wretch poured out, I said:
"Who are you who curse others so?" And he:

"And who are *you* who go through the dead larder
of Antenora kicking the cheeks of others
so hard, that were you alive, you could not kick harder?"

"I *am* alive," I said, "and if you seek fame,
it may be precious to you above all else
that my notes on this descent include your name."

"Exactly the opposite is my wish and hope,"
he answered. "Let me be; for it's little you know
of how to flatter on this icy slope."

I grabbed the hair of his dog's-ruff and I said:
"Either you tell me truly who you are,
or you won't have a hair left on your head."

And he: "Not though you snatch me bald. I swear
I will not tell my name nor show my face.
Not though you rip until my brain lies bare."

I had a good grip on his hair; already
I had yanked out more than one fistful of it,
while the wretch yelped, but kept his face turned from me;

when another said: "Bocca, what is it ails you?
What the Hell's wrong? Isn't it bad enough
to hear you bang your jaws? Must you bark too?"

"Now filthy traitor, say no more!" I cried,
"for to your shame, be sure I shall bear back
a true report of you." The wretch replied:

"Say anything you please but go away.
And if you *do* get back, don't overlook
that pretty one who had so much to say

just now. Here he laments the Frenchman's price.
'I saw Buoso da Duera,' you can report,
'where the bad salad is kept crisp on ice.'

And if you're asked who else was wintering here,
Beccheria, whose throat was slit by Florence,
is there beside you. Gianni de' Soldanier

is further down, I think, with Ganelon,
and Tebaldello, who opened the gates of Faenza
and let Bologna steal in with the dawn."

Leaving him then, I saw two souls together
in a single hole, and so pinched in by the ice
that one head made a helmet for the other.

As a famished man chews crusts—so the one sinner
sank his teeth into the other's nape
at the base of the skull, gnawing his loathsome dinner.

Tydeus in his final raging hour
gnawed Menalippus' head with no more fury
than this one gnawed at skull and dripping gore.

"You there," I said, "who show so odiously
your hatred for that other, tell me why
on this condition: that if in what you tell me

you seem to have a reasonable complaint
against him you devour with such foul relish,
I, knowing who you are, and his soul's taint,

may speak your cause to living memory,
God willing the power of speech be left to me."

Notes

3. *which bears the weight of all the steeps of Hell:* Literally, it is the base from which all the steeps rise; symbolically, it is the total and finality of all guilt.

10. *those Ladies of the Heavenly Spring, etc.:* The Muses. They so inspired Amphion's hand upon the lyre that the music charmed blocks of stone out of Mount Cithaeron, and the blocks formed themselves into the walls of Thebes.

28-29. *Tanbernick . . . Pietrapana:* There is no agreement on the location of the mountain Dante called Tanbernick. Pietrapana, today known as *la Pania,* is in Tuscany.

32-33. *season . . . gleaning:* The summer.

35. *the part at which they blushed:* The cheeks. By extension, the whole face.

41-61. *two clamped together:* Alessandro and Napoleone, Counts of Mangona. Among other holdings, they inherited a castle in the Val di Bisenzio. They seemed to have been at odds on all things and finally killed one another in a squabble over their inheritance and their politics (Alessandro was a Guelph and Napoleone a Ghibelline).

61. *him whose breast and shadow, etc.:* Modred, King Arthur's traitorous nephew. He tried to kill Arthur, but the king struck him a single blow of his lance, and when it was withdrawn, a shaft of light passed through the gaping wound and split the shadow of the falling traitor.

63. *Focaccia:* (Foh-KAH-tcha) Of the Cancellieri of Pistoia. He murdered his cousin (among others) and may have been the principal cause of a great feud that divided the Cancellieri, and split the Guelphs into the White and Black parties.

66. *Sassol Mascheroni:* Of the Toschi of Florence. He was appointed guardian of one of his nephews and murdered him to get the inheritance for himself.

68. *Camicion de' Pazzi:* (Kah-mih-TCHONE day PAH-tsee) Alberto Camicion de' Pazzi of Valdarno. He murdered a kinsman. *Carlin:* Carlino de' Pazzi, relative of Alberto. He was charged with defending for the Whites the castle of Piantravigne (Pyahn-trah-VEE-nyeh) in Valdarno but surrendered it for a bribe. He belongs therefore in the next lower circle, Antenora, as a traitor to his country, and when he arrives there his greater sin will make Alberto seem almost virtuous by comparison.

70. *And leaving him:* These words mark the departure from Caïna to Antenora.

73. *the center of all weight:* In Dante's cosmology the bottom of Hell is at the center of the earth, which is in turn the center of the universe; it is therefore the center of all gravity. Symbolically, it is

the focal point of all guilt. Gravity, weight, and evil are equivalent symbols on one level; they are what ties man to the earth, what draws him down. At the center of all, Satan is fixed forever in the eternal ice. The journey to salvation, however, is up from that center, once the soul has realized the hideousness of sin.

78. *against the face of one:* Bocca degli Abbati, a traitorous Florentine. At the battle of Montaperti (cf. Farinata, Canto X) he hacked off the hand of the Florentine standard bearer. The cavalry, lacking a standard around which it could rally, was soon routed.

107. *What the Hell's wrong?:* In the circumstances, a monstrous pun. The original is *"qual diavolo ti tocca?"* (what devil touches, or molests, you?) a standard colloquialism for "what's the matter with you?" A similar pun occurs in line 117 "kept crisp (cool) on ice." Colloquially *"stare fresco"* (to be or to remain cool) equals "to be left out in the cold," i.e., to be out of luck.

116. *Buoso da Duera:* Of Cremona. In 1265 Charles of Anjou marched against Manfred and Naples (see Canto XIX), and Buoso da Duera was sent out in charge of a Ghibelline army to oppose the passage of one of Charles' armies, but accepted a bribe and let the French pass unopposed. The event took place near Parma.

119. *Beccheria:* Tesauro dei Beccheria of Pavia, Abbot of Vallombrosa and Papal Legate (of Alexander IV) in Tuscany. The Florentine Guelphs cut off his head in 1258 for plotting with the expelled Ghibellines.

120. *Gianni de' Soldanier:* A Florentine Ghibelline of ancient and noble family. In 1265, however, during the riots that occurred under the Two Jovial Friars, he deserted his party and became a leader of the commoners (Guelphs). In placing him in Antenora, Dante makes no distinction between turning on one's country and turning on one's political party, not at least if the end is simply for power.

121. *Ganelon:* It was Ganelon who betrayed Roland to the Saracens. (See Canto XXXI.)

122. *Tebaldello:* Tebaldello de' Zambrasi of Faenza. At dawn on November 13, 1280, he opened the city gates and delivered Faenza to the Bolognese Guelphs in order to revenge himself on the Ghibelline family of the Lambertazzi who, in 1274, had fled from Bologna to take refuge in Faenza.

130-1. *Tydeus . . . Menalippus:* Statius recounts in the *Thebaid* that Tydeus killed Menalippus in battle but fell himself mortally wounded. As he lay dying he had Menalippus' head brought to him and fell to gnawing it in his dying rage.

Canto XXXIII

CIRCLE NINE: *Cocytus* — *Compound Fraud*

ROUND TWO: *Antenora* — *The Treacherous to Country*

ROUND THREE: *Ptolomea* — *The Treacherous to Guests and Hosts*

In reply to Dante's exhortation, the sinner who is gnawing his companion's head looks up, wipes his bloody mouth on his victim's hair, and tells his harrowing story. He is COUNT UGOLINO and the wretch he gnaws is ARCHBISHOP RUGGIERI. Both are in Antenora for treason. In life they had once plotted together. Then Ruggieri betrayed his fellow-plotter and caused his death, by starvation, along with his four "sons." In the most pathetic and dramatic passage of the Inferno, *Ugolino details how their prison was sealed and how his "sons" dropped dead before him one by one, weeping for food. His terrible tale serves only to renew his grief and hatred, and he has hardly finished it before he begins to gnaw Ruggieri again with renewed fury. In the immutable Law of Hell, the killer-by-starvation becomes the food of his victim.*

The Poets leave Ugolino and enter PTOLOMEA, so named for the Ptolomaeus of Maccabees, *who murdered his father-in-law at a banquet. Here are punished those who were TREACHEROUS AGAINST THE TIES OF HOSPITALITY. They lie with only half their faces above the ice and their tears freeze in their eye sockets, sealing them with little crystal visors. Thus even the comfort of tears is denied them. Here Dante finds FRIAR ALBERIGO and BRANCA D'ORIA, and discovers the terrible power of Ptolomea: so great is its sin that the souls of the guilty fall to its torments even before they die, leaving their bodies still on earth, inhabited by Demons.*

The sinner raised his mouth from his grim repast
and wiped it on the hair of the bloody head
whose nape he had all but eaten away. At last

he began to speak: "You ask me to renew
a grief so desperate that the very thought
of speaking of it tears my heart in two.

But if my words may be a seed that bears
the fruit of infamy for him I gnaw,
I shall weep, but tell my story through my tears.

Who you may be, and by what powers you reach
into this underworld, I cannot guess,
but you seem to me a Florentine by your speech.

I was Count Ugolino, I must explain;
this reverend grace is the Archbishop Ruggieri:
now I will tell you why I gnaw his brain.

That I, who trusted him, had to undergo
imprisonment and death through his treachery,
you will know already. What you cannot know—

that is, the lingering inhumanity
of the death I suffered—you shall hear in full:
then judge for yourself if he has injured me.

A narrow window in that coop of stone
now called the Tower of Hunger for my sake
(within which others yet must pace alone)

had shown me several waning moons already
between its bars, when I slept the evil sleep
in which the veil of the future parted for me.

This beast appeared as master of a hunt
chasing the wolf and his whelps across the mountain
that hides Lucca from Pisa. Out in front

of the starved and shrewd and avid pack he had placed
Gualandi and Sismondi and Lanfranchi
to point his prey. The father and sons had raced

a brief course only when they failed of breath
and seemed to weaken; then I thought I saw
their flanks ripped open by the hounds' fierce teeth.

Before the dawn, the dream still in my head,
I woke and heard my sons, who were there with me,
cry from their troubled sleep, asking for bread.

You are cruelty itself if you can keep
your tears back at the thought of what foreboding
stirred in my heart; and if you do not weep,

at what are you used to weeping?—The hour when food
used to be brought, drew near. They were now awake,
and each was anxious from his dream's dark mood.

And from the base of that horrible tower I heard
the sound of hammers nailing up the gates:
I stared at my sons' faces without a word.

I did not weep: I had turned stone inside.
They wept. 'What ails you, Father, you look so strange,'
my little Anselm, youngest of them, cried.

But I did not speak a word nor shed a tear:
not all that day nor all that endless night,
until I saw another sun appear.

When a tiny ray leaked into that dark prison
and I saw staring back from their four faces
the terror and the wasting of my own,

I bit my hands in helpless grief. And they,
thinking I chewed myself for hunger, rose
suddenly together. I heard them say:

'Father, it would give us much less pain
if you ate us: it was you who put upon us
this sorry flesh; now strip it off again.'

I calmed myself to spare them. Ah! hard earth,
why did you not yawn open? All that day
and the next we sat in silence. On the fourth,

Gaddo, the eldest, fell before me and cried,
stretched at my feet upon that prison floor:
'Father, why don't you help me?' There he died.

And just as you see me, I saw them fall
one by one on the fifth day and the sixth.
Then, already blind, I began to crawl

from body to body shaking them frantically.
Two days I called their names, and they were dead.
Then fasting overcame my grief and me."

His eyes narrowed to slits when he was done,
and he seized the skull again between his teeth
grinding it as a mastiff grinds a bone.

Ah, Pisa! foulest blemish on the land
where "si" sounds sweet and clear, since those nearby you
are slow to blast the ground on which you stand,

may Caprara and Gorgona drift from place
and dam the flooding Arno at its mouth
until it drowns the last of your foul race!

For if to Ugolino falls the censure
for having betrayed your castles, you for your part
should not have put his sons to such a torture:

you modern Thebes! those tender lives you spilt—
Brigata, Uguccione, and the others
I mentioned earlier—were too young for guilt!

We passed on further, where the frozen mine
 entombs another crew in greater pain;
 these wraiths are not bent over, but lie supine.

Their very weeping closes up their eyes;
 and the grief that finds no outlet for its tears
 turns inward to increase their agonies:

for the first tears that they shed knot instantly
 in their eye-sockets, and as they freeze they form
 a crystal visor above the cavity.

And despite the fact that standing in that place
 I had become as numb as any callus,
 and all sensation had faded from my face,

somehow I felt a wind begin to blow,
 whereat I said: "Master, what stirs this wind?
 Is not all heat extinguished here below?"

And the Master said to me: "Soon you will be
 where your own eyes will see the source and cause
 and give you their own answer to the mystery."

And one of those locked in that icy mall
 cried out to us as we passed: "O souls so cruel
 that you are sent to the last post of all,

relieve me for a little from the pain
 of this hard veil; let my heart weep a while
 before the weeping freeze my eyes again."

And I to him: "If you would have my service,
 tell me your name; then if I do not help you
 may I descend to the last rim of the ice."

"I am Friar Alberigo," he answered therefore,
 "the same who called for the fruits from the bad garden.
 Here I am given dates for figs full store."

"What! Are you dead already?" I said to him.
 And he then: "How my body stands in the world
 I do not know. So privileged is this rim

of Ptolomea, that often souls fall to it
before dark Atropos has cut their thread.
And that you may more willingly free my spirit

of this glaze of frozen tears that shrouds my face,
I will tell you this: when a soul betrays as I did,
it falls from flesh, and a demon takes its place,

ruling the body till its time is spent.
The ruined soul rains down into this cistern.
So, I believe, there is still evident

in the world above, all that is fair and mortal
of this black shade who winters here behind me.
If you have only recently crossed the portal

from that sweet world, you surely must have known
his body: Branca D'Oria is its name,
and many years have passed since he rained down."

"I think you are trying to take me in," I said,
"Ser Branca D'Oria is a living man;
he eats, he drinks, he fills his clothes and his bed."

"Michel Zanche had not yet reached the ditch
of the Black Talons," the frozen wraith replied,
"there where the sinners thicken in hot pitch,

when this one left his body to a devil,
as did his nephew and second in treachery,
and plumbed like lead through space to this dead level.

But now reach out your hand, and let me cry."
And I did not keep the promise I had made,
for to be rude to him was courtesy.

Ah, men of Genoa! souls of little worth,
corrupted from all custom of righteousness,
why have you not been driven from the earth?

For there beside the blackest soul of all
Romagna's evil plain, lies one of yours
bathing his filthy soul in the eternal

glacier of Cocytus for his foul crime,
while he seems yet alive in world and time!

1-90. *Ugolino and Ruggieri:* (Oog-oh-LEE-noe: Roo-DJAIR-ee) Ugolino, Count of Donoratico and a member of the Guelph family della Gherardesca. He and his nephew, Nino de' Visconti, led the two Guelph factions of Pisa. In 1288 Ugolino intrigued with Archbishop Ruggieri degli Ubaldini, leader of the Ghibellines, to get rid of Visconti and to take over the command of all the Pisan Guelphs. The plan worked, but in the consequent weakening of the Guelphs, Ruggieri saw his chance and betrayed Ugolino, throwing him into prison with his sons and his grandsons. In the following year the prison was sealed up and they were left to starve to death. The law of retribution is clearly evident: in life Ruggieri sinned against Ugolino by denying him food; in Hell he himself becomes food for his victim.

18. *you will know already:* News of Ugolino's imprisonment and death would certainly have reached Florence, *what you cannot know:* No living man could know what happened after Ugolino and his sons were sealed in the prison and abandoned.

22. *coop:* Dante uses the word *muda,* in Italian signifying a stone tower in which falcons were kept in the dark to moult. From the time of Ugolino's death it became known as The Tower of Hunger.

25. *several waning moons:* Ugolino was jailed late in 1288. He was sealed in to starve early in 1289.

28. *This beast:* Ruggieri.

29-30. *the mountain that hides Lucca from Pisa:* These two cities would be in view of one another were it not for Monte San Giuliano.

32. *Gualandi and Sismondi and Lanfranchi:* (Gwah-LAHN-dee . . . Lahn-FRAHN-kee) Three Pisan nobles, Ghibellines and friends of the Archbishop.

51-71. UGOLINO'S "SONS": Actually two of the boys were grandsons and all were considerably older than one would gather from Dante's account. Anselm, the younger grandson, was fifteen. The others were really young men and were certainly old enough for guilt despite Dante's charge in line 90.

75. *Then fasting overcame my grief and me:* i.e., He died. Some interpret the line to mean that Ugolino's hunger drove him to cannibalism. Ugolino's present occupation in Hell would certainly support that interpretation but the fact is that cannibalism is the one major sin Dante does not assign a place to in Hell. So monstrous

would it have seemed to him that he must certainly have established a special punishment for it. Certainly he could hardly have relegated it to an ambiguity. Moreover, it would be a sin of bestiality rather than of fraud, and as such it would be punished in the Seventh Circle.

79-80. *the land where "si" sounds sweet and clear:* Italy.

82. *Caprara and Gorgona:* These two islands near the mouth of the Arno were Pisan possessions in 1300.

86. *betrayed your castles:* In 1284, Ugolino gave up certain castles to Lucca and Florence. He was at war with Genoa at the time and it is quite likely that he ceded the castles to buy the neutrality of these two cities, for they were technically allied with Genoa. Dante, however, must certainly consider the action as treasonable, for otherwise Ugolino would be in Caïna for his treachery to Visconti.

88. *you modern Thebes:* Thebes, as a number of the foregoing notes will already have made clear, was the site of some of the most hideous crimes of antiquity.

91. *we passed on further:* Marks the passage into Ptolomea.

105. *is not all heat extinguished:* Dante believed (rather accurately, by chance) that all winds resulted from "exhalations of heat." Cocytus, however, is conceived as wholly devoid of heat, a metaphysical absolute zero. The source of the wind, as we discover in the next Canto, is Satan himself.

117. *may I descend to the last rim of the ice:* Dante is not taking any chances; he has to go on to the last rim in any case. The sinner, however, believes him to be another damned soul and would interpret the oath quite otherwise than as Dante meant it.

118. *Friar Alberigo:* (Ahl-beh-REE-ghoe) Of the Manfredi of Faenza. He was another Jovial Friar. In 1284 his brother Manfred struck him in the course of an argument. Alberigo pretended to let it pass, but in 1285 he invited Manfred and his son to a banquet and had them murdered. The signal to the assassins was the words: "Bring in the fruit." "Friar Alberigo's bad fruit," became a proverbial saying.

125. *Atropos:* The Fate who cuts the thread of life.

137. *Branca d'Oria:* (DAW-ree-yah) A Genoese Ghibelline. His sin is identical in kind to that of Friar Alberigo. In 1275 he invited his father-in-law, Michel Zanche (see Canto XXII), to a banquet and had him and his companions cut to pieces. He was assisted in the butchery by his nephew.

Canto XXXIV

NINTH CIRCLE: *Cocytus*	*Compound Fraud*
ROUND FOUR: *Judecca*	*The Treacherous to Their Masters*
THE CENTER	*Satan*

"On march the banners of the King," Virgil begins as the Poets face the last depth. He is quoting a medieval hymn, and to it he adds the distortion and perversion of all that lies about him. "On march the banners of the King—of Hell." And there before them, in an infernal parody of Godhead, they see Satan in the distance, his great wings beating like a windmill. It is their beating that is the source of the icy wind of Cocytus, the exhalation of all evil.

All about him in the ice are strewn the sinners of the last round, JUDECCA, named for Judas Iscariot. These are the TREACHEROUS TO THEIR MASTERS. They lie completely sealed in the ice, twisted and distorted into every conceivable posture. It is impossible to speak to them, and the Poets move on to observe Satan.

He is fixed into the ice at the center to which flow all the rivers of guilt; and as he beats his great wings as if to escape, their icy wind only freezes him more surely into the polluted ice. In a grotesque parody of the Trinity, he has three faces, each a different color, and in each mouth he clamps a sinner whom he rips eternally with his teeth. JUDAS ISCARIOT is in the central mouth: BRUTUS and CASSIUS in the mouths on either side.

Having seen all, the Poets now climb through the center, grappling hand over hand down the hairy flank of Satan himself—a last supremely symbolic action—and at last, when they have passed the center of all gravity, they emerge from Hell. A long climb from the earth's center to the Mount of Purgatory awaits them, and they push on without rest, ascending along the sides of the river Lethe, till they emerge once more to see the stars of Heaven, just before dawn on Easter Sunday.

"On march the banners of the King of Hell,"
my Master said. "Toward us. Look straight ahead:
can you make him out at the core of the frozen shell?"

Like a whirling windmill seen afar at twilight,
or when a mist has risen from the ground—
just such an engine rose upon my sight

stirring up such a wild and bitter wind
I cowered for shelter at my Master's back,
there being no other windbreak I could find.

I stood now where the souls of the last class
(with fear my verses tell it) were covered wholly;
they shone below the ice like straws in glass.

Some lie stretched out; others are fixed in place
upright, some on their heads, some on their soles;
another, like a bow, bends foot to face.

When we had gone so far across the ice
that it pleased my Guide to show me the foul creature
which once had worn the grace of Paradise,

he made me stop, and, stepping aside, he said:
"Now see the face of Dis! This is the place
where you must arm your soul against all dread."

Do not ask, Reader, how my blood ran cold
and my voice choked up with fear. I cannot write it:
this is a terror that cannot be told.

I did not die, and yet I lost life's breath:
imagine for yourself what I became,
deprived at once of both my life and death.

The Emperor of the Universe of Pain
jutted his upper chest above the ice;
and I am closer in size to the great mountain

the Titans make around the central pit,
than they to his arms. Now, starting from this part,
imagine the whole that corresponds to it!

If he was once as beautiful as now
he is hideous, and still turned on his Maker,
well may he be the source of every woe!

With what a sense of awe I saw his head
towering above me! for it had three faces:
one was in front, and it was fiery red;

the other two, as weirdly wonderful,
merged with it from the middle of each shoulder
to the point where all converged at the top of the skull;

the right was something between white and bile;
the left was about the color that one finds
on those who live along the banks of the Nile.

Under each head two wings rose terribly,
their span proportioned to so gross a bird:
I never saw such sails upon the sea.

They were not feathers—their texture and their form
were like a bat's wings—and he beat them so
that three winds blew from him in one great storm:

it is these winds that freeze all Cocytus.
He wept from his six eyes, and down three chins
the tears ran mixed with bloody froth and pus.

In every mouth he worked a broken sinner
between his rake-like teeth. Thus he kept three
in eternal pain at his eternal dinner.

For the one in front the biting seemed to play
no part at all compared to the ripping: at times
the whole skin of his back was flayed away.

"That soul that suffers most," explained my Guide,
"is Judas Iscariot, he who kicks his legs
on the fiery chin and has his head inside.

Of the other two, who have their heads thrust forward,
the one who dangles down from the black face
is Brutus: note how he writhes without a word.

And there, with the huge and sinewy arms, is the soul
of Cassius.—But the night is coming on
and we must go, for we have seen the whole."

Then, as he bade, I clasped his neck, and he,
watching for a moment when the wings
were opened wide, reached over dexterously

and seized the shaggy coat of the king demon;
then grappling matted hair and frozen crusts
from one tuft to another, clambered down.

When we had reached the joint where the great thigh
merges into the swelling of the haunch,
my Guide and Master, straining terribly,

turned his head to where his feet had been
and began to grip the hair as if he were climbing;
so that I thought we moved toward Hell again.

"Hold fast!" my Guide said, and his breath came shrill
with labor and exhaustion. "There is no way
but by such stairs to rise above such evil."

At last he climbed out through an opening
in the central rock, and he seated me on the rim;
then joined me with a nimble backward spring.

I looked up, thinking to see Lucifer
as I had left him, and I saw instead
his legs projecting high into the air.

Now let all those whose dull minds are still vexed
by failure to understand what point it was
I had passed through, judge if I was perplexed.

"Get up. Up on your feet," my Master said.
"The sun already mounts to middle tierce,
and a long road and hard climbing lie ahead."

It was no hall of state we had found there,
but a natural animal pit hollowed from rock
with a broken floor and a close and sunless air.

"Before I tear myself from the Abyss,"
I said when I had risen, "O my Master,
explain to me my error in all this:

where is the ice? and Lucifer—how has he
been turned from top to bottom: and how can the sun
have gone from night to day so suddenly?"

And he to me: "You imagine you are still
on the other side of the center where I grasped
the shaggy flank of the Great Worm of Evil

which bores through the world—you *were* while I climbed down,
but when I turned myself about, you passed
the point to which all gravities are drawn.

You are under the other hemisphere where you stand;
the sky above us is the half opposed
to that which canopies the great dry land.

Under the mid-point of that other sky
the Man who was born sinless and who lived
beyond all blemish, came to suffer and die.

You have your feet upon a little sphere
which forms the other face of the Judecca.
There it is evening when it is morning here.

And this gross Fiend and Image of all Evil
who made a stairway for us with his hide
is pinched and prisoned in the ice-pack still.

On this side he plunged down from heaven's height,
and the land that spread here once hid in the sea
and fled North to our hemisphere for fright;

and it may be that moved by that same fear,
the one peak that still rises on this side
fled upward leaving this great cavern here."

Down there, beginning at the further bound
of Beelzebub's dim tomb, there is a space
not known by sight, but only by the sound

of a little stream descending through the hollow
it has eroded from the massive stone
in its endlessly entwining lazy flow."

My Guide and I crossed over and began
to mount that little known and lightless road
to ascend into the shining world again.

He first, I second, without thought of rest
we climbed the dark until we reached the point
where a round opening brought in sight the blest

and beauteous shining of the Heavenly cars.
And we walked out once more beneath the Stars.

Notes

1. *On march the banners of the King:* The hymn (*Vexilla regis prodeunt*) was written in the sixth century by Venantius Fortunatus, Bishop of Poitiers. The original celebrates the Holy Cross, and is part

of the service for Good Friday to be sung at the moment of uncovering the cross.

17. *the foul creature:* Satan.

38. *three faces:* Numerous interpretations of these three faces exist. What is essential to all explanation is that they be seen as perversions of the qualities of the Trinity.

54. *bloody froth and pus:* The gore of the sinners he chews which is mixed with his slaver.

62. *Judas:* Note how closely his punishment is patterned on that of the Simoniacs (Canto XIX).

67. *huge and sinewy arms:* The Cassius who betrayed Caesar was more generally described in terms of Shakespeare's "lean and hungry look." Another Cassius is described by Cicero (*Catiline* III) as huge and sinewy. Dante probably confused the two.

68. *the night is coming on:* It is now Saturday evening.

82. *his breath came shrill:* CF. Canto XXIII, 85, where the fact that Dante breathes indicates to the Hypocrites that he is alive. Virgil's breathing is certainly a contradiction.

95. *middle tierce:* In the canonical day tierce is the period from about six to nine A.M. Middle tierce, therefore, is seven-thirty. In going through the center point, they have gone from night to day. They have moved ahead twelve hours.

128. *the one peak:* The Mount of Purgatory.

129. *this great cavern:* The natural animal pit of line 98. It is also "Beelzebub's dim tomb," line 131.

133. *a little stream:* Lethe. In classical mythology, the river of forgetfulness, from which souls drank before being born. In Dante's symbolism it flows down from Purgatory, where it has washed away the memory of sin from the souls who are undergoing purification. That memory it delivers to Hell, which draws all sin to itself.

143. *Stars:* As part of his total symbolism Dante ends each of the three divisions of the *Commedia* with this word. Every conclusion of the upward soul is toward the stars, God's shining symbols of hope and virtue. It is just before dawn of Easter Sunday that the Poets emerge—a further symbolism.